Praise for the work of
USA TODAY bestselling author
Jennifer Greene

"A book by Jennifer Greene hums with an unbeatable combination of sexual chemistry and heartwarming emotion."
—*New York Times* bestselling author
Susan Elizabeth Phillips

"Jennifer Greene's writing possesses a modern sensibility and frankness that is vivid, fresh, and often funny."
—*Publishers Weekly* on *The Woman Most Likely To*

"Combining expertly crafted characters with lovely prose flavored with sassy wit, Greene constructs a superb tale of love lost and found, dreams discarded and rediscovered, and the importance of family and friendship."
—*Booklist* on *Where is He Now?*

"A spellbinding storyteller of uncommon brilliance, the fabulous Jennifer Greene is one of the romance genre's greatest gifts to the world of popular fiction."
—*Romantic Times BOOKclub*

"Ms. Greene lavishes her talents on every book she writes."
—*Rendezvous*

Jennifer Greene

Jennifer Greene sold her fist novel when she had two babies in diapers. Since then, she's become the award-winning, bestselling author of more than seventy novels. She's known for warm, natural characters and humor that comes from the heart. Reviewers call her love stories "unforgettable."

You can write Jennifer through her Web site at www. jennifergreene.com.

JENNIFER GREENE

Sparkle

SPARKLE

copyright © 2006 by Alison Hart

isbn-13: 9780373881000

isbn-10:   0373881002

This edition published by arrangement with Harlequin Books S.A.

® and TM are trademarks of the publisher. Trademarks indicated with
® are registered in the United States Patent and Trademark Office, the
Canadian Trade Marks Office and in other countries.

TheNextNovel.com

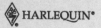

PRINTED IN U.S.A.

From the Author

Dear Reader,

When we're kids, we dream of being all kinds of things when we grow up—from president of the United States to the scientist who cures cancer, from being an Oscar-winning actress to being a major trendsetter.

Then we grow up. We don't stop dreaming, but we learn some realism, and give up the dreams that we know are just too impossible.

I'm a believer that good people should get what's coming to them. Maybe the meek and gentle don't always inherit the earth, but darn it, there should be some payback for all the people who wake up every morning just trying to be good people, good lovers, good parents, good friends.

It ticks me off mightily when this doesn't happen.

So I created this story…about two women who'd put on their realistic grown-up lives and never gave their old dreams another thought. About two women who keep getting put down for having extraordinarily good hearts. About two women who deserve a lot more than jewels and gems.

But after I gave them the jewels, I tried to give them something else. Something that mattered a lot more.

I hope you like this story!

All my best,

Jennifer Greene

To Jennifer—
I keep trying, but no heroine I've ever created comes
close to you. I want to be you when I grow up.
Love, Mom

Just as Maude Rose glanced at the kitchen clock, she felt a sudden fierce tightening in her chest. She ignored it. She wasn't a woman to cater to pain, never had been. More to the point, it was finally past eleven. The bars wouldn't serve liquor until noon, but by the time she got her old butt in gear, the time'd be close enough.

She was already wearing her favorite caftan—the purple with the gold and green threads. The slippers were an elegant satin green, not exactly perfect for walking in a September drizzle, but hell, she couldn't fit any other shoes over her hammertoes anymore anyway.

She made up her face, patting a pretty circle of rouge on each cheek, then slathering on a bright, cheerful lavender lipstick. She just couldn't seem to manage coloring her hair anymore—these last couple months, her arthritis had been a blinger—so her hair seemed to be two-tone these days. Half orange, half white. Truth to tell, she kind of liked it. She swept it up in an elegant style, give or take.

For a finishing touch, of course, she added jewelry. A good pound of gold and silver around her neck and then sparkles of all kinds on her wrists and fingers.

The only place to hide a secret, Maude thought, was in plain sight. Everybody knew that. The kicker in Righteous, Virginia, was that nobody realized that Maude Rose knew that, too.

On the other hand, there were only two women in this town worth sharing a secret with.

She grabbed her cane, let herself out the apartment front door and paused to light a cigar. That feeling of a sharp, tight fist in her chest came back to haunt her, but she determined to ignore it. The pain would go away. Or it wouldn't. Same with all the other aches and pains that a girl her age was stuck with.

She set out. Predictable as taxes, heads showed up in windows as she passed. Lots of people in Righteous took daily pleasure in sniffing their noses at her. Maude Rose didn't make friends, didn't have friends. Truth was that nobody had been in her corner since Bobby Ray died, and that was better than twenty years ago. He'd stood up for her, taken her out of The Life.

Once he'd died, that was that. It was back to loneliness again. Just as well, since anybody she'd ever needed had let her down anyway. There always seemed somebody dying to judge her. It had taken her years to figure out that the way of handling the judgers was to let them. Flaunt what they thought they knew right in their faces.

She passed by Righteous Elementary School—which was right next to Righteous Academy. Kids scrambled all over the playground in spite of the steady drizzle coming down. Both schools had turned her down when she'd offered to volunteer. A teacher looked protectively at her clutch of kids when Maude passed. The little twit.

Past the schools, she eased her cane over the curb, flicked her cigar ash, took another long pull and then headed upstream. The newspaper, *Our Way*, was housed on the next block. She didn't glance at the newspaper office, hadn't ever since they'd refused to print any more of her letters to the editor. This wasn't exactly a town that was pro-choice or tolerant of gays—or, for that matter, appreciated hearing that the mayor needed the shit kicked out of him. Righteous was a place that wrapped its personality around its name.

A dozen times Maude Rose had considered leaving, but now it was too late. And anyhow, it was home. She passed by Marcella's Expert Hair Salon—another place she used to go all the time. Now she did her own. When she got around to it, anyway. She hadn't stepped foot in there again, not since Marcella told her she looked like a cheap tramp, wearing all that gaudy jewelry all the time.

Past Marcella's was another curb. She had to wait for a red light. Finally, though, she could see Manny's Bar—it was still a ways yet, several long blocks' distance, but the trek was all downhill now. Not like she had anything better to do, even if it was a long hike, and she couldn't very well drive when she didn't have a car. Or a license, for that matter.

Halfway across the road, she felt that clenching pain in her chest again—this time sharp enough to steal her breath. In that instant when she couldn't seem to move, stood there frozen, she noticed the drizzle was letting up. A peek of sun was even showing through the clouds. A car horn beeped at her impatiently. Another scandalized face looked out a window and shook a prissy finger at her.

That sun seemed to gently beam down on her wrinkled face, though, and made her smile. The sun felt so...kind.

Kindness was vastly underrated in this world, but not by Maude Rose. The way she saw it, she was tough. She hadn't let anyone hurt her in a long time. Since yesterday at least.

She just wanted to get to Manny's, get that first drink put in front of her. She didn't need or want revenge against all the people who'd been mean to her. Once she got a few belts in her, she stopped feeling needy altogether. Lately, though, she'd gotten a little obsessed with wanting to pay back the few people in this life who'd been decent to her.

There were only three, and since Bobby Ray was long dead, that left a short list of two women Maude Rose felt she owed a thanks.

The really funny thing was that the two girls likely had no idea how much they'd meant to her.

But they would.

Oh, yes. They surely would.

CHAPTER 1

"Now look, sweetheart. I totally understand why you don't want a stranger washing your balls. But we're not strangers, now, are we? I love you. You love me."

Georgina Loretta Thompson—Poppy—tried to breathe, but it was difficult with a hundred and eighty pounds of dead weight lying on her chest. Something dripped on her nose. She was pretty sure it was drool. Drool was the most logical assumption, when the big black oaf sprawled on her in a snoozing heap was a Newfoundland.

"I don't want to have to get tough about this," she crooned affectionately. "I know you're tired and you've been good forever. More than any human has a right to expect. But honestly, love bug, you're wet and heavy and we have to finish up. Your owner's going to be here in another hour."

Beast seemed to realize she was unhappy with him. He reached down with a tongue longer than Poppy's whole face and, eyes closed, slathered a slow, wet kiss down her cheek.

"I love you, too. Really. But remember how we talked about this? I'm the alpha dog in the pack. That means you're supposed to obey me. In fact, you're supposed to cower in my presence. You don't just get to flop down on top of me whenever you want your own way."

"That's it, Poppy, you tell that dog who's boss."

Poppy winced. Naturally she recognized the gruff, humored voice in the doorway. She was too old to be humiliated this way. Or so she'd been telling herself ever since she'd taken the job with Webster O'Brien four years ago.

"I suppose you think I can't get this dog off me," she said darkly.

"It wouldn't be the first dog who had you buffaloed."

"Beast does not have me buffaloed. I'm letting him take a little break. He's been good as an angel for hours. You saw him when he came in. He was a mess. Naturally he got tired of being groomed and cut and shampooed and fussed with all day."

"Uh-huh. So he lay on top of you to take a nap. And to drool on your face. But that's totally your choice, right?"

"There was a reason I permanently gave up men and took up dogs," she told Beast. And then to her boss she said, "Did you come in here just to pour grief on my head or did you have another purpose?"

"I did. A serious purpose, actually. And I promise I'll tell you in a minute, but honest to Pete, I have to do this first." Her vision was blocked by Beast's big, heavy head, but she heard the click-click-click of a camera. "There now. That should be blackmail power for at least three months—"

"Did I mention recently that I think you're low-down pond scum?"

"I don't think it came up…since yesterday anyway." He

snapped his fingers. "Now I remember why I first came in. You had a phone call."

Poppy normally had more patience than Job, but Beast's heavy, damp weight was starting to get a wee bit claustrophobic. She tried a tactful shove. It had the same effect as dust moving a mountain. "Since when would you interrupt your day to tell me I had a phone call?"

"Well, Tommy had homework, so I told him he could go home, and Lola Mae left a half hour ago. And King Tut's owner finally came in to pick him up, so I was getting ready to leave myself when the phone rang. I knew you were tied up with Beast here, but your caller didn't want to leave a voice mail. He was real urgent about wanting you to call him back, still today or tonight if you can."

"That's weird."

"Yeah, that's how it sounded. And it was a lawyer, besides."

"The only lawyer I know has a pit bull," she started to say, and Web obviously couldn't let that go.

"The only lawyer I know *is* a pit bull." He laughed at his own joke and then peered over her head with that big, shaggy St. Bernard head of his. "Would you like some help?"

"Have you ever seen me need help with an animal? I'm completely in control of the situation." Damn it. She was forty-two years old. Her clothes were soaked. Her hair and skin were damp and smelled like dog. Her back hurt. Her knees hurt. She'd never given a hoot about her appearance—what was the point when she was homelier than a coyote? But right now she'd be downright embarrassed to be seen in public—even if the only public around was Web.

"I could get him off you," the vet said mildly.

"I'll get him off when I'm good and ready. Exactly what did this lawyer say he wanted?"

"Just for you to call him back. It was Cal Asher. You know, next to the newspaper office?"

"Sure." Everyone knew Cal. He looked like a reincarnated version of Mark Twain because of the white hair and moustache. And because Cal was an institution in Righteous, people tolerated his little problem with alcohol. He was a bright man. A good guy. People just knew to make an appointment with him before noon—and to get off the road if they saw his car. "That was the whole message? For me to call him? I can't imagine what he'd want from me."

"Beats me," Web said peaceably. "Anyone suing you?"

"Not that I know of."

"You suing anyone?"

"Not that I know of."

"You smack any men around lately?"

"No one who didn't deserve it."

Web threw up his hands. "Guess you'll have to call him back yourself to figure it out, then. I'm going home. So this is your last chance to beg for help."

"I don't need help." She added quickly, "You're coming in early tomorrow to check on Lucky and Devil's Spawn, aren't you?"

"Yeah. So the longest you could be trapped here is until seven in the morning." But then Web, just because he had an evil sense of humor, suddenly whistled.

Beast immediately lifted his huge black head and

bounded to his feet. Everybody loved the vet. Canine, feline, human, didn't make any difference. Poppy loved him, too— the damn man was the best vet she'd ever known—but sometimes he was so aggravating she could smack him.

It hadn't been her best day. Beast had come in with a tangled mess of swamp spurs. Her two younger brothers had called to insist on her participation at a family party. Her laptop was sick. Her favorite jeans had blown out a knee.

The call from the lawyer was a bright spot, though. Why a lawyer, any lawyer, could conceivably want to get in touch with her was unguessable.

But Poppy had always loved a mystery.

Bren Price was polishing the altar candlesticks when the church door opened, letting in a sudden burst of late-September sunshine. Late Thursday afternoons, she often cleaned the altar, because invariably no one was using the church at that time. Right off, though, Bren guessed the reason for the interruption. A miserably distraught Martha Almond spotted her and all but ran up the aisle.

Bren met her at the base of the pews, her arms already opened wide. "So…it's bad, is it?" she asked softly.

Bren already knew the story. Martha's sixteen-year-old son had been in a car accident. It looked as if he was going to lose his leg. On top of that, the teenager was to blame for the accident because he'd been drinking and partying with a group of friends.

"Everyone's blaming me," Martha wailed. "Thing is, I'm blaming me, too. I just don't know how I could have stopped him. No matter what I ever said or did, he was just determined…"

Bren let her pour. It was the typical mom-of-a-teenager list of complaints, but the typical teenager usually managed to slip around fate. Martha's son hadn't. In time, things would get better, but right now Martha couldn't see a ray of sunshine anywhere. She was exhausted and scared and shaken.

Bren came through with tissues, a listening ear, the warmth of someone holding her. Martha wasn't the best mom or the worst. Like everybody, she tried her best, and yet sometimes her best wasn't good enough. Finally Martha's tears eased up and she sank limply against Bren's shoulder, as if just needing to gather up some strength before letting go.

At least, until the door to the chancellery opened and Charles shot through the doorway with an impatient scowl. "Bren, I've been looking all over for you—" His expression changed from night to day. He turned back into the pastor his parishioners loved, his eyes kind and his voice a gentle, easy baritone. "Why, Martha, I didn't realize you were here."

Two hours later, Bren was just putting a bubbling crock of Brunswick stew on the table when Charles walked in. One look at his face and she could feel a sick feeling in the pit of her stomach. Lately that sick feeling seemed to be there more often than not.

"Don't you think it's a little hot for a heavy meal like this?" he demanded.

"Yes, actually," she admitted wryly. "But I knew I had a full afternoon, so I was trying to put something on that we could just come in and eat whenever we were both free."

He said nothing then, just sat down and snapped his napkin open. She served iced tea, then took the salad from the refrigerator and sat down across from him. He neither looked at her nor acted as if she were in the same room. The yellow overhead revealed the sharp lines on his normally handsome face. His posture was unrelentingly stiff, his mouth forbidding.

"Now, Charles, I can see you're annoyed with me," she said carefully. "But honestly I have no idea why if you don't tell me."

"You know perfectly well what's wrong, so don't try that game."

Okay. So it wasn't going to be one of those times when she could coax him into a better humor. "Tell me anyway, all right?"

He slammed down his iced tea glass, making the liquid splash and spatter. "I've told you before. When a parishioner comes in with a problem, you're to call me. I'm the minister, not you, Bren. I'm the one they're here to see. Not you."

She felt slapped but tried not to show it. "You're angry because I was talking to Martha Almond?" she said, confused. "Charles, she was crying. I just offered another woman's shoulder—"

"You drew attention to yourself, that's what you did. You make yourself important." The chair clattered back when he stood up, his face turning pale as ice. "You've always got an excuse. I'm tired of excuses. You *know* what we're dealing with. The Baptists have no end of funds. The Methodist church just added a wing. We're struggling to survive, and here when I need you on my side, I find you doing things to sabotage me. You've let me down, Bren. Again."

He stalked off in the direction of his study, with Bren still sitting at the table. The steam from the Brunswick stew gradually disappeared. Both his plate and hers stayed untouched. The dusk outside slowly turned pitchy black, somehow making the old, worn kitchen look shabbier.

Finally Bren stood and started carting dishes. The enamel sink was chipped, the counter scarred from decades of different pastors' families over the years. The olive-green color would never have been her choice, nor the mismatched giveaway dishes, but as Charles always said, they shouldn't be focusing on material goods. Whatever they had should be given to those with real needs.

Bren agreed completely. The hunger for nice things shamed her, made her feel selfish and small.

When the dishes were done, the kitchen scoured within an inch of its life, she stood in the sink window nuzzling two small fists at the ache in the small of her back. She knew her flaws. Her secret wish for pretty clothes, for dishes she'd chosen herself, for living room furniture that didn't sag and poke. She wasn't as patient as she should be. And sometimes she stretched the truth.

She didn't used to, but lately she seemed to be truth-stretching with her husband all the time. It was the only way she could find to keep the peace. Charles was going through a terrible time. He was wonderful, as always, to the parishioners. It was her. She couldn't seem to breathe right, do right, think right. Everything about her seemed to annoy him, no matter how hard she tried.

The stress of struggling to keep the church afloat was the

core problem, she thought. But there was also the childless issue. They'd both wanted children, but at thirty-nine, Bren had quietly given up on the possibility. So had Charles, she'd believed, until he'd had some tests a couple years back and discovered he was sterile. It was those test results that seemed to turn on an angry switch inside him. No one ever saw it but her. No one would believe it if she tried to tell them—which, of course, she wouldn't.

Lately, though, she'd realized that nothing she'd done had pleased him for years. Everyone in town thought Charles was the gentlest, kindest man in Righteous.

So had she. Once upon a time.

Now it seemed as if she woke up scared and went to bed scared. Some days she felt as if she were a stranger in her own life. She even...

The phone rang on the far kitchen wall—the line that connected to the rectory office, as well. Immediately she leaped to answer it before Charles could be interrupted.

"Church of Peace," she answered swiftly.

"This is Cal Asher. I need to speak with Mrs. Price."

"That's me." She frowned curiously. She knew the name Cal Asher. Not personally—she'd never had a reason to seek out a lawyer for anything—but he cut a colorful reputation in Righteous, both for his drinking and his lawyering. He'd never stepped foot in Charles's church that she knew of, though. "Are you certain you don't want my husband, Mr. Asher—"

"No, no, it's you I'm looking for. I wondered if there was a convenient time you could come in to my office."

"What is this about?" she asked, confused.

"It's a legal matter, Mrs. Price. I'm representing a client. You're mentioned in her will on an issue that she wanted to be kept private. It won't take me long to give you the information, but I'd prefer to do it in the privacy of my office, unless that's impossible for you."

"No, no, of course it's not impossible," she said, but a fresh knot was already tying tight in the pit of her stomach. "It's a little difficult for me to pin down my husband right now. He's just so busy—"

"No, no, you're misunderstanding. It was expressly my client's wishes that I see you alone. Later, whatever you choose to tell your husband or anyone else is up to you, not my business. But for my part in this, I need a short one-on-one meeting with you to convey the issue in my client's will."

Bren started to say that that was impossible. The whole thing sounded hokey. Nothing secret was ever legitimate, now, was it? And more to the point, she never did things—serious things—without consulting Charles. She didn't have that kind of marriage.

"Mrs. Price?"

"Yes, I'm here." She clapped the receiver tighter to her ear.

"So…can you meet sometime next week? Say Monday morning, ten o'clock?"

"Yes," she said.

When she hung up the phone, she was still bewildered how or why she could possibly have agreed.

Of course, she could go right in and tell Charles about the call this very minute.

She decided to do just that. She even took a brisk step

forward—and then suddenly leaned back against the counter. She stood there without moving for a good long minute. Some instinct held her back. Maybe it was as simple as not wanting to interrupt Charles when he was already in an ornery mood.

Maybe it was something else.

She didn't know. She couldn't explain this silly, inexplicably strong intuition that she keep this information to herself…at least for now.

CHAPTER 2

When Poppy clomped up the steps to Cal Asher's office, it was five minutes to ten. She was crabby at having her Monday workday interrupted and she'd forgotten her thermos. No one—at least no one who knew her—could possibly expect her to be civil without her caffeine quota, and she'd been too darn busy this morning to guzzle it.

She charged in the gloomy vestibule and promptly found another reason to scowl. She wasn't alone. Someone else had obviously arrived ahead of her and was waiting to see Cal.

More annoying yet, the lone woman sitting there was…well, Poppy couldn't immediately remember her full name, but she was pretty sure the last name was Price and that she was a minister's wife.

Poppy liked to think of herself as tolerant, but in her heart she knew perfectly well she was allergic to churches. She had no problem with religion. Hell, she even had some herself, even if she tended to be quiet about it. But something seemed to happen to a lot of people when they attended church. They started turning into serial sinners, tended to claim their beliefs were the only right ones and then felt obligated—for God knows what reason—to push those beliefs on everybody else. Poppy knew everybody else hadn't noticed it, but as far as she could tell, something about chronic church attenders turned normal people mean, besides. They took cuts in line. Shoved in the grocery store. Demanded to be taken care of first at the vet, the doctor, the dentist, as if their problems were more important than everybody else's.

In principle, Poppy didn't care what anybody did as long as they treated their pets well. But wasting a good work morning in a lawyer's office with no one to talk to but a pastor's wife...well, it sucked.

She plunked down on a hard-back chair and glanced at her Swiss Army watch, willing the minute dial to hustle along. She'd always been very good at doing, very bad at waiting. She hadn't dressed up for this shindig because she was going straight back to work, but her one pride and joy— her mane of thick russet hair—was freshly washed. And she'd taken the trouble to throw on a sweatshirt without holes and jeans more reputable than most. Naturally she hadn't bothered with makeup because she didn't own any.

As a young teenager, she remembered believing all the advertisements zealously pushed on girls to make them think that makeup had the power to change their looks. Eventually she'd recognized that scam for what it was. Nothing was going to make her pretty. Makeup made her more vulnerable instead of less, because it drew attention to her potatoes-plain face. Better for people to think she didn't give a damn about her looks than to reveal she was sensitive about them.

Poppy glanced at her watch again, discovered less than forty seconds had passed and jumped to her feet. Might as well look around, since she couldn't sit still.

Cal Asher still practiced law in the old family home on Main Street. Everybody knew the story about how he'd been the sole holdout when the town council fought to renovate the rest of Righteous. The tall, skinny brick home was tucked between *Our Way*—the town newspaper—and various other commercial ventures, from Silver Dream to Marcella's Expert Hair Salon.

Cal's house stood out like the eccentric he was, inside and out. The parlor/waiting area may have seen an update in the '80s, but that would have been the 1880s, as far as Poppy could tell. All the furnishings would have looked elegant—in another century. Doubtful it had been dusted since. The big room was crowded with character—lots of furniture with feet, lots of cracked crown molding and blistered woodwork, lamps with fringe and dangling crystals. She accidentally caught a glimpse of a funny-looking woman with a disheveled mane of reddish hair—realized it had to be her in that wavy, gilt-framed mirror on the far wall and swiftly turned away.

She wasn't ignoring the pastor's wife. Just couldn't see a point in starting a conversation with someone she had nothing in common with. And she kept fretting who Cal was going to see first—yeah, the woman had arrived before her, but Poppy was the one who had a ten o'clock appointment. For which she'd been early. And for which Cal was now two minutes late.

The far double doors were opened by a scrawny little guy wearing a bow tie. "Miss Thompson and Mrs. Price, come this way, please."

Poppy tossed a startled look at the pastor's wife. The woman shot an equally startled look back at her—then smiled. "I didn't expect we would be called in together," the woman said.

"Neither did I. I don't understand anything about this," Poppy admitted.

"Me either. I have no idea what I'm even doing here."

Okay, Poppy thought. So the Price woman wasn't the stiff-as-dried-mud preachy type she'd instantly assumed. But they were still from alien planets. Price was wearing a mid-calf-length dress, a print with little flowers and a tidy belt. Her wheat-pale hair swayed just to her shoulders, curling under, a style that suited her perfectly. Her posture was perfect. In fact, she could have aced the course in modesty and decorum—which Poppy couldn't do if her life depended on it—and most aggravating of all, the damn woman was beautiful.

Their ages were similar; she had to be late 30s, early 40s. But she was one of those classic beauties, great bones, striking blue eyes, a tall, reed-slim figure. No hips. How could Poppy ever relate to someone who didn't know what a hip was? And the darn woman looked that good without any makeup or artifice in sight. It was enough to make Poppy want to smack her upside the head, just on general principle.

Once ushered into Cal Asher's office, Poppy quickly took the far leather chair and stretched out her legs, work boots and all. Ms. Prissy Price took the chair next to her and sat as if she were happy with a ruler up her spine.

Cal was just putting something out of sight in a side desk drawer. Poppy wasn't born yesterday; she saw him rub an arm across his mouth, clearly wiping the last traces of liquor from the swig he'd just stolen. He smiled at both of them, looking much like a genial Mark Twain from a century by-gone—give or take the rheumy eyes. "Ladies, if you don't know each other, Poppy, meet Bren, and vice versa."

They did a mutual obligatory nod, then quickly ignored each other. "I hope this won't take too long, Cal, I've got a ton of work waiting," Poppy said briskly.

"Ah, yes. Don't we all." With a dramatic flair, Cal slowly stood, shifted a bad print of hunting dogs to the side and turned the dials on a large wall safe. Eventually he pulled out two boxes—they looked like plain old children's shoe boxes—and set them on his desk. "Do you ladies know an old woman named Maude Rose?"

"This is about Maude?" Bren said bewilderedly. "But she died several weeks ago."

"Exactly. I was her attorney. Her estate was somewhat complicated because, well, Maude Rose tended to be a little on the complicated side herself. Certain situations had to be ascertained and resolved before I could contact either of you, even though you were both directly mentioned in her will." Cal settled back in his old leather desk chair. "The state has always had the peculiar idea that a person's bills should be paid and that no lien should remain on property or belongings before any legacies can be given away. Also, no one thought Maude Rose had any relatives, partly because she mentioned none in her will and no one ever saw anybody visit her. But that had to be verified, as well, before I could contact either of you. As you might suspect, when there's money involved, it's amazing how many shirt-tail relatives can suddenly show up out of the woodwork just in time to make claims."

"Mr. Asher," Bren said quietly, "if Maude Rose mentioned me in any way in her will, you can just give it to charity. I'm certainly not entitled to anything."

Poppy rolled her eyes. How sanctimonious could you get? Not that she wanted anything of Maude Rose's either. The town had treated the poor old woman like dirt. It had always infuriated her.

And Poppy was quickly guessing what this meeting was really about. Rose had no one, so obviously someone had to clean up her place and dispose of all her junk.

Hell. She'd roll up her sleeves if she had to. Better than have strangers—or people who'd been mean to her—paw through Maude Rose's private things.

"Did you hear me, Poppy?" Cal asked.

"Nope. Sorry, I drifted off there for a second." She straightened up, determined to pay more attention. The last thing she wanted was to cause this meeting to drag out any longer than it had to.

"Well now…Maude Rose felt folks treated her like a pariah. Of course, she was quite a liberal for these parts, marching for women and homosexuals and abortion and atheists and what all."

Poppy didn't want to interrupt, but damn, she could hardly let that go. "Uh, Cal? Being a supporter of women doesn't exactly label one as a wild-eyed liberal these days."

"Maybe not for you, Poppy. Your family has only been in this area for three or four generations," he said with utter gravity. "But the point I was trying to make was, you know what people thought when they saw Maude Rose. It wasn't just her politics. It was her walking down the public street in her bedroom slippers, wearing all kinds of gaudy jewelry, hanging out hours in Manny's Bar. And though most weren't aware, she'd been losing her sight for some time. Truth to tell, that might have contributed to how flagrantly she dressed sometimes and why folks were so sure she'd lost her noodles."

"If she'd lost her mind—or her sight—that was even less excuse for how some treated her," Bren said gently.

Cal Asher nodded. "Believe me, I know. Several times, the town council tried to have her put away. Had her tested to see if they could institutionalize her against her will. And then she was arrested twice last year for disturbing the peace. The mayor didn't take it too kindly when she chose to burn her underwear in his front yard." Cal scratched his chin. "I seem to have forgotten exactly what that was all about, but it sure got this town buzzing. Anyway…let me read you the paragraph in the will that Maude wrote specifically to you two."

Cal opened his desk drawer, fumbled for his glasses and eventually found a pair to prop on his nose. Poppy doubted anyone could see through the lenses, they were so smudged up, but Cal was clearly into drama and he seemed determined to draw this out.

"'People liked thinking the worst of me from the day I was born,'" Cal read. "'Just like everybody else, I'd have lived decent if I'd had the chance or the choice. But I never did. My mom died too young and my daddy was a crook. I was selling my body before I was twelve to put food in my mouth, and I'll be damned if I should feel guilty for fighting to survive. One person loved me for all I was, all I wanted to be, but Bobby Ray died a long time ago. Since then, I stopped caring. But sometimes it scraped hard when people were so mean. They didn't know me. They didn't try to know me. They were just in an all-fired hurry to decide who I was without ever even knocking on my door.'"

Cal glanced up to make sure they were paying attention, then read on. "'But there was an exception. Two women in Righteous.'" Cal whispered, "She spelled *exception* wrong and quite a number of other words, too, but—"

"Just go on, Cal," Poppy said. "We already know she wasn't a Rhodes scholar."

"I am, I am." Cal cleared his throat and put on his speech voice again.

"'The same two women stood up for me more than once. And for all the choices I never had, I'd like to give them each a choice or two. It isn't payback, because kindness never pays back in real life. But I'm dead now, so I don't have to worry about real life. And I like the idea of giving you two something for no other reason than that you was both good to me.'"

Cal glanced up again. He looked as if he'd like to spin this out a while longer, but it seemed he only had one more thing to say. "Short and sweet, she left you her jewelry, ladies."

"Her jewelry?" Poppy's jaw almost fell to the floor. She well remembered all the gaudy stones Maude Rose had piled on from her neck to her wrists to her ears and fingers. If there was a cheap rhinestone ever made, Maude Rose seemed to own it.

"Her jewelry?" Bren echoed and then abruptly chuckled. "I'm sure she meant well, Mr. Asher, but of all the people in the universe who have no use for costume jewelry—"

"It's not costume." And suddenly Cal stopped smiling. "There's a story behind Maude Rose. Years ago, she had one of her regular johns pay her in bank stock. Seemed that bank stock belonged to his grandpa and it was for a bank that he thought folded during the Depression. Anyhoo…that's what Maude Rose thought—that the stock was worthless— and she just put it in a box and forgot about it. But later, when her Bobby Ray died, she needed to clean up things, so she brought me this whole grocery bag worth of papers to sort through. It seems that bank had long revived, got a new name, been building interest for years. So it was at that point she knew she had some decent money. She wasn't going to have to worry about her future anymore."

"But I don't understand," Poppy interrupted. "I know she had that one-room apartment, but she always looked like a bag lady. No car. We've all seen her pay for groceries with change she'd count out one dime at a time. If she had money—"

"She was afraid." Cal answered the question that no one

had directly asked. "Once her lover died, she was afraid she'd be prey to thieves and gold diggers. So she chose to live in a way that would protect her from anyone knowing how much she had."

He pushed one box toward Bren, the other toward Poppy, but then cautioned them both. "We're not talking millions here, so don't be getting your hopes up too high. All those baubles aren't real. But even so, I think you'll be plum surprised at what she left you. *But…*"

Before either could open their boxes, he waggled a finger at them. "I can't tell you what to do, but I'm telling you this. Maude wanted you two to keep this quiet. She didn't want your spouses or friends or family or anyone else to know about this. That's why she insisted I set up this meeting with you two alone. Maude trusted no one. You can understand. People always used her roughly. And that was exactly why she wanted you two to hear about this in the privacy of this office with no one else here—so you'd have something you didn't have to share. That no one knew about, so they couldn't take it away from you. Something you could use for a little nest egg or to protect yourself or for something you never dreamed you could have otherwise. I can't tell you how strongly she felt about this. She didn't want anyone to try to influence you as to how you used your legacy from her."

Enough speeches. Poppy couldn't wait any longer to push the lid off her box. Hearing the whole story had almost made her believe the contents would be gorgeous…but no.

She'd seen all this cheap-looking crap on Maude Rose a zillion times. There were a couple of rings as big as her knuckle, earrings so heavy they'd tear out an earlobe. One bracelet looked like a cuff worn by a prisoner in a state pen, and a whole bunch of sparkly, glittery pins shaped like bugs and reptiles.

If it would save a puppy's life, Poppy would happily walk down a street naked. It wasn't as if she had any reason to be invested in appearance issues, with her looks. But man, it would have to be Halloween—and she'd need a snootful of Jack Daniel's—before she'd ever wear any of this stuff.

"You're sure this isn't junk?" she insisted. "It's hard to believe any of this is worth last year's newspaper."

"Some of it is definitely worthless. But not all."

"But..." Poppy glanced at Bren, who finally couldn't resist opening her box either. The jewelry was all different, but the array of dazzling sparklers in Bren's box looked as if it came off the same Cracker Jack assembly line. Tasteless, bulky, big stones in an array of eccentric and crazy-shaped bracelets and brooches and rings.

Although Poppy normally couldn't imagine having anything in common with the pastor's wife, the two women shared a mirrored look of helplessness and humor.

"I think," Bren confessed, "that I'm just too stunned to say much of anything."

"If I might offer some advice," Cal said, "I suggest that both of you take these things immediately to a jeweler to have them appraised. And then take them straight to a lockbox until you're certain what you wish to do with them."

"For my part," Bren said, "I want to give them to a charity—"

"And of course you can do whatever you like," Cal said. "That's not my business. But I'd ask you to remember Maude Rose's wishes. Most of her life, she felt trapped. She had to do things she never wanted to do. Because you were good to her, she wanted you to think about something you really wanted in your life that you never thought you could have. And to use the value of the jewelry for something that you really, really wanted."

Poppy stood. She felt odd, as if she'd been slapped by a kiss. Not that there was anything bad about this unexpected windfall, but it was still a shock. She needed some time to wrap her mind around this whole goofy thing. Bren Price looked as if she couldn't come up with anything more to say either.

Cal had a few more lawyer things to rant about before they could leave. "I need you both to sign some papers before you take the boxes. And I want to give you both a key to her apartment. The rent's paid through the end of the month, and then—unless one of you wants the place—I'll get a Realtor to do something with it. Until then, though, ladies, don't be foolish. Get yourselves to a reputable jeweler as soon as you have a chance. And keep this to yourselves until you do."

The women walked through the vestibule and out the front door at the same time. Once in the fresh air, Poppy took a healthy gulp of oxygen. Bren, quiet as the breeze, took a long second to catch her breath, as well.

"I just can't seem to believe this," Poppy said bluntly.

"Me either."

"I can't possibly go to a jeweler right now. I've got a whole day of work scheduled."

"So do I. My husband doesn't even know where I am. I can't just disappear for another couple hours, not right now." Bren added, "I keep thinking this is some kind of joke. That in another minute or two someone's going to tell me the real punch line."

"I have no use or interest in her apartment. But I'll check it out as soon as I can get some free time. I don't know if there are things to be cleaned up or if she has any personal, private belongings still in the place."

"The same problem occurred to me," Bren agreed. "I don't like the idea of going through her personal things. But it just seems…respectful…to have someone who cared about her do the job. Assuming it hasn't already been done."

Poppy wouldn't have used the word *respectful,* but she felt the same. "I don't care if you do it or I do."

"Same here."

Neither seemed willing to push the other to a decision. They stood on the porch for a while longer until the awkward silence between them stretched like a too-taut rubber band. Poppy couldn't think of anything to say to the other woman. It just felt weird leaving her, almost as weird as the impossibly strange last hour they'd just spent together.

Craziest of all—even kind of funny—was that Maude Rose must have thought the two were similar if she'd chosen them out of the whole population in Righteous to give her special legacy to. Poppy felt as much in common with Bren as a can of peas and had no doubt the other woman felt the same way.

"Well," Bren said finally, "I have to get going. I'm sure you do, too, Poppy. Good luck to you."

"Same back."

And that was that, Poppy thought. She stashed the infamous box on the passenger seat of her mint-green VW and headed out of town—which only took a couple of minutes. Righteous was built in the curl of a hillside, with three main streets curved in a semicircle. Past Cal Asher's office and the short sweep of stores, came the Baptist church, then Righteous Academy—a parochial high school—and then zip. Open road.

Two miles out of town, tucked in a nest of curly maples, was the sign for Critter Care. Web's house stood a few hundred yards beyond the clinic. He could have walked to town, but the nature of the property made the place look secluded and protected.

Conscience nagged at her—the attorney was probably right about her needing to see a jeweler or at least to put the jewelry in some kind of protective place. But when Poppy climbed out of the car, she just felt stubborn about the whole thing. You couldn't drop a bomb on a woman's head and expect it to gently sink in. At least, nothing ever sank into *her* head that easily. She needed a few minutes to take it in, think about what it all meant. Besides which, she was already twenty minutes late for an appointment with Bubba.

An extraordinary number of dogs in Virginia were named Bubba. This one happened to be a thirteen-year-old black and tan with a really mean case of arthritis.

Heaven knew where the receptionist was—Lola Mae seemed to need a cigarette break every fifteen minutes—but Web was bent over the front desk when she charged in. Typically he looked as if he'd just wakened from a tryst with a lover—his jacket was wrinkled, his shock of dark hair rumpled, his chin haphazardly shaved. He shot her one of those God's-gift-to-women grins. Poppy didn't waste time taking offense, because Web couldn't help looking like a George Clooney clone.

"It's been hell on wheels around here since you left, Poppy. So what was the deal with the lawyer?"

"I can't wait to tell you. It was just unbelievable." But she could see at a glance there was a crying cat and a bluetick hound waiting for him, and her plate was just as full. "I'll catch up with you later, okay?"

She headed straight in, past the reception desk. Her two rooms were off the left, with an outside entrance. Four years ago—after his second divorce—Web had plucked her from a life of misery behind a desk in an insurance office and conned her into being a part-time groomer for him. He'd kept adding hours as the clinic grew and her skills with it. Heaven knew, she had no formal education or training the way he did, but she'd long felt secure that she was a valued part of the clinic team. Primarily she focused on grooming, training and re-hab—and jumping in whenever they had a difficult critter to handle. She loved the tough ones. And Web kept raising her salary, until she didn't have time to spend the salary she had.

Truth was, Poppy had realized for some time that she loved animals more than people. More than herself, when it came down to it. And Web gave her a ton of freedom and encouragement to try things that worked. In this case, what worked for Bubba was a treadmill under water.

The contraption looked like a bathtub set below floor level—because she couldn't very well lift the heavier animals. Bubba was a love. This was his third time, and initially he'd liked standing in the lukewarm water. Getting him to walk on the underwater treadmill was a way of giving him exercise without putting any pressure or weight on his old hips. It worked like a dream to limber him up.

The only slight problem was that most dogs couldn't be coaxed into doing it until she got in the water with them. She didn't exactly mind. But ten minutes into the session with Bubba, she was wetter and stinkier than he was—and that wasn't too complimentary, considering how much stinky hound was in Bubba's genetic heritage.

Web stopped by a few minutes later but just to chortle in the doorway. "Tell me again—who's that exercise pool for, you or the dog?"

She ignored the insult. She was used to it. "Look how good he's doing!"

Web stepped in then and hunkered down at the dog's level to watch how Bubba moved in the water. "I never thought this was going to work when you made me build the damn thing," he admitted.

"I don't know why you keep doubting me. I've told you and told you that I'm always right." Though she easily teased him back, Web wasn't on her mind. The dog was. Damn, but the old love was able to move with so much more ease in the water. Bubba was even wagging his tail—which contributed mightily to Poppy and the floor being extra wet, but it wasn't as if she gave a damn about irrelevant stuff like that anyway.

"You have a helluva gift, Poppy," Web murmured seriously.

Sometimes she thought she did. Animals made so much more sense to her than people. A critter never stood you up and rejected you or made you feel like dirt. Give an animal love, they gave back.

When she glanced up, Web had gone back to his other patients. She did the same, finishing with Bubba, then taking on a Jack Russell named Sergeant. Sergeant's owner had been bringing him in weekly for grooming. The dog didn't need grooming, he needed training. But since his owner couldn't face up to admitting failure, Poppy called it "grooming" and just did the job.

Sergeant was smarter than most men—not that that was any exceptional accomplishment—and he took pleasure in testing all the humans in his realm to the far reaches of their patience whenever possible.

Poppy could outpatience him with no sweat, but she was whipped when her hour with him was over. By then it was two o'clock, and she was close to death from starvation.

If anyone had asked, she'd have claimed that the box locked in her car trunk hadn't given her a moment's worry. But it had. She yanked on a clean long-sleeved T-shirt, because she was too disreputable to be seen in public— even by her own loose standards.

Then she drove back into town, taking Willow Street, past all the blue-and-silver banners at the high school, past Pete's Pharmacy and Clunkers Shoe Store and Baby Buttercup Clothes for Tots. Link's was next, one of her favorite takeouts because it had great fresh deli.

She was still munching on a pastrami-on-rye when she pulled into the parking lot next door, behind Ruby's Rubies. The name was hokey, but the owner's last name was actually Ruby, so it wasn't his fault. And of the three jewelry stores in town, everyone seemed to inherently know that Ruby's was the best.

That wasn't why she'd chosen the place, though. Anonymity was. One of her younger brothers was a sheriff deputy and the other volunteered with the fire department—which meant they heard all the Righteous gossip almost before a juicy story could even happen. When Poppy wanted to do something on the Q.T., she had to be sneaky enough to slip under their radar.

She was already known here, although heaven knew, not because she'd ever purchased any jewelry.

She popped in the front door, the box under her arm. The bells jangled over the door, but initially she saw no one and called out, "Hey, Ruby!"

Ruby was a one of a kind. Agewise, he had to be somewhere between forty and a hundred. He had a nose so hooked it could have caught fish, hair that streamed down his back in wiry strings and quiet gray eyes. He'd never cracked a smile that Poppy had ever seen, but he had a framed photograph over his door. It said Nature's Most Savage Predator and showed a five-week-old orange-striped kitten peeking fearlessly over the side of a wicker basket.

Poppy had met Ruby when he'd brought the kitten in to the vet for the first time. She'd seen how he acted with the baby. Didn't have to know him better than that to know he was a trustworthy kind of guy.

His store, though, was an alien planet. Two rows of counters gleamed with baubles and glitter. Lots of watches. Lots of wedding rings. Lots of rainbow-colored junk to dazzle the eye. Poppy heard a woman's voice in the back room and realized Ruby must have a customer back there—but before she could duck out the door, he suddenly showed up in the workroom doorway.

She opened her mouth to say what she needed, when he simply said, "Come on back," as if he already knew.

He couldn't, but she really didn't want to display the contents in the public front of the store anyway, so she trailed him into the back room. And then lifted her eyebrows in surprise.

Bren Price was already there. Her jewelry goodies were spilled out on a velvet scarf, where Ruby had obviously been studying her pieces.

"I had to know, too," Bren said as if they'd been carrying on a conversation.

"I can do this via separate appointments if you want," Ruby said in his deep, quiet baritone. "But I'm guessing you both have similar kinds of questions. I can do a short, cursory appraisal for you both right now—at least, if we're not interrupted by customers."

"I don't know what questions either of us have. But I'm okay with your handling us together, if that's all right with Bren," Poppy said frankly.

"It's all right with me," Bren affirmed.

After that, neither woman spoke for quite a while. Poppy figured she wasn't *that* surprised to find Bren there. They were both women, after all.

No female alive could survive a major dose of curiosity indefinitely. Although Poppy couldn't believe this could possibly be a serious financial legacy—and probably neither did Bren—she just plain had to know what all that gaudy jewelry was worth so she could put her curiosity at ease.

Clearly Ruby had been working for some time on Bren's cache of sparklers, because there was stuff all around him—paper, pencil, a monocle, some kind of fancy microscope. Once he went back to concentrating, Poppy could see a pattern emerge. He kept looking at the jewelry, then his instruments, then Bren. "Jesus," he said.

And then, "Jesus," he repeated.

By the time he spun his stool to Poppy's stash and dived into her mother lode, he seemed to have that mantra down pat. The only variance in his vocabulary seemed to be an occasional, "Jesus, Mother and Mary."

Poppy asked once, "How's the Lion, Ruby?" referring to Ruby's kitten, but he completely ignored her. Truth to tell, he didn't seem to give a particular hoot if either woman was in the room.

That didn't bother Poppy, but even for an irreverent antichurch person like herself, his choice of words started to get to her. Eventually she had to interrupt. "Look, I couldn't care less if you use four-letter words until the cows come home, but you know Bren's a minister's wife, right? I mean, I realize she isn't objecting, but I'd think…"

He just whispered, "Jesus," again in an awe-filled tone, as if the two women weren't even there.

A customer came in—all of them heard the bell—but Ruby jogged out to the storefront, said something, ushered the customer out and hung up his Closed sign.

In Righteous, no one turned down customers. Business was never that good.

"All right," Poppy said finally, "you're scaring me, assuming you aren't scaring Bren. I sure as hell don't want to interrupt your concentration. The sooner this gets done the better. But if you could just give us some idea what's going on here…?"

He couldn't be rushed. Poppy kept looking at her watch. Bren kept looking at hers.

Finally Ruby lurched off his stool and stood up, knuckling the ache at the small of his back as he gave them the bad news. He started with Bren, going through the handfuls of jewelry piece by piece. "Now all these beads here, they likely came from a five-and-dime at best. But then you see the yellow one? This one? That's a blond diamond."

"I never heard of a blond diamond."

"That's because most folks in these parts don't tend to shop on Fifth Avenue. And you see this brooch?"

"The one with all those rhinestones and the strange peach stone shaped like a tongue?"

The brooch in question was Bren's, but Poppy leaned closer to get a look, too. It was almost as ugly as the stuff in her hoard. The weird pink stone really did look like an animal's tongue hanging out.

"That ain't a tongue," Ruby said. "It's a conch pearl. And those rhinestones are diamonds. I need some time, but at first guess I believe that brooch is worth somewhere near a hundred grand."

"Excuse me?" Bren's voice was as faint as a mile-away whisper.

"A hundred thousand dollars."

"Excuse me?"

"Then there are these long earrings here. The ones with the pink tourmaline and black gold and peridots and diamonds and all…" He held up the trashy, flashy things. "I can't give you an exact price until I've studied 'em more, but off the cuff I'd say they're worth in the ballpark of fifty grand."

"Excuse me?"

Ruby said to Poppy, "You best get her a chair before she falls over."

Poppy went chasing after another stool. As an afterthought, she rolled a third stool over from the back of the store for herself.

Bren plunked down on hers, looking as pale as if she'd been stung by a wasp and was experiencing the first waves of shock.

"We'll give her a minute to breathe," Ruby said to Poppy and then started playing with her stash. "I can't say I care for this particular pin. It's as big as a padlock, for Pete's sake. Just don't know where a woman could wear it. But the platinum and diamonds are something else. I never seen anything like her. I'm not committing it to paper until I've studied it more, but don't think there's any question we're talking around a hundred and fifty grand."

"Say *what?*" Poppy said.

"And this cuff bracelet. Lots of those little stones are just chips, nothing that's gonna save the farm, so to speak, but those two big stones at the end are kunzite. Good kunzite. Don't know much about the stone, but anybody can see they're really good quality. I'd throw out twenty-five thousand for an initial guess."

"*Say what?*"

"The tanzanite beaded necklace, now, isn't quite as good as you'd think—"

"Trust me, Ruby, I'm not thinking."

"I'm just saying. People know of tanzanite being rare, so they generally assume it's more valuable than it is, when tanzanite is too soft a stone for a lot of applications. This one's in a protected setting, though. It's all right. Good stones. An interesting piece, but I still have to say I don't think it'll be worth more than ten K."

"Say what?"

"Look, ladies. I need time with pieces like this to give you a true appraisal. And I'm not too proud to admit, I may have to consult with some other jewelers, check the market. Not like I'm regularly exposed to pieces like this. But offhand I'm guessing you each have jewelry valued somewhere in the two-hundred-thousand-dollar price range."

CHAPTER 3

Two hundred thousand dollars. Bren stood at the gas pump, filling the church van before she headed home. Typically almost everyone stopping for gas was a face she knew, so she waved and smiled and did some chitchat. But her mind was still roller coastering up and down the mental hills of two hundred thousand dollars. Two hundred thousand dollars. Two hundred thou. Two hundred K. Two hundred grand.

Anyway you said it, it was beyond anything she'd imagined.

As a child, she'd grown up safe financially. But that was the last time she remembered not worrying about every dime and every bill.

"Hey, Mrs. Price, how you doing?" Joey greeted her when she plucked a few bills from her cracked wallet. He'd galloped out of the station to clean her windows the instant he'd seen the church van. She had to give him something.

"Doing just fine, Joey. How's your mom? Her foot any better?"

There was no way to escape the conversation. She knew Joey and his sister, knew their mom, knew what a rough road the family had had ever since the mom had been laid up with foot surgery. She'd carted over dinners herself the first week. Charles had added prayers for them in his church sermon. People mattered more than money, so darn it, caring just couldn't be rushed. But when Bren finally climbed back into the church van, she hoped God would forgive her—and the Virginia cops, too—because she sped out of town as fast as the old engine would let her.

Giddy euphoria danced in her pulse. She couldn't wait to tell Charles about their good fortune. She could picture the relief on his face. Picture them sharing a moment of joy together. Picture that harsh look of stress ease on his face for the first time in months.

She wheeled through yellow lights at Willow, then Main, then wheeled left on Baker Road. She supposed it didn't make too much sense to speed past the courthouse, then past the police and fire stations, as well. But there wasn't a policeman in town who didn't know her, so if one was going to do something wrong, Bren figured she might as well do it in plain sight. Past all that busy part of town, of course, was their Church of Peace.

A little neighborhood of houses clustered around their church. Maybe someone thought the area would become a bedroom community of D.C. back in the fifties, but that kind of prosperity never discovered the area. People were hanging on, raising their kids, but this side of Righteous was visibly struggling.

Their church looked as wilted as the rest of the structures. She was just a white frame building, long and narrow, with their house—the parsonage—just beyond the parking lot. Charles often used their home for different gatherings; so did she. The church basement was also huge, ample for events like bible readings and meals and craft sales and all that kind of thing. Even had an old, spotless kitchen down there. Bren had planted bushes and flowers when they could afford them, taken care that the church was always polished and spotlessly clean. So maybe it didn't look like much on the outside, but inside it was safe and peaceful and had that warm-glow welcoming feeling.

Or it used to. Before things got so tight.

She parked at the house but hightailed it immediately toward the office at the back of the church, assuming she'd find Charles there. But no. She found nothing but dust motes dancing silently in the sunlight. The message light blinked on the answering machine. Charles's jacket still hung on the old pine tree. A sermon in progress sat half-finished on the desk.

He must have taken off for some reason, and she wanted to head straight for the house, to check there. But first she grabbed a pen and paper and took the messages. Whenever Charles came back, he'd want to know who had called and why, and often enough, she could field questions on her own, without bothering him.

That done, she hustled toward the house, realizing with a half laugh that she was out of breath, had been probably since she'd left the jeweler's. "Charles!" she called as she pushed open the screen door to the kitchen and then stopped abruptly.

Charles had his white shirt rolled up, hands on his hips. He swiveled around abruptly when he heard the door open.

She had the impression he'd been pacing. Her heart sank fifty-seven feet—and fast—when she saw the straight-lipped, tight-jawed expression on his face.

"Where were you?" He asked it in that certain tone. The tone that claimed he had tons and tons and tons of patience and now was completely out.

She tried to calm her panicky pulse, but that particular tone always rub-burned her nerves. She couldn't *think* when he was irritated with her. And though she'd always valued honesty, she heard a half-truth babble from her mouth. "I was just talking to a woman in town—"

"What woman?" he demanded, again his tone sharper than ice.

She couldn't explain why she hedged telling him the whole truth. It's not that she wanted to lie to him—ever, ever—but when she felt that anger coming at her, some instinct took over. She wasn't thinking about lies or truth. She was just thinking about doing whatever she could to mollify him. "No one from the church, Charles. No one you would have felt you needed to talk to yourself. Just a woman who stopped to chat with me. I didn't think there was a problem. I had no idea you were waiting for me—"

He yanked out a chair from the kitchen table, making a scraping noise that made her jump. She understood he wanted her to sit down, which seemed a fair idea, for them to try sitting and talking together—only Charles didn't sit.

Once she was parked, he loomed over her and started talking in that tone again. The acid tone. The acid-angry scary-quiet tone. "I took you in when you were an orphan.

You had nothing and no one, remember that? Just your dad in a hospital bed and no way to take care of him or yourself. You didn't have a roof over your head. I still remember how beautiful you were. How lost. Seventeen, and so crippled on the inside to lose your mother and sister in the same accident. But I came through for you, didn't I, Bren? Didn't I?"

"Yes. I know you did. And I've always been grateful—"

"*This* is how you show me how grateful you are?" He yanked out another chair, just to make the squeaky noise again, just to vent more of that rage. Maybe just to make her jump again. "By disappearing for hours at a time?"

"But, Charles, I had no idea you needed me for anything this afternoon—"

"Right. How could you know when you didn't even bother to ask?" He switched subjects faster than an eye blink. "I had the pastor breakfast this morning—assuming you could bother remembering. Everyone's doing a fund-raiser for the hurricane in the south. We need to put on a fund-raiser, too. A bigger one. A lot bigger and better one than the Baptists are putting on."

"All right." She was thrilled to change the subject. Even though she knew that part of his anger was nerves and stress and not necessarily *about* her, somehow he made her feel…small. When he started ranting like that, she just wanted to sit tight with her knees together and her arms pressed at her sides and her head tucked, so that she took up the tiniest amount of space possible. It was kind of a goofy sensation. Just wanting to make herself as close to invisible as she could get.

She should be listening to her husband and working on the problem, working on and with him, instead of hiding out in some goofy mental corner. It shamed her that she wanted to disappear like a child instead of handling the real problems between them. But right then, God help her, she just wanted him to calm down and lose that icy look.

"Whatever you've been spending your time on, it isn't as important as this. I want you to spearhead this fund-raiser. I need ideas for something different. Something that will really grab the community's attention and interest. Not the same old bake sale or craft sale. Something *good*."

She'd put on the last bake sales and yard sales and craft sales. All of them had brought in hefty donations, she'd thought. Just not enough to satisfy her husband. But it wasn't his fault that times were so hard.

"Okay, I'll be glad to," she said.

"I want some kind of plan to discuss by dinner tonight."

She didn't look at her watch, didn't dare, but thought it had to be already past three. Charles was still circling the table, finding things to thump around, but at least he'd stopped looming over her.

"Then I'll include information about it in the sermon this Sunday, put it all together, start to get our parishioners excited about it. We need to look proactive."

She lifted her head, feeling a spark of enthusiasm catch her now, too. "I couldn't agree more. We should be proactive in times of trouble like this. And maybe you could put just a little less fire and brimstone in your sermon. Concentrate more on themes about coming together, on—"

God. She'd blown it again. He surged around the table faster than the lash of a whip. "Excuse me? Were your criticizing my sermons?"

"No. No, of course not, Charles. I just—"

"You think I don't know how to write a good sermon? That I need *advice* how to do my job?"

"Charles…" She couldn't maintain this razor-sharp level of anxiety. It was just too crazy. "Charles, come on. For heaven's sake. Lately you're angry at me for anything I say. I was just trying to make a suggestion—"

The next seconds passed in a blur. She doubted he'd heard her. He wasn't listening; he was charging around the table toward her like an angry bull.

She saw him lift his hand. Saw his hand was folded in a fist. Saw the dark, livid color shooting up his neck.

As crazy and ridiculous as the thought was, for that second she actually believed he was going to hit her.

Her heart stopped. Not just her heart, the physical organ, but the core of her emotions suddenly seemed to go still, deep down. She felt as if something died, some feeling, some hope, nothing she could name…yet the sense of loss was as real as her own pulse.

"Oh, for God's sake," Charles said abruptly. He lowered his arm, dropped that fist. Then said nothing else, just stormed out the back door. The screen door slapped behind him.

Bren sat statue-still for a few more minutes…until the oddest thing happened. She saw a vague silhouette of a reflection in the kitchen window. It had to be a stranger, that cringing woman with the submissive bent head. It couldn't be her. How could it possibly be her?

For that brief second she felt like a stranger in her own life.

But then, of course, she got a grip. Stood. Started dinner, started brainstorming fund-raising events.

Charles was going to be terribly upset and apologetic when he came to his senses, realized how mean he'd been to her. She was sure of it.

Three evenings later, it was pouring buckets when Bren turned the key on Maude Rose's apartment. The place was on Willow, with a private set of stairs over Ms. Lady Lingerie and Clunkers. Everyone knew there were apartments above the retail shops, but who ever thought about them? Until she'd known Maude Rose, she'd never considered what those apartments looked like or who lived in them.

A naked lightbulb illuminated the dingy stairs—not enough to make the lock easy to see. Once inside Maude's door, she fumbled around the wall for a switch. Lightning crackled just as she located the overhead. Slowly she slipped off her damp jacket, startled at her first look at the place.

Charles often spent one night a month in Charlestown with elders of the church, a prayer retreat sort of thing with a dozen other pastors. It never crossed Bren's mind to check out the apartment until he'd been on the road. Then the impulse hit. There was no one to question or argue with her if she chose to come here tonight.

For the first time since she could remember, she had a completely private spot to think. Maybe that was part of what had spurred the impulse to come here. More than that, though, she really wanted to know more about the woman who'd given her such a generous legacy—especially because Bren had no idea Maude Rose even knew she'd stood up for her now and then.

And now, as she glanced around, the first shock was discovering the pale pink living room walls. Not red, not neon, not splashy or vulgar. But a quiet, clean pastel, recently painted. As far as Bren could tell, the apartment only had a bedroom, a bathroom and then this one big L-shaped room.

The fat part of the L had windows overlooking the street below. The skinny part of the L was the kitchen and eating area. Or it had been.

Bren heard the clomp of footsteps on the noisy stairs and spun around. Hard to tell who was more surprised, her or Poppy.

"I'll be damned. Who'd have thought we'd have the same idea on the same night?" Poppy asked wryly, but her grin was wary. "Hey, if you want the place to yourself, go for it. I can come back another time—"

"I think it's great you're here. It'll give us a chance to put our heads together and figure out what to do with the place at the same time."

Poppy nodded. "I don't even know why I came tonight. The curiosity bug just keeps getting to me. Who Maude Rose really was. How and why she picked us to give that stuff to, when I don't remember her even speaking to me. In fact, I didn't know she realized I'd defended her now and then. And I just…those jewels, you know? That whole thing's still bowling me over."

"I know. Me, too." Bren, all her life, had felt easy around people, loved people in all their facets and colors and rainbow choices of personalities. But Poppy was a puzzle.

She'd looked nervous as a newborn colt when she'd first stepped in. Shed a dripping rain jacket at the door, dropped it. She was such a character, Bren thought. A full-grown rag-amuffin. Gorgeous hair, all red and gold and blond, thick and glossy—but she wore it shaggy and rumpled, washed and dried as if it were polyester. The clothes appeared to be rejects from a rag bag—the jeans were too tight in the behind, dirty in the knees, thready at the hems; the flannel shirt was twice too big for her frame.

Poppy's face fascinated her the most, though. Her dark eyes were bright with intelligence and sassy humor. She had a long, wide mouth, skin softer than a baby's. The nose took up too much space. So did the chin. But there were so many contradictions in that face, so much character. Poppy seemed shamelessly irreverent, hopelessly blunt…so much her own woman, the way Bren had always wanted to be herself. Everything about Poppy seemed to capitalize a strong woman, unafraid to fight for whatever mattered to her…yet that essential gutsiness was shadowed by something else. Anger, Bren was almost sure.

Somewhere inside that brash, artsy package was a lot of anger at something. The way she walked, the way she moved, Poppy always seemed braced for someone to cut her or hurt her—and ready to lash out when and if anyone tried.

"*Pink?* You gotta be kidding me," Poppy said when she saw the walls. She pushed out of her wet shoes, tromped around barefoot.

Bren hadn't felt comfortable at baldly opening cupboards and drawers, but sheesh, as long as Poppy was doing it, she indulged in her curiosity, too. "Apparently it was rented furnished."

"You guessing that by the crappy furniture?" Poppy said wryly. "Yeah, I'd guess the same thing. Thinking about an old lady trying to ease her tired bones on a cheap futon kind of makes me sick." She spun around. "Did you see this?"

Bren nodded. She'd already noticed the picture on the far wall. It wasn't a good print or even a poster. Just a picture cut out from a magazine of a stone hearth with a blazing fire. It put a lump in Bren's throat. "Maude Rose never had the warmth of a real fireplace, I'm guessing."

"Everything around this damn place makes me think she was so damn lonely that I'd like to hit someone. Pardon my French." Poppy opened a kitchen cupboard. Bren came up behind her to view the contents. The two women exchanged glances.

The shelf held two plates, two cups, two saucers—all cheap, chipped pottery. But also on the shelf sat a half-used candle, rose-scented.

"Damn it," Poppy said again.

Bren didn't say it, but she felt the same way. The candle still had a whiff of that soft, vulnerable scent. Again she hurt for the old woman's loneliness. For something inside Maude Rose that so few had ever seen. A softness. A yearning for something pretty, something gentle, something feminine.

"I've got to quit saying *damn it* around you," Poppy grumped. "I think it's because I know you're a pastor's wife. I mean, I swear. But not every two seconds."

"It's all right."

Poppy started spinning around again. "Pretty obvious the furniture comes with the place. But I don't think we should rent this place out—or let anyone else see it—until we've taken out some things. Like the candle. And the picture. And whatever else we find that belonged to Maude Rose that's..."

"Personal." Bren nodded. She shuffled through a handful of books on the stand by the TV. Dilbert. Garfield. Not reading books, just cartoons. On a wall shelf, she found records. Not CDs or tapes but old records—the kind that had to be played on a turntable. Only there was no turntable. Just the big, black disks. She read the labels to Poppy. "*Night and Day*, Frank Sinatra. Who's Montavani?"

"Don't know."

"Cal Tjader. Ella Fitzgerald. Miles Davis. Wes Montgomery." Bren recognized some of the names, not all. "I'd hate to think she loved this music and then had no way to play it."

"Bren?"

"What?"

Poppy stood in the doorway of the bathroom. "I think we need a glass of wine. Or beer."

"Oh, I can't sta—" Bren clipped off her knee-jerk response. It must be the stranger living in her life that said,

"Actually, I can stay for a while. And I think a little drink's a good idea. Hmm, I'm trying to think of the closest place that might sell a bottle of wine—"

"Manny's Bar. Maude Rose's hangout. Which seems fitting. I'll spring for it."

By the time Poppy returned, she was soaked all over again, laughing at what a rotten, blustery night the storm had turned into. By then, Bren had filled a couple of grocery bags with things of Maude Rose's. She wasn't sure what to do with them but left them for Poppy to see so they could decide together.

"I guess I should have asked if you'd rather have a soda instead of something alcoholic," Poppy said.

"You know," Bren said mildly, "just because I'm married to a minister doesn't mean that I don't drink, don't swear or can't have a bitchy mood just like anyone else."

"You just said *bitchy*."

"Yes." Bren glanced out the window. "And I see quite a bit of lightning, but none of the lightning bolts seemed to have shot me down, so I guess God must be in a forgiving mood today."

Poppy squinted at her. "Was that a joke?"

"Oh, no. I never joke about God shooting me down with lightning bolts."

Apparently that kind of teasing was what it took for Poppy to relax around her. Contrary to Bren's claim, she really didn't drink—at least, not normally. But when she started to sip that first glass, it seemed the right thing to do. It wasn't that easy for her to relax around Poppy any more than the other way around. Slowly, though, they seemed to be finding their way around each other.

"So you left your jewels with Ruby," Poppy said. "Mine, now, they're still in my fridge."

"Your *refrigerator!* You can't be serious."

"Can you imagine a thief opening the fridge for anything to steal? Besides which, I've just been so darn busy. I'll do something serious as soon as I can catch some free time. Anyway, the point is, do *you* know what you're going to do with your side of the loot?"

"No. Not yet." She took another sip of wine, let the dry taste swirl on her tongue. "How about you? When you get that free time…do you have some ideas what you're going to do with the money?"

Poppy was still opening and closing things as she drank, and so far she'd finished three glasses compared to Bren's first three sips. "You know, my first thought on this place is just to find someone who needs a place. A kid graduating from high school, first job kind of thing. Someone wanting to live independent. Or needing to. But someone needing something cheap."

"A girl, not a guy," Bren said.

Poppy nodded immediately. "Yeah. I know we shouldn't discriminate, but…"

"But it'd feel good to do something for a girl who needed help," Bren added thoughtfully. "From what Cal Asher said, Maude had enough funds in the kitty to pay for several more months' rent. So it wouldn't cost us to hold on to the place for a while. Give us the time to find the right person."

"I'm not sure how to guess who Maude Rose might have wanted here. Except…a girl who needs a safety net."

"Yeah. And a girl who needs a little kindness passed along." Bren found it astounding how easily they were talking about this. But she'd definitely noticed how Poppy had initially ducked the question of her inheritance. Before she could ask her again, though, Poppy motioned her closer.

"Bren! Look what I found!" Poppy had just topped her third glass—again—when she sloshed it on the scarred plastic table. Apparently she'd spotted something under an upholstered chair, because suddenly she knelt down and reached deep under there. She emerged with an old wrinkle-edged cigar box.

"Um, doesn't look like much of a treasure. Maybe if you smoked," Bren said doubtfully.

Poppy rolled her eyes. "It's not about smoking, you silly. Cigar boxes are for hiding treasures."

"This is a rule where?" Bren asked wryly, but they both bent over the box to view the contents. Neither touched. They just looked. There was a dried-up daisy. A newspaper with its name cut off, just a scrap of yellowed paper with the cutout date of November 7, 1984. A beach shell, broken. A photo of a couple from the '40s, judging from their clothes, but it was so faded and crackled it was hard to tell. Another photo of a young man—skinny, scrawny, standing by a motorcycle, looking cockily as if he owned the world.

Slowly Bren said, "You're right. They are treasures."

"Impossible to guess what they meant to her."

"No way to know," Bren agreed.

"I guess we should throw it all away."

"I guess we should. What else could we do with it anyway?" Yet Bren looked at Poppy's face, sighed and said, "Okay, let's just put it back under the chair for now. We'll throw it away. Eventually."

"I know we will." Poppy put on her tough, defensive face. "Hell, how stupid to be sentimental about stuff like that. What difference could it possibly make now?"

"You're so right," Bren murmured. She tried to look away from Poppy, but for that instant—whether Poppy knew it or not—her eyes glistened when she saw that cheap dried flower. So had Bren's. But then, Bren had no illusions about herself that she was tough. "Hey, Poppy…I didn't mean to pry before. You don't have to tell me what you plan to do with your jewels. I was just making conversation."

"Hey, I wasn't ducking it."

She was, but Bren wasn't about to call her on it. She watched Poppy toss back the rest of her wine. The Ms. Tough expression was back in place.

"I want to have my face fixed," she said bluntly.

"Your face? What's wrong with your face?"

Poppy rolled her eyes again. "Come on. It's obvious. My whole life, I've been butt-ugly. But I always thought I just had to live with it. Now suddenly I don't have to. And it's not as if I need the money for anything else." She scowled at Bren. "You don't approve."

"It's not up to me to approve or disapprove."

"But you think it's vain. Frivolous. A dumb thing to do with the money."

"I never said that," Bren defended herself.

"You didn't have to. It's all over your expression. But you never had to live with a face like this. You don't have my history. You don't even know me—"

Bren said quickly, "Poppy, I'm sorry if I offended you. Or if you felt I was judging you. You just took me by surprise, that's all. I had no idea what you were going to say."

But Poppy closed down tighter than a threatened clam. She corked the wine, put attitude in her shoulders, carted her glass to the sink. She was obviously making moves toward leaving. "So what about you, anyway? What'd your husband say when you told him about your windfall?"

Now it was Bren's turn to fall silent. Poppy turned. "Bren?"

Bren punched out cheerfully, "I haven't gotten around to telling him yet." It was her turn to leap to her feet. She aimed for the sink, figuring she'd wash both glasses. Oh, and check the contents of the refrigerator. Neither of them had looked inside to see if there was food that needed throwing out.

Poppy hadn't moved. Was still staring at her. "Well, hell. I didn't mean to ask some heavy, loaded question."

"It isn't a loaded question. It's just a little different circumstance. It's hard to explain."

"No need to strain yourself. It's none of my business."

"I'm *going* to tell him. He'll be really happy. I mean, who wouldn't at such an extraordinary surprise—"

"Uh-huh. That's why you didn't tell him immediately, right? Because he'd be so happy."

"It's hard to explain," Bren repeated uncomfortably.

They both left at the same time. Both had keys, lifted a hand to lock the door at the same moment. Went to take the stairs down at the same moment. Hesitated at the same moment before taking off in the pouring rain in opposite directions.

Bren couldn't stop thinking how nice it had been between them for a while. Just talking together, more easily than either could ever have expected. It was as if the bond of Maude Rose had somehow paved the way for a friendship between them. They shared a secret. A secret that seemed to open the doors to communicating, talking about things they wouldn't or couldn't normally.

But that door had sure slammed shut fast.

Bren was still shaking her head—who could ever, would ever, guess that a woman who dressed as ragamuffinlike as Poppy would want plastic surgery? That vanity or looks was even a thought in her head?

And for herself...well, obviously she couldn't just *tell* Poppy about her marriage. You couldn't explain something like that in a single sentence or a couple of seconds.

Heckapeck. Bren had been trying for days, weeks and now months to explain to herself what the Sam Hill was going wrong between her and Charles. If she couldn't figure it out herself, how on earth could she tell a stranger?

CHAPTER 4

A week from Thursday, Poppy came to work with her internal engine on rev. She'd been to a plastic surgeon in D.C. Actually, she'd seen a second one in Arlington, as well. And as soon as she'd poured a mug of sludge from the community caffeine pot, she tracked down Web.

She knew he'd be busy, just wanted to pin him down to a quick conversation later. It wasn't as if they didn't pass each other a zillion times during the average workday, but she didn't want to discuss arrangements in public.

She heard his voice in exam room one and jogged there—yet ended up standing in the doorway without saying a word. Web was with a gorgeous golden retriever—and the retriever's owner.

Pauline was thirty-something, buxom and brunette, pretty enough if you went for the poured-in-jeans type, and was batting her eyelashes at Web as if they were lethal weapons. Poppy had all she could do not to laugh.

All the women went for Web. He couldn't help looking like a hunk, but it was still fun to watch an unwitting Roman being circled by a determined lioness. All Web had to do was smile at a female—any age, zero or ninety, and pretty words seemed to promptly spew from the woman's mouth like bubbly sea foam.

Web, turning to examine the retriever's ears, caught sight of her in the doorway and shot her a please-God-save-me! look. Poppy just heartlessly grinned. Maybe he could get the golden retriever to rescue him, assuming the dog wasn't female and didn't fall head over heels, too.

She finally caught up with him at lunch, more by chance than plan. Web usually took off at noon, but he had a patient coming out of surgery. Mrs. Bartholomew's cat. The cat would have been just fine in the recovery cage, but Web was Web. Took better care of people's pets than they did.

More to the point, about the same second Poppy remembered there was cold pizza in the lab fridge, so did he. Seeing him gave her the excuse to grouch about her last customer. A cocker. The owner only came to her because no one else in a three-county radius would handle the spoiled little snapper.

"But it's not that," Poppy groused. "The dog has every right to snarl and growl when it's miserable. It's just that I don't get why they insist on owning a cocker when both of them like to tromp through the woods. It's just not fair. She always comes back full of prickers and burrs, and you know how cocker fur is to brush…"

Web pretended to listen to this rant—he'd heard it all before—as he helped himself to his share of the cold pizza, the part with the mushrooms. Both dived for the stash of Dr. Pepper. Rain started dribbling down the windows. A serious storm was coming in fast, judging by the darkening sky. Poppy reached up behind her to flick on the overhead.

The so-called break room was really the lab. Blood tests and X-rays and other tests were isolated in one section, but the sink and dishwasher functioned for both. A microwave made it easier to eat inside on bad-weather days, and the cot-bed was used for anyone who didn't feel good—or for Web when he was spending the night for a favorite patient, which, of course, he'd never admit to on his deathbed. The closet had lab coats and at least one change of clothes for anybody who needed them—primarily Web and her. A critical drawer to the left of the sink was reserved for life essentials: Heath bars, jelly beans, butterscotch buttons.

"So did you survive the soccer mom this morning with your virtue intact?"

"The soccer mom?"

"Don't waste your breath playing innocent with me. You know I mean the one with the size-eight jeans squeezed on a size-twelve ass. The one with the retriever." Poppy rose up yet again to reach for napkins, which neither of them ever seemed to remember before they dived into food.

"Pauline. And, hey, you saw I needed help. How come you took off?"

"Because she's cute. And God knows she worships the ground you walk on. I thought you could use a little hero worship this morning. And it's been a while since you've succumbed…I thought maybe you needed to get laid."

Web sighed. And chomped down on more pizza. "You know way, way too much about my private life. Or you think you do."

"What, was that a rash assumption? You don't need to get laid?" she asked innocently.

"Not to or by Pauline. No." For an instant she caught the oddest glint of light in his eyes. But it was probably just a reflection. The window view of the Shenandoah Mountains in the distance suddenly showed a scissor of heavy-duty lightning. "I don't need to be hooked up with any more divorcées—or nondivorcées, for that matter—who think I've got money."

"I hate to tell you this, cookie, but it was never your money drawing the girls. It's your adorable butt."

Web wasn't born yesterday. He put up with so much and then shoveled it back. "You have a cute butt, too, but I don't see you running around getting either laid—or married—all the time."

She laughed, thinking that was just the thing about Web—why they worked together so well, why they talked together so easily. She'd been hurt in her relationships. He'd been hurt in his. The reasons for their respective disastrous personal lives were entirely different, but the point was that they could easily tease each other without fear of it being taken the wrong way.

Web was too good-looking to notice a woman with her physical appearance, besides, making it even easier to banter from their respective sides of the gender fence. After two divorces, Web was so antimarriage he might as well wear a sign. And she'd had it with men who assumed it was okay to treat her ugly just because she physically was.

"Hey." That second piece of pizza had taken the edge off. Web was still diving in. A good time for her to bring up more serious subjects. "I need to ask you something."

"Sure. Shoot." Although he glanced at her warily. "You want me to haul in wood for your fireplace this winter, right?"

"No. Well, yes. But this is a little more serious. I need some time off."

"You're telling me this why? Your schedule is totally up to you. You sure don't need my permission."

"I know that, but…I need a little help." Her tangle with the cocker had left her pale yellow sweatshirt fringed with cinnamon hair. Web's theory was the same as hers, that a meal without animal hair would be like Thanksgiving without turkey—too unnatural to consider. But just once in a blue moon she'd like to stay clean for just a few hours. "I'm going to have a little surgery done. Nothing huge, but…I'm going to need a couple weeks off from work. And I'll actually not be home for about three days. That's the time when I'm worried about Edward—"

"That damned rabbit?"

"Edward is not a damned rabbit. He just has a little problem with anxiety attacks. You would, too, if a human had practically burned off your behind. But the problem is that no one can seem to feed him but me. And, I have to believe, you. And then there's Snickers."

"You don't still have that cat," Web said positively.

"Don't you start on me, cookie. I couldn't take him to the shelter. Who would ever adopt her? She's blind in one eye and doesn't have a nose. She's almost beyond ugly."

"When she first came in after the accident, you could have listened to me. We could have made the intelligent choice and put her to sleep."

"You talk real big," she said darkly, "but wasn't it just last month you took in that scruffy, mangy, derelict-looking mutt—"

"Now wait a minute. That's completely different. I'll find a home for Blue. He just needs to be more recovered..." Web seemed to shake himself. They'd been down this conversational road dozens of times. Which she knew, and which was why she'd started it, to distract him. "Let's backtrack five miles. You know I'll take care of your godforsaken rejects, just like you'd take care of mine. So forget that. What's this surgery about?"

"Just a minor procedure." She glanced at the clock, then popped to her feet.

"Don't give me that shit. What are you having the surgery for? You need someone to be there?"

"No, honestly. You know I have a dad and two brothers. They'd smother me with help if I needed it—and most of the time when I don't." She squished a little dish soap in the sink. There were only a handful of dishes to clean up, but too little for the dishwasher, and it was a sacred rule in the lab to leave no messes. "That's why I asked you to help with the critters. I'd just as soon stay under my family's radar. I don't want them worried. Nothing to worry about."

He scooped up the napkins and paper plates, suddenly quiet, as if he were making his mind up whether to change subjects. "You haven't said anything about your crazy inheritance in a few days."

"Well, I told you about meeting up with Bren Price. We're night and day in personality, that's for sure. But we'll get along as far as figuring what to do with Maude Rose's old place. And as far as the jewelry…"

Web was the only person she'd told about the legacy. Initially she thought she'd go with Maude Rose's advice, enjoy the privacy of no one knowing about her nest egg. But Web was the exception. She trusted him. After working together for four years, she knew she could.

She trusted her brothers and dad, too, of course, but it wasn't the same. Tell them anything, and for the next five hours she'd hear nothing but heated advice and orders and discussion. Web would just let her be. He was always good as a sounding block, but besides their mutual teasing, he never interfered in anything she did—any more than she would in his life.

"Ruby still hasn't come up with a written appraisal, but he must have called a half dozen times. It's kind of funny, really. I think he's shook up about doing this right, wants to be sure he keeps us informed every inch of the way. He's far more worried than either Bren or me."

"Doesn't sound like he's used to handling gems like that."

"He isn't. He keeps saying. But he's honest. That's all that really matters. Even if we don't have the appraisals down in ink yet, he's given us both clear pictures of what the pieces are worth. And Ruby being Ruby, I know what he's told us is conservative." She rinsed the last dishes and then grabbed a cloth to wipe off the table—then saw Web had beaten her to it. "It's just still hard to believe this is real. That a total stranger would suddenly give me something out of the blue. Especially something as overwhelming as this."

"Every once in a while the human race comes through and does something decent."

"I know, I know. But I had no idea she knew who I was." She shook her head, then spun around to glance at the clock again. Their hips bumped at the sink. He glanced at her, but she was no more concerned by the physical contact than he was. The time, she saw, was two minutes to one. She still had to pee and wash her hands before the next client came in.

Web, though, seemed to amble right in front of the door and then park himself. "Okay, so we've covered that waterfront. Now back to the main event. What's the surgery for, Poppy?"

"I told you. Nothing serious."

"Good. Then there's no reason you can't tell me what it is."

Sheesh. It wasn't like him to pry. "It's just awkward, okay? A personal thing."

"So it's about girl parts? I know this'll shock you, but I knew that your half of the planet had girl parts before this. I was even married. Twice."

"It's not about girl parts. At least, not exactly. Sheesh, sometimes you are so full of it!"

"Hey." For a guy who was tall and lean, he sure could block a doorway. "If it's cancer, a serious illness, damn it, you say. Right now. Quit messing with me."

"I swear it's nothing like that." She almost blurted it out, but then stopped herself. She had no fear of Web judging her. It was just that mentioning plastic surgery would draw his attention to her face. Make him look at her.

Web had never looked at her before—not really. Not personally. And they had a darn good working and friendship relationship going. Why put an awkward pin in that haystack?

"Web, I've got a mama bluetick hound waiting."

There. The magic words to make him move. He had critters waiting, too.

Poppy went on with her day and put the conversation out of her mind, although she had the oddest thought. Her last clip was at three, then she figured on a quick grocery run before heading home. But maybe after that she'd stop by Maude Rose's apartment again.

There was no reason to. The idea just stuck in her mind and then itched there. There wasn't much to still discover in Maude Rose's place, but before they did a final cleanup and sublet and got rid of Maude's last things...well, it just didn't seem right to move so fast. It was like letting an old lady disappear as if she'd never existed and never mattered to anyone.

Poppy just figured she'd stop by if she had the chance, that's all.

Even though Bren ran from the van, the rain managed to curl and whip around her. Her raincoat was soaked by the time she pushed open the door to the Righteous Senior Home, and she was gasping—mostly from laughter. On a rotten afternoon, what else could you do?

"How are you, Mrs. Price?" The receptionist smiled warmly at her. "Your dad will be so glad to see you."

"I know. I felt bad that I wasn't here yesterday."

"Well, almost no one manages to come every single day.

He's fine. You know we love him and take good care of him."
The receptionist glanced at her face, then quickly away.

Bren hung up her coat, almost reached up to touch her
bruised cheek and then quickly dropped her hand and
charged down the hall.

There were only two rest homes in Righteous. One was
Peaceful Valley, where you could smell the urine before you
even opened the door. Patients wandered the halls at all
hours of the day and night, and the food was worse than
baby pap. No one, obviously, went there if they had a choice.

And Bren would have had no choice for her father if it
hadn't been for Charles. The bland title of Righteous Senior
Home didn't do it justice. The place was immaculate. There
were crafts and card games and church services and ice
cream socials—something to do every hour of the day, and
someone to coax even the most recalcitrant senior to do it.

Bren paused in the doorway to her dad's room. Two para-
plegics roomed together. Their choice. It gave them someone
to talk to who had the same kind of problems—and the same
interests. Both were addicted to chess, played via a computer
screen. Her dad, Vane, still had use of two fingers, so he could
click on moves that way, where his crony, Mr. Albertson used
a wand between his teeth. When they weren't playing chess,
they were usually arguing politics with each other—occasionally to the point when they didn't speak—for an hour or two.

Her dad's hair had disappeared over the last two years.
His bald head glowed like a target for a daughter's kisses. She
blessed him with one now and loved seeing his eyes light
up. "Nice weather for ducks out there?" he rasped.

"Aw, heck. We need the rain." She walked over to Mr. Albertson's bed and gave him a buss on the cheek. "Aren't you handsome today?"

"Aw, go on with you. Talk to your father. Make him see some sense."

"Ah. We've been talking Middle East politics again, have we?"

She listened to the two of them bristle and expound for a few minutes as she brought out some creams from her bag. They took great care of her dad here. Far better than she could ever afford on her own—far better than Charles could have afforded for her.

But Charles had managed to get her father in the facility when they were first getting to know each other—weeks after the accident that took her mom and sister. Vane was still in the hospital at that time. She'd been seventeen, the only one in the family who hadn't been in the accident, and she'd been so overwhelmed with grief and panicky fear that she'd had no idea what to do for herself—much less her dad.

Charles had. At nine years older than her, he was still a young minister back then, but he'd known the unspoken code in Righteous—that hospitals and health care facilities tried to pull strings for those who did selfless jobs in the community, like the priests and pastors and their families. So Charles had managed to get him in, and Vane had some disability insurance on top of that, so between the two, he'd had a darn near good life here.

She heard the rasp in her father's breathing. Knew how prey he was to infections. But for right now he was doing darn well, all things considered—except for his dry skin. She brought the creams for his hands and feet and elbows. He'd have fussed no end if she tried an all-body rub, but the hands and feet he tolerated.

"We're stuck with a new physical therapist today," Vane told her. "Gonna come in around four, we hear."

"Are you going to behave for her?"

"Not if I have a choice," Mr. Albertson piped in, making her smile.

"Your smile is just like your mother's, Bren," her dad said and then added, "What's that on your cheek?"

Her fingers flew there. "Just a bruise. It just doesn't pay to run into a door these days. Who can figure?"

"You had a bruise on your neck last week," he said.

"I know, I know. Just getting clumsier and clumsier. I guess I wasn't cut out to be a dancer, huh?" She smiled again, rubbing the cream into her dad's hands. She knew he only had feeling in two of the fingers. But his skin was so dry, and it felt good to touch him, to have any excuse to do something for him, to show him how much she loved him any way she could. "Truth is, I've been busier than a one-armed bandit putting together a new fund-raiser. There were so many people left homeless after that last round of hurricanes in the south, you know? Trying to start over from scratch. Struggling to keep their families together—"

"You had your eyes checked?" her dad persisted. "Maybe that's why you're bruising so easy lately. Because you sure aren't clumsy, Bren."

"Spoken like a hugely biased father," she teased him.

"Sure have you fooled, don't I?" And then she said, "Trust me, my eyes are fine, Dad."

She visited longer, met the new p.t. guy, spoke with the nurse on the floor, checked the record on his meds. She left only when the nurse kicked her out for a maintenance run, because her dad didn't like her to see what he went through—as if she didn't know. He asked about Charles, of course, always did.

And she answered with warm, kind words about her husband, because she always did.

When she left the place, though, it wasn't five yet. Charles knew where she was but had no reason to expect her before six because she often stayed longer with her dad. The rain had finally stopped. A hushed sun peeked through the clouds, sneaked behind the turning leaves, glistened on all the wet edges.

She had a hundred things to do but didn't want to go home.

The last few days—the last few weeks—Bren knew she'd been piling a crazy amount of extra chores on her schedule. Anything to avoid going home.

The church van seemed to share the same idea, because just before she reached the light by the newspaper office, she saw a gaping-big parking place right in front of Silver Dream and Maude Rose's apartment.

Maybe it was a sign, Bren thought wryly. Maude had particularly been on her mind because Ruby had telephoned that morning. He'd finished her written appraisal. And Poppy's, for that matter, although he hadn't reached her yet.

She hadn't made time to stop for the appraisal or to pick

up the jewelry, for that matter. But because the legacy had been in her thoughts, maybe it was just natural she found herself pushing the key into the lock on Maude Rose's place.

She let herself in, dropped her bag and raincoat and then just stood there a moment. The silence folded over her like a veil of safety. She could feel the tension leave her shoulders, her heartbeat instinctively slow down.

The apartment was never going to look great. It was hard to make a silk purse from a sow's ear. But it smelled fresh instead of musty now. The old counters shined. She'd cleaned the windows the last time she was here...a few days ago, when she'd sneaked a half hour.

That time, too, she couldn't have said why she stopped by. She and Poppy had agreed to come to some conclusions about the place by the end of the month, if they could. They both thought some cleaning and painting was a good idea. And they both wanted to find the right person to sublet it to—some woman who needed a boost.

Bren had a feeling seep through her just like the last time she'd visited. It was just a snuggling sensation—as if she were a mouse in winter, just looking for a place that was warm and quiet and safe. A place where no one knew where she was.

A place where she could just *be*. For a couple of minutes. Just a couple of minutes...

Abruptly she heard the exuberant bound of footsteps coming from the outside stairs. She jumped—just a knee-jerk response to the sudden sound. When the door pushed open and Poppy blew in headfirst, moving at her usual wild-spirited pace, it was *her* turn to jump.

"Sheesh, could you give a body some warning? I had no idea you were here! Hmm. Come to think of it, why *are* you here?"

Instead of minding the intrusion, Bren found herself relaxing even more. Poppy was just so…brazenly alive. Messy. Rambunctious. She left damp footprints, was wearing a cloche like some artsy free spirit and jeans so worn-out they cased her legs like stockings. If she'd brushed her hair that day at all, it didn't show.

Bren had always cared—what people thought of her, what they said. Poppy so obviously didn't waste a single breath on nonsense like that.

"I don't know exactly what I'm doing here," she admitted with a laugh, but didn't have to further explain that answer because Poppy already had another question.

"Hell. What happened to your face?"

"I danced with a door."

Poppy stormed closer, squinted. "The hell you did," she said with a voice that turned quiet.

Bren shifted away. "Did you get a message from Mr. Ruby today?"

"Yeah, I got the message that the appraisals were done. I was going to stop, but he closed the shop at five, so by the time I got the message it was too late."

"Yet you still found time to come here?"

"Just for a couple of minutes. Oh, my God. A gremlin got in here."

"Pardon?" Bren didn't know what she meant.

"The windows are clean. If it's magic, I wish it'd come to my house."

Bren had to chuckle. "I just had a half hour free the other day."

"When I have a half hour free, I'm probably sipping a beer with the boys at Link's. Or soaking in a tub. Or rolling on the ground with somebody's mutt. Definitely not washing windows."

She was deliberately rubbing it in, Bren thought. Poppy was so...salty. Every time they were together, she seemed to make some comment digging at how prissy Bren was, how she was a free spirit and Bren would never be.

It was so immature. And so unfair.

Oddly enough, though, Bren didn't really mind. For one thing, Poppy was darn interesting. And for another, the only time Bren ever felt she could let her hair down and relax was when she was alone. It was a new experience feeling easy with someone else.

"Well, I don't have a good reason for stopping by here either," Poppy said frankly. She heeled off her damp shoes and then flopped on the spring-risky couch. "I guess I just can't stop thinking about Maude Rose."

"Same here."

"Are you hungry? I could grab some takeout from Link's. Wouldn't take long."

Bren couldn't believe how much she wanted to say yes. To just get some unhealthy carbohydrate- and cholesterol-laden takeout, spread paper plates on the old coffee table. Sit on the floor. Munch. Eat with her hands. "I can't," she said regretfully. "I have to be home twenty minutes from now. Charles will be expecting dinner."

"You could call him—"

"He doesn't know I'm here."

"Okay…" Poppy crossed her ankle over the other knee. "I don't get it. You still haven't told him about the jewelry? About Maude Rose and this place?"

"It was in the will, remember? How Maude Rose wanted us to be quiet. She wanted to make sure we were free to make our own choices about what to do with the legacy, without anyone influencing us."

"Is that how you got that bruise on your cheek? By your husband influencing you?"

"Poppy, you are way, way off base. Charles is a wonderful man. Ask anyone in town. He goes out of his way to help people. People know they can call him at any hour of the day or night and he'll always come. He'd give you the shirt off his back without your even asking —"

"So it's not the first time he hit you, huh?" Poppy asked quietly.

"*No one* hit me."

"Okay, okay." Poppy lifted her hands in one of those aggravating gestures kids make on a playground. She was backing off. But she thought she knew the truth. It was in her eyes, and so was the taunting.

Cripes, she was as mature as a fourteen-year-old.

Bren struggled for the patience to explain, to prove her husband was a far better man than Poppy had rashly concluded. "My parents and sister were in a car crash when I was seventeen. My mom and sister were killed. My dad lived, but his back was broken. Charles didn't even know me when he stepped in and helped me and my dad. *That's the kind of man he is.*"

"Whew. Who'd guess you had all that temper stored up behind those smiles all the time. I'm sorry, okay?" Poppy hesitated, no immature taunting in her expression now. "Look, I mean it. I *am* sorry. I've been known to put my foot in my mouth, but usually it's more like a toe, not the whole heel. When I saw your face, I just thought—"

"Have you thought any more about what you're going to do with your jewels?"

Poppy sprang on the change of subject faster than a tick on a hound. "It's okay. You can say what you really mean, which is, have I changed my mind about getting plastic surgery. And the answer is no. I've had two opinions now, both around D.C. My insurance isn't going to pay for any procedure because it's totally elective."

Bren sat forward, jettisoning the edgy feelings and fooling around. "What exactly do you plan to have done on your face?"

Poppy sighed gustily. "Trust me, it's not worth going into this. There isn't a prayer you'd understand."

"Maybe not. But could you try me?"

Again Poppy sighed. "You've got a beautiful face. So you don't know what it's like to live with this one. My brothers have my looks, too, but somehow they're actually pretty good-looking. The same features seem to do okay on a guy. The big nose. The no cheekbones. The jaw like a bulldog."

"Come on, Poppy. You're making yourself sound ugly, and

that's not true. And you certainly don't remotely have masculine looks. I can't believe you'd think you were ug—"

"Bren." The patience was filtered out of Poppy's voice now. She laid it out bald. "When a guy meets me, he thinks he's giving me a treat by taking me out. That's how it's been since I was sixteen. Aching to go to the prom. Aching to go to homecoming. And I could pretty much always get a date—but the only guys who asked me out figured I'd be grateful. You get me? What I mean by *grateful?*"

Bren reared back. "It couldn't have been that bad. I can't believe there aren't good, decent men who see beyond an—"

"Beyond an ordinary face? See, the problem is that it isn't ordinary. I'd be totally happy with ordinary. Instead this face is homely enough that people notice. It's the kind of face men don't marry. Or love. They might screw. They might borrow money. They might slap me on the back and play poker with me. But no guy looks at me and thinks about a life together."

"I think you're putting a huge amount of weight on physical appearance."

Poppy didn't even blink. "I knew you wouldn't get this. Because you just can't imagine my life, it's so different from yours. Picture a party. Or a group of singles in any scenario—bar, school, any kind of gathering. The single guys will scope the room for possible mates. Then, when they've completely wiped out the possibilities they want, they home in on me. Because they figure a woman who looks like me will be lonely, easier prey. But all the time their eyes are scoping the room for someone better, someone prettier. And I've been a couple. Twice. Not married but close enough to get myself believing it could happen. Only it ends up the same. All the time his eyes—their eyes—are roving around, looking for someone better, someone prettier—"

Poppy stopped talking and suddenly chuckled. "I see you listening to me, Bren. Listening like mad, but your eyes look blank. I knew you wouldn't get it. No one as pretty as you ever would. You just can't imagine living in these shoes."

"All right. I admit it. I can't imagine what you're describing. But…" She lifted a hand helplessly. "If this is really about love—"

"No. God, no. I'm too damned old to believe I need a man to be happy. Or to be *fulfilled*. That's my job, no one else's." Poppy lurched to her feet, spun around, moving apparently because she had energy to burn. "It's just about me. Being tired of living with this face. And for the first time, because of Maude Rose, I've got a choice to change something that's bothered me my whole damn life. What's so terrible about that?"

"Nothing," Bren said gently, but in her heart she thought there was. She thought it was frightening and sad and disturbing that Poppy had invested so much self-esteem in looks she didn't have.

"I don't have to be beautiful. I just want to be…different. Not like this."

"So what exactly would the doctors do?"

"Nothing that complex. Make the nose smaller. Pull up the forehead. Put a couple of implants in my cheeks. Sounds like a lot, but there's nothing fancy or unusual involved. They showed me pictures."

"Who's 'they'?"

"I checked out two different places. Not because I was bargain shopping. But just because I wasn't sure what choices there were. And how much it was going to cost. I decided on this one place—it's just got the best credentials by far. It'll take a good chunk, but I'll still have a lot of the inheritance left over. And there's nothing else I need anyway, nothing else I want."

"You really believe your life will change if you look physically different?"

Abruptly Poppy stalked over to the door to grab her battered rain jacket and push on her shoes again. "I can see it in your expression. The big struggle not to sound judgmental."

"That's not true," Bren said…but she knew it was. It wasn't the vanity thing that bugged her. It was any woman believing that her life would be different by doing no more than making her appearance different.

"I'll tell you what's true, Bren. I'm too damn old to be struggling with self-esteem issues at my age. And so are you. But I'm sitting in a life where I've let my looks affect ninety percent of my choices. And you're sitting in a life where you're letting a guy hit you. So which one of us is better off?"

"No one is hitting me," Bren said sharply.

"Yeah, right. Take it easy." Poppy closed the door with a clip. Not a slam. Not a quiet shut. But a definitive clip.

Bren heard its echo long past the time she heard the fade-out of boot steps down the stairs. And still she stood there, feeling every muscle and tendon in her body tense in frustration. She was dying to defend herself—and Charles. Dying to deny. Dying to argue with Poppy's annoying know-it-all attitude.

Poppy knew nothing. *Nothing*.

CHAPTER 5

There was a teensy problem with her religion allergy, Poppy realized. If you didn't go to church on Sunday, then you were stuck with nothing to do that morning but chores.

By nine o'clock, the dishwasher, washing machine, dryer and vacuum were all going at the same time, threatening to blow fuses and creating an impressive amount of noise pollution. Edward—the burn-singed rabbit—had turned around in his cage and was facing her butt-first, which delicately expressed his opinion of Sunday-morning cleaning. Snickers, on the other hand, who was generally a disgrace to all cats and terrified of her own skin, seemed motivated to attack the vacuum cord at two-minute intervals.

The noise didn't seem to stop Poppy from thinking about Bren. She had friends. Lots of them. Neighbors, family, old school buddies, people she did things with, both male and female. But a strictly girl-buddy, she hadn't really had since high school. And Bren certainly didn't fit that category. Yet the darn woman—and the memory of the bruise on her face—kept gnawing on Poppy. Thinking about her sitting in church with the pastor preaching godliness—if he really had hit Bren—bugged Poppy even more.

Another sweep of the vacuum under the couch brought up an extra five pounds of rabbit and cat fur. When were either of those critters even *under* the couch, for Pete's sake? Thankfully Poppy happened to glance up just in time to see two cars pulling in her drive. The one was noticeably a cop car; the other had a fire department insignia on the side.

She flicked off the vacuum and galloped for the door. The critters burrowed out of sight but then, that was why she'd been stuck adopting them, because they were terrified of people. Besides which, any sane, normal critter would wisely be wary of the two overgrown devils who stomped up her walk.

"Here comes trouble," she greeted her brothers.

Jason slapped her on the back and bussed the top of her head. Zach just cuffed her neck and gave her a noogie. He was the cop. Very scary to think he was in charge of people's lives when he still had the emotional maturity of a puppy. "We're just stopping by to make sure our little sister's okay."

"In other words, your wives had chores for you to do this morning and you were looking for a place to hide out."

They didn't waste time answering her insults, just charged on in, past the long living room and into the kitchen. Unlike how they'd behave in their own houses, they left wet boot prints and cupboard doors gaping ajar as they took out their favorite mugs and poured coffee. Zach lost no time in checking out the inside of the fridge. "Don't you still have some of that great vanilla syrup?"

"Yeah, on the counter, the same place you found it last time," she said drily and then ducked when he took a pretend swipe at her.

"Cookies," said Jase, who knew he didn't have to speak in complete sentences for anyone as lowly as a sister.

"Oreos. Oatmeal-raisin. A few snickerdoodles left. Cupboard on the left, second shelf." Her brothers didn't stop by every single Sunday morning, but close enough that she tended to be prepared. She knew how they liked their coffee—and their sweets.

"Where are my kids?" she demanded, because usually they brought at least one niece or nephew—Jase had a set and Zach had gone for double. Two were still toddling around in diapers, which meant their moms invariably needed a break, and Poppy was the happy stuckee. For the same reason, she kept a couple of open shelves in the kitchen devoted to a mess of toys—building blocks and dolls and trucks and balls and games.

"We both escaped this morning," Jase admitted as if they'd just been freed from prison. He took her bag of Oreos to the kitchen window, monopolizing them as he looked out. "Man, are you going to have leaves to rake a couple weeks from now. Did I warn you before you bought this place? Those maples are gonna shed like I can't believe."

"Does that mean you're offering to help when they all come down?"

She glanced out, too, although she saw an entirely differently view from her brother. She loved those maples. They were just turning red. Sugar-red. Glazy red. The whole back acreage had a lot of bump and roll—what land didn't in Virginia?—but she'd planted a couple of Red Delicious apple trees in a prize sun spot. Closer in, a big old chestnut was just starting to drop nuts. The prickers could tear up her hand in two seconds flat, but there was going to be a heck of a crop. She could already smell the roasted chestnuts in her imagination.

"I'd help with the leaves," Jase said, "but I don't see how you're going to keep in shape and keep your figure if you don't do some physical work now and then."

"Yeah," Zach affirmed. "Way better that you do it yourself."

"Lazy slugs," she muttered and poured a fresh mug of joe for herself, even as she noted the gold eyes staring at her from the cupboard over her sink. Technically Snickers wasn't allowed in the kitchen cupboards, but darn it. The cat was so afraid of humans—at least, normal humans, which seemed to exclude her—that she always aimed for that one hiding spot at the first sign of visitors. Her brothers would have loved the cat to bits. They were only mean to sisters. But Snickers just couldn't seem to trust humans, might never again.

Zach prowled the place like a nosy cat himself. Both brothers had always been more overprotective than parents. Jase passed her place at least once a day, and Zach stopped by a couple times a week. Neither thought she was helpless, but she was still the lone female in the family and living alone besides. For all their insults and teasing, she knew they'd be jostling each other for the right to help her if she ever asked.

Not for the first time, Poppy realized she was a ton more comfortable with them—with men in general—than she'd ever been with her own gender. The thought reminded her of Bren again, which gave the excuse to ask, "Do either of you know Charles Price or his wife Bren? You know, the Church of Peace minister?"

"Sure." Zach knew everyone. And Jason knew all the people Zach didn't.

"He's a good guy. A little preachy for my taste, but what can you say, that's his job."

Jase nodded, scratching his chin—he grew a beard every fall, and the project had begun. At the moment he looked almost scruffy and rough enough to fit in with a motorcycle gang. "If someone's sick or dies from his church, he's always there. Someone in the hospital or an accident, same thing. And if he isn't on the front line, his wife is. She's a real sweetie."

"Yeah, I know her, too," Zach said. "Although she's a hell of a risk on the highway."

"She's a speeder?" Poppy couldn't believe it.

"The opposite. Cranking that old church van up to the speed limit is a miracle, and the damn thing's always breaking down on her. Changed a flat tire for her one time. Tires were pretty bald—that church isn't exactly rolling in it. But if there's a girl in trouble, a pregnant kid, an old woman alone, fire, fight, whatever, that Bren, she's right in there."

"Him, too?"

"Yeah, him, too." Jase was searching high and low for the remote control. She had TVs in both the kitchen and living room—there were no sports events on this early, but Jase couldn't relax without an r.c. in his hand. "What's your interest in the Prices?"

"Nothing. Just wondered." But Poppy thought, *So the*

two of them had reputations for being saints. Bren actually was. But Poppy couldn't fathom how Charles had managed to fool everyone, not that Bren had admitted her husband hit her. And now Poppy wasn't sure if she should rethink her conclusions. Although she didn't much like admitting it, occasionally—rarely, very rarely, but occasionally—she'd been known to be wrong.

"Aw, hell," Zach said suddenly with a glance out her back window. He shot to his feet. "Your vet's coming."

"My ve—you mean Web?" She glanced out, as well. "That doesn't mean you two need to leave."

"Yeah, right." Both of them shoved on their jackets at the speed of light. "I see that trailer full of wood. Got to get home to Sue Ellen."

"Yup, me, too," Jase echoed.

"You need to go home to Sue Ellen?" Poppy teased.

"Of course not. I'm going home to Lisa and the kids. Tons of things she needs me to do today," Zach said righteously.

"You're that afraid he's going to ask you to help unload? Why, you lazy, good-for-nothing slugs— Hi, Web," Poppy said as she opened the door. Her two brothers piled out like six-foot-two puppies, practically tripping over themselves to escape. There were several minutes of "Hey, Webster" and "How's it going?" and "You're still putting up with our sister, huh?" and that sort of thing. But then they were gone, not running for their cars but damn near.

My God, if they weren't a half a foot and fifty pounds per body bigger than her, she'd smack them both upside the head. Twice.

But suddenly everything changed.

She couldn't explain it.

Web hiked up to the door looking as he always looked—edible, with dark sexy eyes and an easy, boyish smile. His loose-limbed stride somehow made an old bomber jacket and jeans look elegant.

She didn't feel weird in her bare feet and scrubby T-shirt and shorts—not with Web, not with anyone. There was no point in a woman with her face trying to pull off girly, and Web greeted her with the same warm, natural smile he always did.

"Okay, you can shoot me for not calling first. Especially if I chased off your brothers. I didn't even know if you'd be home, but when it came down to it, didn't matter. I started to think, if you had surgery coming up, you might need your wood in and done. Also wondered if you need your flue checked, some chemical in the chimney for creosote and all that kind of maintenance stuff."

"God, if you ever decide to marry again, could you ask me?" The joke came as naturally to her as it always did, too. But something was different. Something inside her. A strange kick in the pulse that didn't belong, an odd edginess that shouldn't have been there—not between her and Web. Maybe hormones? She'd already started that perimenopausal crap. That had to be it, she decided and determined to ignore it.

"Come on in. And yeah, I appreciate your bringing the firewood—and I'll help stack it. But I just started a fresh pot of coffee and I got all the crazy jewelry back from Ruby. I'd like you to see it if you have time."

"Are you kidding? Those stones are practically a legend by now. I've *got* to see what they look like. And I wouldn't turn down the coffee."

He'd been here before, just as she'd often been inside his place. Web hosted both a Christmas party and a summer picnic at his house every year. More often, he took in as many sick or abandoned critters as she did, and they both freely called on each other if an animal needed babysitting.

Still, it seemed this morning—because she'd suddenly decided to be weird—that her place looked different to her, as if she were suddenly seeing it from Web's eyes instead of her own.

Web came in the back door—unlike her spoiled brothers—automatically heeling off his boots and tossing his jacket on the mudroom bench. Edward poked his head out of the blanket in his cage where he'd been hiding. Snickers plopped down from the cupboard, recognizing Web, too.

Normally Poppy wouldn't care worth beans, but it seemed she was stuck feeling self-conscious this morning. Knowing it was foolish and unnecessary, she hurled a bra in the dryer out of sight and shifted a towel over her underwear in the dirty clothes bin. "You know where the coffee mugs are. If you'll pour yourself a cup, I'll bring the jewels."

"Sure. You need a fresh cup yourself?"

"You bet."

She scurried. Darn it, she knew the house wasn't much. The thing was, when she'd dumped the last bozo—somewhere in the realm of five or six years ago—she'd realized once and for all that marriage and kids weren't in her cards.

For a while, in fact, she'd tacked a sign over the door: Celibates United, Member in Good Standing.

Long-term, she thought the sign was amusing but the behavior wasn't, so she'd taken it down. Maybe she tended to get stuck with chumps, but a lover now and then was still a necessity in life. A girl couldn't live on vibrators alone.

The point, though, was that she'd figured out That Was It. She needed to make her own life. That meant getting serious about building equity. That meant defining security, and on terms she could provide it for herself. It meant starting to nail down how she wanted to live—*her* dream, living solo and then going for it. So she'd started looking for houses.

God knew, there was tons of farmland around Righteous. Lots of one-acre lots where someone had stashed a trailer, put a few nonfunctioning cars in front and built a doghouse with *Bubba* printed on the roof. She didn't want that. She didn't want suburbia any more than she wanted to live directly in town. She also didn't want neighbors who carried guns with their beer.

And finally she'd found this place. The original owner had been what locals called "an original." Name was Royce. The property went for the price of taxes—although it was far from perfect. It was a little too close to the highway. And Royce still had a functioning still in the back fifteen acres, probably never discovered because it was a wetlands back there, too mucky to farm and to expensive to fix. But the house, when she'd seen it the first time, had been solid, if filthy. And there were four pretty acres around it, with lots of trees and grassy areas, as well as all the wild acres beyond that for privacy.

Before she'd shopped for the first grocery, she'd put out a salt lick for the deer, feeders for the squirrels and raccoons. Even now, she had more bird feeders than she had pairs of shoes. Through the summer and even the cool nights of the fall, she often slept on the deck because it was so darn gorgeous back there. She'd never been one to waste time on loneliness. For one thing, if she didn't exactly have formal pets, she always seemed to be caring for a sick animal. Now she had the place and setup to care for them outside and in.

The property had no garage, but there was an old barn— with big old beams and spooky shadows. But there was ample space to park her car in bad weather, and plenty of room for outside gear, from lawn mowers to a female version of a tool shop to cages.

As Web helped himself to coffee, Poppy kept thinking defensively that she knew the house was small, but it suited her. It was built bungalow-style, with just one giant upstairs loft—nothing up there but her bedroom and a bath, but it was absolutely private from the rest of the house.

A narrow open staircase led down to the living room, which was big, long and open, with an eight-foot stone fireplace and west and south windows so it was wonderfully sunny in the afternoons. She had the usual couch and chair—nothing fancy, but big and overstuffed and mindful of her brothers coming in here with their boots and lazy ways. Tucked in a nook was her grandmother's desk, an antique, precious, where she did bills. And she'd found a round table in her mom's attic, which she'd put in the living room because she always seemed to be doing something that required a sit-down table—crafts or fix-its or whatever.

The living room had accidentally ended up purple. She wasn't sure how, when she'd never been a girlie-girl type, but she'd found the couch she'd wanted on sale—if she'd take it in purple—and the color thing had just reproduced itself from there. She had a couple of oils of mountains at sunset. Obviously there was purple in those. And lavender had been her mom's favorite color, so she had an old lavender throw, pillows, a fluffy foot rug.

A big bathroom cut into the hall that led to the kitchen—which was definitely the core of the place. Web had never seen the kitchen looking spotless. Come to think of it, neither had Poppy.

The main kitchen area had been the only disastrous part of the house when she'd first moved in, but tarnation, after spending a fortune revamping the thing, the room was still hopeless. She'd bought a new sink and counters, for Pete's sake. Spent money on decent appliances.

But somehow a genie seemed to infect her kitchen. She could put forks away tidily in a drawer, but they moved whenever she turned around. Cupboard doors seemed to gape askew, even after she closed them. Glasses didn't walk into the dishwasher, the way she planned. She cleaned the darn table, but by the time she got home from work, it always seemed to load up with mail and purses and earrings and things that just couldn't seem to figure out where else to go. She put napkins in the holder, but still sometimes she found them in odd places, like next to the peanut butter or in the fridge.

At least the kitchen was plain old sturdy. Cocoa and white. The table was big enough to feed eight, but sometimes she did just that—her brothers would come over, their wives, her dad, the kids, and one way or another she ended up putting on a family feed fairly often. Her plates were just white Corning Ware, but she had her Mom's good silver and fabulous wineglasses.

Sometimes other girl stuff seemed to show up, even if it wasn't from her mother's. Too darn often, though, she seemed to be babying some animal or another, so if and when she made the mistake of bringing them inside, it was pretty crazy to have prissy, fragile things when critters tended to claw, shed, stink and take over.

And the thing was, she liked it that way.

There was a plaque over the kitchen sink—I Refuse To Know My Own Place. And another in the mud room—Unfussy. When other people went to "put on the dog", they meant getting fancy. She meant being herself.

"Hey. You suddenly went quiet on me," Web said. "I thought you were going to show me your fancy legacy."

"I am, I am. I was just thinking…my kitchen always looks like I'm a slob."

"What's wrong with your kitchen? I think you've got a great place here."

Dumb. Since she'd put him on the spot, obviously he was stuck saying something nice. Again she told herself to shake off this weird edgy mood, grabbed a mug and plunked down beside him with the box of gems.

Snickers, naturally, had already found her way to Web's lap. He absently kneaded her nape as he studied the jewels, shaking his head as he picked up one piece after another.

"My God, Poppy. I'd never have believed for a minute this wasn't cheap stuff from a dollar store. Except maybe this one." He lifted the cuff bracelet with the big jewels at each end. "It's kind of neat. The jewels are so big they look like bug eyes."

"Oh, thanks. That image is going to stay in my mind now."

He chuckled. Snickers purred, settling in on his lap for a snooze. Snickers, who never went to anyone but her. "When I saw your brothers were here this morning...I was thinking maybe you'd chosen the time to tell them about the surgery. Or the gems."

"Nope. I adore them. I'd trust them with my life. But they were born interfering and overprotecting me—"

"Maybe because you lost your mom so young?"

"That's what I've thought, too. Even though they went through the same loss I did, they always seemed to think I needed more...watching over. Frankly I think *they* do. But whatever..."

"You haven't told them about the gems."

She nodded. "Telling you was different, Web. I *had* to tell someone, even if I wanted to keep quiet. It was just too...wild...not to share. Inheriting something like this. Especially from a stranger."

He'd held up each piece to the light, put it down again. And now those dark eyes centered on her. "I've thought for a long time, Pops…have you ever considered doing some formal animal training?"

She cocked her head. "Half of what I do is training now."

"I know. But you're only getting paid as a groomer, when hell, you're like a dog whisperer. Or a cat whisperer."

"You trying to get rid of me as your groomer?" she asked suspiciously.

"Good grief, no. You're half the reason we've built the practice as big as we have. I just keep thinking that doing shampoos and clips can't be fun or challenging enough for you—not all the time, not when you've got this gift. Maybe you just never thought of it as a possibility before. But now you've got this surprise nest egg."

She frowned. "I don't know. You're right. I never thought about concentrating on animal training before." She didn't want to admit that the only thing she'd thought about lately—relentlessly—was changing her face. Now, though, after doing all the research, she knew there'd be a good chunk of money left over. Until Web spoke up, she just assumed she'd throw it into savings. A retirement nest egg, something like that.

Rather than dump Snickers on the floor, Web scooped her up so he could wander over to pour himself another mug of coffee. "There are all kinds of specialized animal-training concepts. And I assume making it work would require finding your own niche, something you wanted to work with. Lions Club already does great work with guard dogs. State cops do a super job training dogs to sniff out drugs, arson, other crime sort of things. But it's not like there aren't a dozen other niches where you could really be terrific, Poppy. First off, because you've got a knack with problem dogs. And second, because I see real needs in this area. Dogs who could work with the elderly. Handicapped people or people with certain disabilities."

"I do, too. But I wouldn't know how to begin, Web—"

He shrugged. "Maybe the first step isn't finding the obstacles. It's looking really specifically at this area and identifying where the needs are. You know some of the people I've been thinking about. Mr. Minever on Baker Road—the young deaf guy—he could really use a pet with certain skills. And there's an autistic kid lives past the high school, couple roads off Willow. Right pet could be company for him, as well as serve to alert people around him of trouble. We've got a lot of older people where a dog who could open a door or respond to the word *help*…nothing that huge, just something that requires unique training that most pet owners can't do. Poppy, you'd be *great* at that kind of thing."

He rambled on, just mulling the idea with her. Talking was relaxing enough for him. But darn it, for her it was low-down, gut-serious foreplay.

Other women, she suspected, turned on for roses or a love song crooned by candlelight. There'd always been something wrong with her, because champagne had never made her pulse quicken, her cheeks flush. This did. Thinking about a pack of throwaway puppies who just needed a chance. Thinking about angry, hostile dogs who'd lost their ability to be good pets. Thinking about older people—people like Maude Rose—who might be saved from a fire or from loneliness or who just could be enabled after a fall to get help because they had a loving pet who was trained to know what to do. Thinking about ugly mutts who were just dying to be loved, who could be loved, if they had a skill that could make them helpful to humans.

Cripes, it made her orgasmically happy to daydream that kind of stuff. What was wrong with her, that dogs turned her on these days, when thinking about men these last years had just generally made her feel tired?

"You can't tell me these ideas never crossed your mind before, Poppy," Web said.

"Not like you mean. Not like carving out a whole career from it. I never seemed to be ambitious or goal-oriented like the rest of my family. Zach always knew he wanted to be a cop. Jason always knew he wanted into the fireman thing. I was the first one out of school, had the grades to go to college…but my mom was gone by then, money was tight. And I wasn't that school-oriented, so it just seemed a waste."

"You had a good job when I met you."

She remembered that day so well. She'd run across Web by accident—literally. Someone had hit a dog in the road and driven on. She'd seen it, yanked her car to the side of the road, run to the dog and carried it to Web's office…by which time she'd been almost bloodier than the poor mutt. Web had been fresh from his second divorce around then and almost as mean as the hurt dog.

But not with her. And not with the dog.

"I was working in an insurance office, Web. And, yeah, I'd worked myself up the ranks. I was making a good living, and it wasn't bad work, but…" She poked in her brain for the right word. "It wasn't like a calling or anything like that."

"If you're looking for a 'calling,' I think you'd already know animals is it for you. Same as for me but in a different way."

Some things she just couldn't explain to Web. He wasn't female. Until she'd shucked the last loser, she'd been under that old hope umbrella that a marriage would come along. Yeah, she'd probably always work, because that's how it was today. But she'd hoped to have a family, a guy to take care of, that whole traditional ball of wax. And she'd never wanted a particular career more than she wanted that.

A while back, she'd quit trying to turn left from the right-turn lane. A guy wasn't going to be in her picture. That was that. But just maybe she'd forgotten that the rest of her life ideas could use a little redecorating and alterations, too.

She scraped back her chair. "You want more coffee? I just realized I've been jawing with you all this time, stealing your whole Sunday. But I can help unload the wood."

"Good," Web said wryly. "Too darn much work for me alone." He motioned to her cache of jewels. "You've got a good place to lock those away here?"

"Yeah." She opened the fridge and motioned. "The vegetable bin. Nothing else in there for sure." Shooting him a grin, she jogged around the corner and grabbed her oldest fleece. "Actually, I'm taking two of the pieces back to Ruby. It's just the rest I want to keep locked up for a while, until I know what I want to do with them. I'll definitely think about what you said. The whole idea's got my mind buzzing."

"You already know what you're going to do with half the money, then?"

"Yeah. The surgery." Aw, hell, she thought. She hadn't meant to open up that can of worms again and hoped Web would drop it.

Outside, on her back porch, she sucked in a lungful of fresh air. That's what had been wrong with her weird mood, she decided. She'd been cooped up all morning. No air, no exercise. And it was one of those leaf-shuffling fall Sundays, made you happy just to breathe, just to smell all that rusty gold in the air.

Web, though, had a lot of hound in him. He thumped out behind her, hands slugged in his jacket. "Poppy, quit fooling around. Just tell me what the surgery's for."

She sighed, but that didn't put Web off either.

"Come on, for Pete's sake. Just spit it out. What are we talking about—a hysterectomy, something like that? You have a lump? I know damn well you haven't got a prissy bone in your body, so I don't get why you can't tell me. You *know* me. And I hope to God you know I'm a friend, not just someone you work with. I've got every right to worry about you."

"Jesus, would you quit? There's *nothing* to worry about."

"Then just say it. Put it on the line."

She raised her hands in an exasperated gesture. "I'm getting my face fixed. That's all. That's the whole deal. Now forget it."

She stomped off to the trailer heaped with wood behind his truck.

"You're *what*?"

She knew fireplace fires weren't efficient, but she was a sucker for them. The nights hadn't dropped below freezing yet, but they were starting to cool down. There was nothing like coming home after a long, physical day and sprawling in front of a crackling fire with a warm body snuggled next to her. In her case, the warm body was invariably a rabbit or a cat or a dog, rather than a guy, but what the hey. A warm body was better than no body.

The point, though, was that she'd set up a sturdy cradle for firewood. Naturally she didn't want it to touch the house and risk termites and mice and all that nonsense. So the cradle was a couple feet distance from her back door. She started carting the wood.

Web, carrying a load behind her, sounded as exasperated as she'd ever heard him. "You mean to tell me you're having plastic surgery?"

"Yeah. Now forget it."

"I thought you had cancer, for God's sake. Something serious. Something real."

Something real? She rounded on him. "That's why I didn't say anything. To you. To anyone. You, particularly, have no possible way to get it."

"Don't get what?" That quickly, he'd already carted three armloads of wood in the cradle to her one, and she was no wimp. "That by not saying anything, you had me thinking you were seriously ill?"

"Damn it, Web." Her hands were already scratchy with wood scraps and bark. "You're handsome as the devil and you know it. You know what my brothers used to call me?"

"What?"

"Butt-ugly. It was a joke. The way brothers tease. Only it wasn't a joke, and I'm tired to hell of it. Tired of living with this face. I don't give a damn if I'm beautiful. In fact, I couldn't care less. But I want a face that's less—" She pin-wheeled her hands.

"Less *what?*"

"Less like my face, that's what," she said furiously.

He wiped a grimy hand over his face, leaving a dark streak on his cheek. "You want a face that doesn't look like you? Have I got that right?"

It wasn't funny. He wasn't exactly making it funny, but he was sure as hell making light of it. And that made her want to smack him, even though she never lost her temper. Never. Ever.

Not since last month at least.

"Forget it. It's not your problem, not your business—" She turned away, only to hear his leaf-crunching footsteps rounding on her.

He grabbed her arm, spun her back. "You think you're *ugly?*" he demanded as if he were talking to a half-wit.

"Just leave it alone," she said in a voice starting to shake. There was a good reason she hated losing her temper. Because she was lousy at it. Because when she really got wound up, the words came out with spit and shaky sputters. She *hated* getting really mad.

Web knew it because he'd seen her lose it several times. Her Achilles' heel was always animal owners who mis-treated their pets. And more than once Web had intervened before she'd done something seriously close to taking out those kinds of people.

This time, she caught the sudden sharp frown between his brow. Saw him look at her for that millisecond in the oddest way. And then he muttered, "God, I can't believe you're this much of an idiot."

Before he kissed her.

CHAPTER 6

Poppy could have coped if a roof came out of the sky and crashed on her head. She could have coped if her brothers showed up for dinner without warning at five forty-five. She could have coped if a pissed-off bear showed up in her backyard—which, truth to tell, was known to happen now and then in the Shenandoah Valley.

But there was no way in the universe she could have guessed Web was going to kiss her.

He didn't think about her that way. She didn't think about him that way either—or she'd never allowed herself to think of him that way. Yeah, he was adorable. Just because she'd resigned herself to celibacy didn't mean she was hormone-dead. But sex-symbol type guys never glanced at women who looked like her.

More important—far, *far* more important—was that they *liked* each other. It was a revelation and a joy to Poppy. How much she liked Web. How much fun they had working together. How much she valued their work, her job, the whole super environment at the clinic.

And now he was ruining it all.

Out of the blue.

For no reason whatsoever.

But man, was he good at it.

For that first millisecond, his palms framed her face and he just took and took and took her mouth. Her lungs deflated completely of oxygen, but the need to breathe struck her as vastly unimportant just then. He tasted like coffee and exotic male. His arms surrounded her in a magic perfume cloud of pure, zesty testosterone. His mouth was smooth as butter, but he applied pressure—just that little sizzling suggestion of dominance that made her want to sink to the ground for the thrill of it.

Of course, she was kiss-starved. And doubly kiss-starved for a man who knew how to kiss. Come to think of it, she wasn't dead sure she'd ever come across any guy who kissed as well as Web.

She intended to punch him clear across the backyard. In just a second.

Her arms swooped around his waist, just to hold him closer for that one more second. So she was being stupid. Life would just have to go on. She wanted to feel her breasts mooshed against his chest, feel her groin tighten, feel how that whole, rare sensation of intense arousal delighted and drugged. She wanted to feel that hard male body, the heat of it, the power of it, the iron of it.

And after that, she fully intended to pull back and punch him. Only he angled his head a little differently and came back for another pressure-cooker kiss, and this one involved tongue.

She decided all life as she knew it wouldn't end if she procrastinated slugging him for a little while longer.

There were tongues and tongues. Overall, she'd never been all that excited by ultramessy kisses. It wasn't the swapping-saliva thing. Hell, she swapped saliva with dogs and cats—not always willingly—but it wasn't as if she was prissy about much of life. It's just that guys who were gooey kissers had never done much for her. It was more like they thought tongue kisses were a required appetizer before they could push on to the main course.

Not Web.

Damn Web and double damn Web, because he just seemed to like kissing. He took her mouth as if the shape of her, the taste of her, the texture and smell of her had gone to his head. As if he'd just sat down on the last Thursday of November and the only thing in his mind was a good, long, lazy feast.

His tongue found her teeth. Her tongue. He sipped. He tasted. He eased up on pressure and then applied more.

And then slowly he lifted his head. Possibly he'd cut off the kiss because he just couldn't keep leaning over her for that long a time. His back had to be killing him. Something was sure wrong, because there was suddenly a fresh frown line between his brows, an expression of complete confusion on his face.

Then, a little late, she remembered she was going to slap him clear across the yard.

Her knees happened to be a little shaky. And her lips felt wobbly, as well. She managed to form a couple of fists, but then propped them on her hips instead of punching him. "What the hell was that for?" she demanded.

He seemed to have trouble finding his voice, as if his vocal cords had taken off for Alaska and hadn't found their way home yet. He started to answer. Then had to try a second time. "There was a reason I did that," he assured her but then seemed to have to think about it again.

"What, you suddenly felt sorry for me?"

"Sorry for you?" He shook his head like a mutt drying off after a rain. "Why in hell would I feel sorry for you? I did it because…because you were talking about getting plastic surgery."

"Sure, like that makes sense."

He scratched his chin. "It did a minute ago. I thought you were saying…you thought you weren't attractive. I thought…how stupid could you get. I thought I'd show you that there's nothing wrong with how you look, Poppy, that you're great the way you are."

No, she wasn't going to melt. Damn it. He'd just made her even madder.

"Let me translate that to some cold-turkey truth. You thought I was hard up for some action. Because I admitted wanting that plastic surgery."

"I didn't think that."

"Yeah, you did. Because that's what guys think when they look at me. That I'm hard up. And you know the truth of it? I *am*. And that's one of the things I'm sick to bits of. Not sick of being deprived of sex, for God's sake. Sick of men jumping to that conclusion."

"Wait a minute. Wait a minute, Poppy—"

"To hell I will. You listen to me, buster. I don't want pity kisses from anyone—and never, *never* from you. You ever do that again and I swear I'll knock your block off."

He stared at her for a long, hard minute and then turned around and aimed for the trailerload of wood. "Whatever."

"I mean it, Web. Damn it. Don't you mess with me. We work together like a dream team. I love my job. You screw with that and I swear I'll—"

"I heard you, I heard you. You don't need to make any more threats. I think the plastic surgery idea is stupid, but—"

"Did I ask you?"

"You are who you are, Poppy." This time when he turned around with an armload of wood, he looked almost as furious as she was. "You're great the way you are. You're the only one who doesn't see it. And plastic surgery can't fix a woman who refuses to see what's right in front of her eyes."

"That's it," she said. "If you say one more word—"

But he didn't say one more word. He stacked wood. She stacked wood. And when the trailer was empty—the whole cord of wood tidily stacked in record time—Web stalked off, climbed in his truck and drove out.

She wanted to do exactly the same thing. Elegantly stalk off in a dignified way and take off. Only, damn it, it was her house. So she had nowhere to take off to.

Bren was standing on stage in the high school auditorium when she glimpsed Poppy walking in the far entrance. Temporarily she couldn't run down to greet her. She was stuck at the edge of the stage.

In the center, with a microphone in her hand, was a

twelve-year-old named Julia Robbins. Julia's mother had clearly taken her daughter to a beauty salon to get big hair for this talent event. Her skirt, unlike some of the other contestants', covered her little behind—at least when she wasn't shaking it. The top glistened with spangles and beads, which echoed the glittery purple bead in the youngster's belly button.

Bren refrained from rubbing her temples, but it was getting harder to ignore the cyclone-size headache. When she'd first conceived this fund-raising idea—a talent contest, sort of an *American Idol* scaled down a million times to a Righteous Idol level—she'd never dreamed the community would go crazy for it. Tonight, it was already eight forty-five, for a competition that was supposed to have been over by seven. Yet the gym was still filled—in fact, the bleachers were packed to the gills, just as they had been for the other two competition tryouts.

To add insult to injury, little Julia was belting out "We Are the World" so flat, so off-key flat, that Bren could almost hear the scream-scrape of chalk on a blackboard. The volume that little honey could get out of a microphone was not only terrible but almost powerful enough to break the sound barrier.

Bren acknowledged that might be a slight exaggeration. But only slight. The last contender had been worse—past awful, past unbelievably terrible, with a voice that only had a future in Ripley's for the worst singing in the history of the known universe. When it came down to it, realizing a human being could even produce that sound from basic vocal cords was an issue of awe.

In the audience, parents of other auditioning children listened with rapt attention. When the little girl finally wound down, her mom and dad both leaped to their feet and thundered applause. The mother *was* crying. From joy and pride.

Bren was close to crying, too. From joy that she could finally steal the microphone away from the child. "Thank you so much, everyone, for participating tonight! I'm sorry we ended up running so late. I know it's a school night! We just never guessed there'd be this many auditioners for our Righteous Idol fund-raiser. We're delighted and hope you and the judges are, too! The next event is next Tuesday, seven o'clock, same place. Thanks, everyone!"

At this late hour, she expected them to stampede for the exits—especially since it had started raining and the October night had turned black and slippery and gloomy. Instead parents blocked the aisles, gathering all the debris it took parents to attend any function longer than fifteen minutes, bragging on their kids, gossiping, not even trying to herd their caterwauling hellions.

Their adorable children, Bren mentally corrected herself. There had to be over a hundred parents here. Wouldn't you think one of them might have a child who could sing? Anything? On key?

She plucked her purse from a chair behind stage and folded her old plaid raincoat over an arm. Still she couldn't leave. People stopped to talk to her, all abuzz. Praising Charles for coming up with the singing competition. Applauding Charles for thinking of such a fun and fresh fund-raising idea for the community. Supporting Charles for finding a way to help the victims of the terrible storms but in a way that brought all the people of Righteous together, even if they weren't all of the same church or faith.

"That's so exactly the point. Good hearts coming together," Bren affirmed, almost flinching when Buzz Harding patted her extra hard on the shoulder. Certainly he only meant a supportive *atta girl*, but beneath her sweater she had a bruise there the size of a baseball. In the last two days it had gotten prettier than a rainbow, all purples and greens and blues, and barely still hurt—unless someone accidentally pressed the spot.

"Well, you tell Charles we all sure appreciate how much he's doing for the community," Buzz said heartily, with his itty-bitty wife nodding like a mad thing beside him.

"I will, I will. I know he'll appreciate hearing it," Bren said warmly.

Finally the crowd and noise thinned out—and she spotted Poppy again, wending her way up to the stage. Bren wanted to chuckle. Naturally, for a public event, she was wearing attire appropriate for a minister's wife—practical shoes, a below-the-knee skirt, a pretty enough burgundy cardigan. She liked her clothes well enough. She just normally never thought about them and certainly never aspired to Poppy's choice of style.

But Poppy was always so much *fun*. As always, she looked irrepressible. The jeans were just jeans, but the old bomber jacket could have been resurrected from WWI, and her neck brandished a snuggly purple scarf that almost reached her ankles—the color a wild contrast to her burnished bright hair, besides. Her boots clicked up the stage steps, full of attitude, just like her.

"Here I thought you were a woman of God and now I discover you have a cruel streak, Bren," were her first words.

"Pardon?"

"From what I heard in the crowd, this whole sing-along competition was your idea. Do you have no mercy in your soul? Did you feel some personal need to punish the entire community? I only heard the last singer, but her voice could have curdled milk."

Now that everyone else was either gone or out of earshot, Bren could freely laugh. "Wasn't it terrible? I never dreamed it would go this far. And the worse the kids are, the more the whole town seems to be loving it."

"What's that about? When you have a kid, you turn deaf, dumb and blind? Those parents actually thought that kid could sing. Can't you put people away for delusions like that?"

Again Bren laughed, feeling—for the first time all day and maybe all week—a silly kind of lift. She loved her work in the community, loved almost everything a pastor's wife could get involved with. It was just that lately tension haunted her like an inescapable shadow.

Funny how being with Poppy for even a few minutes lessened that stress. But even if they were a snake and a mongoose in temperaments and personality, Poppy was so honest. Bren couldn't imagine needing to be diplomatic or politically correct anywhere near her. "Charles asked me to come up with a fund-raising idea for the storm-relief efforts—but something different than the other churches and organizations were doing. It's not like this idea is original. You know how popular that *American Idol* program is."

"Yeah, but I can't imagine why people would pay money to be involved in this."

"Crazy, huh? But they're betting on who's going to win in. And betting separately on who's going to stay in after each competition. The winner gets to sing at the Thanksgiving program—but in the meantime, we've raised more in the last couple weeks than for any fund-raiser we ever tried." And truly Bren couldn't be more gratified at the community's wildly enthusiastic response.

She just wished Charles were as happy with it.

Poppy kept looking around, hands on hips. "I haven't been inside the high school in years," she said.

"Well, the school was nice enough to donate the gym—as long as we didn't need it on sports event nights." Her smile dropped a notch. "Poppy, I'm glad to see you, but when I left a message on your voice mail, I just meant for you to call back when you had time. I feel bad if you thought you had to come out on an awful night like this all this way—"

"It's hardly a long distance. And when you left the message that you'd be here tonight…well, I wasn't sure if you really wanted me calling you at home," Poppy said bluntly. "If Charles answered, I didn't want him asking you questions if you hadn't told him about the inheritance. Or anything else I could save you from, for that matter."

Bren wanted to leap in to defend Charles, knowing perfectly well that Poppy was implying Charles's temper was a problem. But the truth was, she still hadn't told her husband about the legacy. And she was having enough trouble with her conscience on that score without trying to explain it to someone else. Besides which, standing this close, she suddenly noticed the dark shadows under Poppy's eyes, the rare look of weariness.

"Are you doing okay?" she asked Poppy.

"Of course. Why wouldn't I be?"

She could have guessed Poppy'd get prickly if anyone tried to express caring. Bren murmured, "It's so odd. When I first met you, I couldn't imagine one thing we'd ever have in common. Yet things keep popping up. Like you don't want anyone's help. I don't either. You don't want anyone even *thinking* you need help. And I'd climb a mountain to avoid anyone thinking that, too."

"Huh?"

Before Poppy could get any more annoyed, Bren cut to the chase. They both walked toward the back outside door behind the stage. "I called because I wanted to talk to you about the apartment."

"Okay. Shoot." Poppy pushed open the door. Almost no one was left in the school now—a good thing, since the evening rain had turned into an exuberant downpour. Curtains of black needles sluiced on the parking lot. Blinding lights echoed as the last parents' cars left the lot. They could both run out in it, but that would obviously end any chance of a conversation. Poppy reclosed the door.

"I talked to the landlord," Bren said. "Not because I

would have made any decisions without you. Just to ask some questions. I'd like to paint the bedroom and living room, just to freshen it up. The landlord said he'd deduct the rent for any improvements we did. He also said he didn't care one way or another if we kept the place or sublet it."

Poppy leaned against the cement wall, slugged her hands in her pockets. "Are you thinking about keeping the apartment now?"

"No. Not me. Not for me. But I came across a girl—Mary Sue Chapman. She's nineteen. Been on her own since she was sixteen, a long history of trouble. A single mother who didn't do much mothering. Mary Sue started by skipping school, then there was a pregnancy. Lost that baby, but she had one boyfriend after another who—"

"Who was bad news." Poppy had no trouble filling in that blank.

Bren nodded. "Ultrabad news. She needs a fresh start." Before, Bren hadn't buttoned up. But now, knowing the weather, she buttoned to the neck and wrapped the sash on her old raincoat. "She's living with a boy. She didn't admit it, but I believe he's selling drugs. She doesn't have anywhere else to go—or that's what she believes. She's got a job waitressing at Grits and Grub—"

"I think I know her. Tiny little redhead?"

"Yes, that's her. So she has a job, but she's not earning enough to boost her into an independent bracket. If she could live for, say, six months without rent money going out the door, she'd have a shot at getting some savings in the bank—"

"Sure."

"She's young. She still thinks she can't make it without a guy in the picture. If she just had a chance to believe she could survive on her own, then she might make better choices—"

"Sure."

"I mean, she—" Bren was still trying to explain when Poppy cut her off.

"Bren, you don't have to sell me. I like the idea. What were you thinking—that after Maude Rose's rent is all paid up, the two of us would chip in for a few months for the kid?"

"Well…that would be one way. I thought we could offer her a six-month sublet. I don't see offering more than that, in case it doesn't work." She hesitated. "And it might not. In fact, we could be on the hook for the damage deposit. And damages, for that matter, if—"

Again Poppy cut her off, not sounding impatient but simply curious. "Are you always this way? Afraid to bring up an idea without a dozen justifications? We already talked about this, B. About doing something that seemed right for Maude Rose. I'm cool with it."

Bren lifted a hand. "I just wanted to ask you in person. Because I didn't want you to feel on the spot to say yes. There's no reason you have to do this if you don't want to. You could need your money for something else."

"I'm not up for giving away the farm, so to speak. But this is hardly a big financial risk. We're only talking a few gallons of paint and a few months' rent on that little place. I don't mind. In fact, it kind of feels like it's a little giving back to Maude Rose."

"That's exactly how I felt." Bren sucked in a breath. Weariness was starting to fray all her edges. It had been a long evening, long day, long week. "Are you still planning on the plastic surgery?"

Immediately she saw Poppy stiffen and shook her head quickly. "No, Poppy, I wasn't going to criticize you or talk about that again. I just wondered if you were going through with it. If you'd set a date. If you could use some help."

Poppy pushed away from the wall, obviously getting antsy to leave now. "Yeah, the date's set. I'll be gone from next Tuesday through Saturday. The place is like a...spa. I think. I've never been to a spa before. But it's kind of an all-service health and medical and lifestyle thing for women. I hooked up for the whole program. That's why I'll be gone so long." Before Bren could comment, she added, "I realize you think the whole idea is vain and frivolous. Cripes, I think the whole idea's vain and frivolous, too. I don't care. I don't want to hear any grief about it."

"How odd," Bren said mildly. "Because I don't like hearing a bunch of unasked-for opinions about my private life either."

For a moment the two just stared at each other in the shadowed hallway, and then Poppy's face suddenly cracked into a chuckle. "Damn it, Bren. Could the two of us actually be becoming *friends*?"

"Impossible," Bren reassured her.

"That's what I thought. It's just too goofy to imagine. We're complete opposites in every way."

"Totally. In fact...I haven't done the 'girlfriend' thing or the 'best friend' thing since I was in junior high."

"Me either. Just never had the time or chance. Or else I was too ornery," Poppy admitted.

Again the two smiled at each other—and again chuckled. Moments later, they both pelted outside in the deluge to take the last lone vehicles in the school parking lot.

As Bren started the van, she kept mulling over their conversation. In her life, she'd never had secrets—never did anything worth keeping a secret about. So it was just so unusual to find herself sharing a serious secret with a woman so unlike herself.

Odder yet, she realized that she trusted Poppy.

Trust wasn't a word she ever thought about…until lately. The drive home took less than ten minutes. She'd barely pulled in the driveway before feeling a too-familiar thud in her pulse, a too-familiar tightening in her shoulders. She let herself in the back door, almost soaked through just from the race to the house.

For a few moments the warmth of the kitchen reached out to enfold her. She slipped off her damp shoes, then hung her raincoat on the hooks by the back door. The sink light cast a soft yellow pool of warmth in the shadowed room. She could smell the Burgundy pot roast she'd made for dinner, the cinnamon-apple strudel, the mint she'd been growing on the windowsill.

"You finally home?"

She jumped when she heard Charles's voice, spun around to find him standing in the doorway. "Yes. It went great, Charles."

He said nothing. The silence only stretched on for a few

seconds, yet when he turned away, walked back into the den, she found her fingers intertwined like knitting needles. She trailed after him, her voice bright and cheerful.

"There were tons of people there, lots of parents. All of them passed on comments to you. They wanted to thank you for the idea, the support—"

"It wasn't my idea. It would never have been my idea to support gambling." Charles settled in his customary chair in the living room and snapped a newspaper open. "Or to promote children displaying themselves on a stage. At least, unless the music was church music. But I realize you didn't think of any of that—"

"Charles, we're raising a ton of money and bringing attention to our church, as well. And I understand your objections, but people have been totally happy about the project. There's no negative that I can see. You asked me to come up with a project. You told me to take the ball and get it done and not bother you. To—"

"Yes, I did. But I didn't expect you to come up with a concept that involved gambling or principles that you know perfectly well I'm opposed to. But then, you don't think about much but yourself these days, do you? You're loving the attention. Everyone's talking about the pastor's wife and how darling she is."

He snapped the paper again, then disappeared behind it.

Or maybe it was Bren who disappeared. She stood there in their familiar living room, with her damp feet and her hands still knitting themselves into a frenzy, and felt that sensation again. As if she were a stranger in her own life.

She felt fear and frustration and a thick dread sensation in her stomach. She felt as if she were galloping toward the edge of a cliff and had no way to brake. They were all alien sensations. All sensations she'd never expected to feel with Charles.

Their marriage had been good for so many years. She just didn't know what had changed. She was more than willing to take her share of the blame, but the harder she tried, the further away she seemed to move from this man she'd once loved so completely.

She didn't know what to do, what to think, what to try next.

Except that how they were living together right now couldn't continue much longer. Slice by slice, he was breaking her heart.

The next day, Poppy arrived at Critter Care an hour early, knowing she had a hell of a wild morning schedule and hoping to get a head start. The only other vehicle in the lot was Web's. She jogged for the door, assaulted by a blustery October wind. Leaves thrashed through the air. Branches bucked and tossed. The temperature had one of those rattling chills to it.

Inside, though, it was snuggling warm. She heard a cat squalling from one of the back rooms. The front reception counter wasn't manned yet, but the phone already blinked with emergency calls. The room smelled faintly of antiseptic and dog treats. The floor was freshly mopped and shined, and the shelves were temporarily all tidily stocked with an array of pet products.

None of it was fancy, but Poppy loved every smell and sound, always felt a sense of coming home when she walked through the door. At least she used to.

She charged back for her work area, wanting to be well prepared before Barney—alias the Infamous Basset Hound from Hell—got here.

This feeling of being rattled and edgy was new. Poppy always thought she was too ornery to waste time on nervousness. But somehow the plastic surgery plans had exploded on her. The surgery itself wasn't going to be that expensive, she'd discovered. But somehow the pretty basic surgery had exploded into a full-blown spa experience.

It all made so much sense when she'd been researching it all. She'd picked the doctor because of his credentials, but he happened to practice at this fancy place outside D.C. that offered so much *stuff*. Who knew? Poppy had just started checking things on the list, and before she knew it, she'd signed up for the seaweed-and-mud wrap. The cosmetic consultation. Somebody who did highlights and hairstyles. And she wasn't exactly sure what a "personal shopper" was, but she seemed to have signed up for having her entire wardrobe and look overhauled, right down to her underwear.

Now, as she set out her clippers and towels and brushes, she glanced down at her holey jeans and battered sweatshirt. With three canine wash-and-grooms scheduled this morning, there seemed no point in wearing anything nicer. She'd be soggy and haired up lickety-split.

After that, she remembered, she had a training hour with a shepherd who'd suddenly turned scared of strangers.

Overall, it'd be an interesting morning, she thought. Except that she couldn't stop thinking about next week—and still wasn't sure if she was more excited or more scared.

Hells bells, if a woman wanted to change, why shouldn't she do it whole hog? It was the first and only time she'd ever done anything totally selfish, something just for her. Granted, she was a little edgy about how people would react when they saw the change, but, as she kept reminding herself, other people weren't the point.

She was tired of this face. Tired of all the memories that went with it.

She'd just never dreamed that she'd have the means to do anything about it.

In the lobby, pets and owners started to arrive. She heard Web's deep voice and instinctively braced—but only for a second. Lola Mae had shown up; the two of them were going through all the night call-ins. Poppy finished up her preps. Seconds later Web showed up in the doorway.

"Morning," he said.

"Morning," she sang back, just as cheerful as a magpie. But that was it. No more sharing a mug of joe to start the day in the break room, with jokes and laughter and animal stories. No more squabbling over the last Dr. Pepper or dried-up piece of pizza at lunch.

He'd screwed it up with that kiss.

She still felt the loss. Web—who could have guessed?— had somehow become the closest, the most compatible, the most interesting and challenging friend she'd ever had.

The cloud chasing Poppy's great mood was suddenly

darker than mud. The chances were a million to zero that she'd ever forgive him for screwing that up. A million *zillion* women would be thrilled to be kissed by Web. He'd never had to pick on her. Never had to do the whole hormone game with her.

Before she could let that problem fester up into a major daylong blister, she determinedly banished Web from her mind. She heard Barney's mournful, desperate howl from the parking lot and knew her first client was coming in...but at the same time she heard something else. Other sounds. Wrong sounds.

The clinic had two back doors, one for an emergency entrance and the other used as an exit for surgery patients. The sounds Poppy heard came from the emergency door, which meant someone was likely bringing in a badly hurt animal. From the raised and frantic voices, it sounded as if the crisis was going to end up on the wrong side of a happy ending.

She heard Web's voice in the middle of the fray, at first saying something soothing and calming. Then his voice changed, the tone taking on a crisp, authoritative note.

Poppy immediately whipped around and charged out. Barney would have to wait. She knew that particular tone of Web's. He was never a domineering order giver unless things were going wrong.

In a single glance, she realized things had gone bad, bad wrong. Four people, along with Lola Mae and Web, were all jammed near the door, clearly trying to carry in a hurt and bleeding Newfoundland. Newfs were probably the gentlest giants on the planet, not prone to any temperament problems, but this one looked well close to two hundred pounds, and from the amount of blood, had to be shocky. The dog was way too panicked to be a good boy for anyone.

His owners were frantic, both talking nonstop, crying nonstop, trying to communicate to Web what happened. But all the noise and confusion wasn't helping the dog—nor was it getting him moved.

Poppy silently ran forward. Web saw her. The kiss was forgotten.

This was about life now, something that really mattered.

"Clear out, everyone," Web snapped. "Right now we need only one thing—to get this dog in a secure place where we can treat him. I don't need all the talking. Not until we get him in and stabilized. Everything else is secondary."

"He's going to die," the older man said—the one with blood all over his L.L. Bean jacket. "He was trying to save my life, and now…" He broke down, which made the woman next to him, clearly his wife, start crying too hard to talk again.

"Maybe he will. Maybe he won't. But the sooner we get him quiet and secured, the faster we've got a shot at saving him," Poppy said soothingly.

Web clipped out, "Jay, open the far door on the left there. And Mary, I want you standing at the door to the lobby so no one else can get back here."

Poppy shot Web a look. They both knew the routine. Give people something to do besides stand around and howl, and everybody started behaving better. Nothing was worse than feeling helpless.

"X-ray," Web mouthed to her. As if she didn't already know.

Shirley, Web's surgical assistant, never worked more than part-time, but she was always in by ten. Poppy pitched in the off-hours, always had. Even when Shirley was there, Poppy sometimes joined the team. A third person could be needed to handle an especially difficult or large animal.

And sometimes—not often, but definitely sometimes— she was even better than Web at handling difficult critters.

This was one of those times. They fixed a blanket beneath the dog to carry him into X-ray and the surgical table. The owner had had an accident with a chain saw. When he'd called out, his valiant pet had tried to help him and ended up getting sliced up himself. Poppy didn't need to be told that it would take a small miracle to save the dog—and take a downright mighty miracle to give him any use of the leg again.

She set up near his head. Everything took time, too much time, she worried. Getting him settled on a flat surface. Getting the bleeding stopped. X-rays taken. An IV. It was easier to give a human painkillers than an animal, because many meds reacted more unpredictably on a critter, so it was always safer to give less—safer, but that didn't mean the animal was happier. Poppy did what she always did, holding his head, talking to him, soothing him, promising him a thousand treats if he could just stay still for her. And finally he went quiet.

"Hell," Web said once. "Sometimes I can't believe what you can make an animal do."

"It's not me. He knows you're helping him." Poppy knew

that was true. Newfoundlands were smart. Not like her Basset from Hell—who was still baying in the lobby and who would invariably sabotage anything anyone tried to do for her. The Newf was miserable, but he knew he was in good hands. Poppy told him over and over, told him all about Web, how much Web loved animals, how much Web loved him, how much Web was going to make him feel better, what a good, good, good dog he was.

She talked nonsense. It wasn't about the words. It was about the tone, about the trust.

It took well over an hour before Web finally pulled off his surgical gloves and heaved a tired sigh. Shirley jogged in, frantic that she'd missed an emergency like this, and was filled in about what happened. The older woman's gaze took in the Newf with the same look Web and Poppy shared. "You did it. Pulled off a miracle," she said quietly.

"Yeah, we did. And it feels damn good," Web said, then seemed to look at Poppy and himself and had to laugh. "I don't think we'd better be seen in public for a few minutes, though."

Poppy glanced down, too. The two of them were covered, almost everywhere, with blood and fur and various kinds of messes. They did look on the far side of ghastly. Yet she met his eyes and smiled, one of those smiles that was hopelessly, helplessly straight from the heart.

He smiled back at her—with the same smile.

Damn, but she loved that man. Not *love*, like thinking marriage or relationships or sex or any damn fool thing like that. But whether she wanted to or not, apparently she was going to have to forgive him for that screwed-up kiss. She just couldn't imagine giving this up—the rare kindred-spirit feeling she had with Web, the wordless understanding, the big-heart love for animals. They even had the same being-able-to-look-like-absolute-hell-and-still-laugh-together feeling.

Something broke the spell—that looking at each other, pinned-by-a-smile spell. Probably the baying of the basset hound and a harried Lola Mae coming in to whine about how late they were running for the morning's appointments. The moment was gone.

Poppy hustled back to work, feeling both relieved...and warned. There'd be no more kisses between them. She wouldn't risk losing what she had with Web ever again.

CHAPTER 7

Fragrant steam rose from the pot on the stove. Humming, Bren gave the stew a stir—after testing a sip. This morning her kitchen was a zesty, chaotic mess of scents and tastes because she had a zillion different things going on. There were two brand-new moms in the church, so she was taking them both batches of stew. Another church member was ill and lived alone—she had a batch of vegetable soup bubbling for him. Then the preschoolers' program at church this coming Sunday was building up for Thanksgiving, so she was preparing a wonderfully messy, fragrant dough ball of snickerdoodles for the kids to work with.

Maybe her kitchen was a disaster, but she hadn't hummed like this in a long time. She hadn't felt…easy…in a long time. She loved doing stuff for people, always had, but this morning Charles was sitting at the table, doing bills and bookkeeping—usually a source of worry and stress. But not today.

For the first time in ages she knew they were in good financial shape. The fund-raiser wasn't just bringing in great money for the cause. It was bringing people back to the church, and they'd been generously donating to the church, as well.

Obviously a few weeks of good revenues didn't solve any

long-term problems, but at least the numbers had put them in the black for now, and that gave them some oomph going into the Advent and Christmas season. In between stirs— and hums—she kept glancing at Charles, waiting for him to finish, waiting for a look of pleasure on his face when he realized they'd climbed out of this last tight financial corner.

Guilt still simmered on her conscience. She *knew* she could chip in her inheritance. That amount of money could really bring the church's financial situation around. By her own standards, she knew that was what a good wife would do. She should be doing things to show not only that she wanted to stand up for the church and her faith but for her husband.

Yet she still hadn't told him. Still hadn't done a thing with even a dime of Maude Rose's legacy.

She needed a slap upside the head—which she'd mentally told herself at least a dozen times since that first meeting with Cal Asher. But right now her heart was just glad the fundraiser and other efforts were working. Maybe she was flunking the loyalty course, but it would have been worse if Charles critically needed the money and she'd failed to come through.

She glanced at the clock and abruptly realized the Bible study group was due any minute. This was the guys' group, and although they used to meet in the church, Charles preferred them coming to the house. That way they could put up their feet and pursue their discussions in a warmer, more comfortable setting.

Swiftly she plugged in the coffee and took the plastic wrap off the fresh cinnamon-apple coffee cake.

She'd barely finished and turned around before she saw

Charles pound a fist on the table and stand with a look of frustration.

"What?" she asked quickly.

"We're not bringing in enough. Not to pay the bills. Much less to turn this church around. I can't keep going under this kind of impossible pressure."

Her lips parted to say something, but for an instant she was too confused to know what to say. She knew what the receipts were. She knew what the bills were. If they were still in some kind of serious financial crisis, she didn't know the how or why of it.

But just then the phone rang, and she hustled to grab it. Of all the voices she'd expected to hear, it certainly wasn't Poppy's.

"You're still doing okay, aren't you?" Bren had called Poppy's house until she'd gotten an answer late last Saturday. So she knew the surgery had gone fine, that Poppy was on the recovery track and that Web had fed her animals until she'd gotten home. But she hadn't heard anything since.

"I'm okay. And I'm sorry to call the house. Even sorrier to be asking you for a favor—so if you can't, you can't. Don't worry about it. But if it's possible for you to stop by for an hour or two, I'd appreciate it. It doesn't have to be immediately or anything like that. There are just a couple things I'm really having trouble coping with on my own—"

"Of course I'll come. In fact, it couldn't be easier for me to come this morning. I'll already be out and about, delivering some things to a few parishioners." Her eyes narrowed on the pot of stew, wondering if the volume would stretch to three batches instead of two. "I can stop by your place when I'm through. Just tell me how to get there. And what can I bring you?"

She hung up moments later, staring at the phone for a second in bemusement. They were making progress as friends if Poppy had been willing to ask her for help.

"Who was that?" Charles demanded.

When she spun around again, he still looked tight as a knot. The bookkeeping that should have reassured him seemed only to have agitated him further. That white look around his mouth wasn't a good sign.

"It was a woman named Poppy. She needed a bit of help, asked if I could come over for a short visit. And it's easy for me to add another stop. While you have the men over, I was planning on taking food around to various parishioners anyway." As if her voice wasn't calm and cheerful, as if she wasn't saying things she tended to say every day, he pounced on the one thing she was hoping to slide past.

"Is this woman a member of the church?"

"No. But she's alone, just recovering from some surgery. So I'll just take her some stew—"

"You're wasting time on someone who isn't in the church? And if that phone call had come in when I wasn't here, would you have even told me about it?"

His leaping to such a conclusion confused her. "I don't understand. Someone called and asked for my help. There's nothing unusual about that. Since when do we only help people who belong to the church?"

"The more relevant question is when did you start doing things behind my back?"

Oh, God. She *had* been doing things behind his back. The legacy. The apartment. The talks with Poppy.

Yet Bren couldn't have answered him straight at that instant to save her life. He'd stomped closer. Close enough that she felt the sudden beat of fear in her pulse. She'd been just about to ladle the hot stew and soup into containers she could cover. Now she instinctively put down the ladle, moved steps away from the hot stove.

She wasn't *that* afraid, she told herself.

She didn't really think he would do anything…crazy.

This fear thing—she was building a mountain out of a molehill. Overreacting. Her hormones had been haywire for a year now, even though technically she shouldn't be anywhere near menopause. It wasn't that Charles had a regular problem with anger. It was just recently that he'd exploded a few times….

She saw the look in his eyes and moved another few inches from the hot stove. And then the doorbell rang.

The first of the Bible study group arrived, Amos Byrd, his burly form stomping through the doorway, and Ridley McKenna hiking in just behind him.

Bren greeted them both, and when she turned round, Charles's expression was jovial and warm. My Lord. It was like watching Jekyll turn into Hyde. He surged forward, his greetings to the men warm and sincere. He clutched Amos's shoulder, pumped Ridley's hand. His pleasure at seeing them had to be obvious to the men.

His behavior was so Charles. At least, so like the Charles she'd always known.

The rest of the guys arrived. She served coffee and the coffee cake and, quiet as she could possibly be, finished preparing the hot food to take out. She spilled some of the stew, had to shove her hand under running cold water for a second. Idiot clumsiness.

Of course, she'd always been clumsy, but right now that wasn't the reason for her agitation. No one saw the side of Charles that she was seeing behind closed doors lately. She kept trying to grasp what was happening.

Had he stopped loving her? Where was all that anger coming from? Was he even aware of how much his behavior had changed toward her? Could he be ill?

How she was supposed to know what to do without even knowing for positive what the problem was?

It was ages before she finally got to Poppy's. She couldn't drive fast because she had all the hot pots in the back of the van, and even though they were covered and taped, she didn't want to risk a messy spill. And she had to visit with each of the people, coo over the two new babies, make sure old Mr. Marzke was functioning okay on his own.

By the time she'd turned off Baker Road, headed past town, she started searching for Poppy's address. She knew the general location—the hill country beyond town, somewhere between the hard-core horse-and-farm country and the last county-line bars. She hadn't stopped worrying about Charles by then, but curiosity had sneaked up on her.

She'd wondered where Poppy lived, what it'd be like. As she pulled in the drive—and naturally she missed the turn

the first time; she never could find her way out of a bucket—
the view snared her attention first.

It was like a private hideaway. Tall, regal woods bordered
the far back of the property. Closer in, a meadow area was
covered with tall grasses. Nothing was flat. All the land rolled
and curved. A double row of tall lilacs wrapped the driveway
and house in privacy. She could see a tidy barn out back, wood
neatly stacked for the winter. Tons of red and gold and apricot
trees…the leaves were hurling down in today's wind, making
a sea of crusty leaves in the long backyard.

The house itself was neither new nor big. But there
were potted plants on the porch, a couple of big old Adi-
rondack chairs.

She wrestled the stew from the van floor, trying not to
spill, yet it was hard to keep her gaze from nosing around.
She used hot pads to carry the pot, blew a strand of hair from
her cheek as she carried it to the front door, put it down.
Knocked, then didn't wait—she didn't want Poppy rushing
to be near the draft of an open door anyway, so she just
turned the knob and pushed.

"It's just me, Poppy!"

When she didn't immediately hear a response, she started
to call out again and then stopped. Stunned shock seemed
to paralyze her vocal cords. In fact, she almost dropped the
stew altogether when she saw all the purple.

Quickly she put the pot on tile floor, tore off her jacket
and heeled off her damp shoes. Still her gaze stayed nailed
on the couch. It was just so…purple. Such a girl-color
purple. So unlike anything she'd expected Poppy to have.

And it wasn't just the couch that was a shocker.

She took a single quiet step forward, when suddenly an animal streaked past her. It had to be a cat—or at least a cat in another life. The poor thing was missing one ear and all its nose, giving it the oddest flat face.

The cat might have distracted her attention, except that it streaked out of sight lickety-split…leaving Bren free to gape at the room again. A picture hung over the fireplace, not a print but an oil—a gorgeous scene of the mountains at sunset, all smoky mauves and sapphires and more of that velvet-purple color.

And in the far corner was an antique secretary. Not a guy piece of furniture but strictly girl-sized, small, feminine and pretty, made of wild cherry in a polished burl grain.

Bren had lived on hand-me-downs and parsonage furniture since she'd been married. She didn't covet material things. She *didn't*. But sometimes it was impossible not to imagine how she might have decorated a place of her own. It wasn't just the money of it but the freedom to have things around her that she'd chosen, that she loved…and no, she wouldn't have chosen Poppy's things. But the so-feminine choices were so different than the personality Poppy showed the world.

Other things caught her eye. A mirror sat on the coffee table—an odd place to put a mirror. The huge TV made Bren think of a bachelor apartment. The one and only thing she'd expected was messes, and thankfully there was a ton of clutter and mess. Newspapers, magazines, a shoe here, a mug there, stuff. Still. It was a lived-in, loved-in room. A room that revealed more of Poppy than Bren had guessed before—at least, a vulnerable side of Poppy she'd never guessed before.

And then a woman walked through a far doorway, startling Bren just as she was lifting the stew pot again. Foolishness. She had no reason to be startled just to find someone else here. Bren had just blindly assumed Poppy was alone because she'd asked for help.

"Hi, I'm Bren Price," she said warmly. "I'm just here to see Poppy for a minute. And I'll just take this stew in the kitchen if you'll tell me where to—"

"For heaven's sake, Bren. It's *me*."

The voice was familiar. The hazel eyes. And one way or another, Bren seemed to run across almost everyone in Righteous sooner or later, so she knew everybody, yet for the life of her she couldn't seem to place a name. The woman was her basic age, with a trim, slim figure, a stylish top with a bit of a wicked V neck and really pretty hair—kind of red, sassy styled, just snug under the chin. "I'm sorry," she said with a laugh, "I know I know you, but—"

And then the light hit the woman's face.

And Bren, who hadn't sworn in years—even when she hit her thumb with a hammer—whispered a helpless, "Holy shit!"

"Uh-oh. Did I scare you that much just to look at me?" Poppy asked. Snickers had broken into the bathroom to get her, a sure sign someone had knocked on the door, even if she hadn't heard it. The cat was now cuddled on her shoulder, head poked right into her neck, a posture she seemed to assume meant no one could see her.

"There's nothing *scary*, Poppy. I was just so startled. For a second there I really didn't recognize you."

"Well, I'm stuck with the bruises for a while yet. In fact, I'm afraid people'll think I've been in a bar fight for at least another ten days." Man, she'd felt so weird about calling Bren. Worried about calling her at home, where Charles could answer. Fretting what an imposition it might be. She just wasn't comfortable with needing a girlfriend. But...it turned out fine.

Better than fine. There were just some things she couldn't have asked her dad or brothers. Or a guy friend. There's no way she wanted to see anyone male in the population right now.

And Bren, maybe she should have guessed, was impossibly natural in this kind of situation. She just...moved in. Took the stew to the kitchen, put it on the stove, turned it on. Started looking in cupboards for mugs to make tea. Filled the sink with soapy water and dishes before Poppy could possibly stop her.

"Quit it," she said. "I didn't ask you over to clean up the place. I asked you over..."

"Why?" Bren prodded her.

Poppy let out an enormous embarrassed sigh. "Because I can't stand the dirty hair. I can't get the stitches on my face wet. And since no one's going to see me, the hair shouldn't matter. But it *does*. It's driving me out of my mind. I *know* that's a crazy reason to bother you, but—"

Bren was studying her speculatively. "Dirty hair drives me bananas, too. I can't stand it either. So, okay. Obviously you can't wash it in the shower if you can't get the stitches wet. Can't just lean over the sink, because that'd get your face wet, too. Hmm. I know—how about if I clean off this whole counter so you could lie on your back right here? I could wash it that way."

Poppy had never been a babbler. Sure, she talked. She loved to talk. She wasn't shy. But she generally only got wound up when she had something to say.

Yet the longer Bren stayed, the more froth kept bubbling out of her mouth. She was just so unused to someone taking care of her, doing for her. And Bren never said anything, she just kept *doing*. And somehow because she kept doing, Poppy started spilling how the whole last week had gone and couldn't shut up.

"I don't know what I expected. But this was like some place where movie stars or rich people go. No one like me. I walked in the door and they just started…pampering me. Treating me as if I couldn't walk a step on my own. At first I thought it was horrible…but it was embarrassing how fast a woman can get used to being spoiled—do you want me to change positions or move or something?"

"No, you're just fine the way you are." Faster than a thief in a flea market, Bren had made the dirty dishes disappear, then all the clutter on the counter. No one had to sell her tickets, for sure. She didn't ask where the shampoo and towels and all were, although Poppy realized that wasn't so odd. People tended to keep those things in the same obvious places in every house. "So keep talking. What'd they all do to you? What was it like?"

Poppy told herself that she felt laid out on the counter like a slab of meat. But it wasn't true. No one had ever washed her hair outside of a salon that she could remember. And somewhere Bren had unearthed a pitcher and was now rinsing her hair with soothing warm water, slowly, carefully.

She had to close her eyes, and when she did, images of the fancy spa flashed in her mind. The luxurious, soothing aquarium-blue everywhere. The plush carpeting. The staff in bare feet and yoga pants, soft in voice, easy in manner. Every smell in every room was a good one, fresh, enticing.

She struggled to explain to Bren, but it was like explaining an alien world. "These people were working for a living, you know? Just like everyone else? Only they never acted as if they were doing a job. They just acted like they existed just for you. It was surreal. And goofy. But what was not to like?"

"So...you got there and then what happened?"

"Well...first there was just talk. Interviews. Questions. Not prying. Just setting everything up, the schedule of events, where to go, how, what was going to happen. The first thing they actually did was a seaweed-and-mud wrap. It took hours. The smell—who knew? And I loved to play in mud when I was a kid. But the whole place was so wonderful. Soft lights, pretty colors everywhere, gentle music—not elevator music, just soothing, quiet stuff. Water and fountains everywhere you turned. And then you just lay there with the seaweed drying on you...."

When she sat up, Bren had already wrapped a towel around her head to start drying her hair. But damned if she didn't feel mortifyingly dizzy.

"I would never have guessed I'd be any kind of sissy about anything—"

"You're not, Poppy, quit apologizing. You probably haven't eaten much. And you've been taking medication. And you just had surgery, so there are drugs you're recovering from, too—"

Bren seemed to find all kinds of excuses to justify her behaving like a goose. And by the time she'd finished making excuses for her, Poppy was helped down from the counter, installed in a chair, fed a fat cup of stew and then urged to get on with the story.

"It was just…an experience I'd never dreamed of going through before. A world I didn't know existed. Everything about it was different than anything I knew. For damn sure, I've never been remotely spoiled like that…."

"Uh-huh."

"Then there was this style person. A personal buyer or something like that—not sure I got the job title right. But this woman sat with me, discussed what I wore, what I wanted to wear, what my self-image was. As if I'd ever wasted time thinking about what in hell a self-image was. Anyway, I didn't know where they were going with this. I mean, I'd signed up for it. I wanted new clothes. A different me. I wanted the whole program. But I didn't have a clue how that was going to work. You think this top is weird?" She plucked at the top over her jeans.

"I think it looks terrific on you."

She met Bren's eyes. "So do I. It's so strange. I rarely spend two seconds thinking about clothes, but then I put this on and thought, damn. I like this. Who'd have thought?"

The minute she'd finished the stew, Bren scooped up the bowl. "Okay, now I want to get your hair dry—I'm assuming the blowing heat of a hair dryer would feel rotten on those stitches, but we can really carefully towel-dry it a lot better than it is now. But I'm putting on a fresh pot of tea first. Just stay there."

It was so unnerving to have someone ordering her around that Poppy didn't know what to do. Except keep talking. "They didn't force bows and ruffles on me. They seemed to actually hear what I said. That I'm a jeans-and-sweatshirt person. They just kind of upgraded me. I'm not much of a shopper—"

"Neither am I."

"But this was different. They did the shopping. Almost everything they brought actually looked like me. Only better. It was so much fun—"

"Sounds like everything was fun," Bren said.

"Not the surgery, but all the rest—it really *was* fun. And then there was the hair." At that moment Poppy's eyes were closed again. Bren had a brush in her hand, was slowly brushing and drying her hair at the same time. She felt like a child again. Her mom used to do this, sit behind her and brush her hair.

The memory touched something that Poppy hadn't let loose in a long time. That hunger to be touched. Not the way a man touched a woman, not that kind of hunger. But the sweet girl-longing to be fussed over, the way her mom used to cosset and fuss over her, all the girl talk, all the girl touches. All the memories of her mom were seeped in her childhood, precious treasures still.

And when she'd lost her mom, they were simply gone.

"When I walked in," Bren said, "the first thing I noticed was your hair. It's really pretty, Poppy."

"I don't know about 'pretty.' But the cut—I'd never have known to ask for it. And the color, adding the streaks and lights and all. I don't quite get it, why it made such a difference, but it really seemed to—Bren, that stew was delicious."

"Glad you liked it. Had enough nutrition for now? Need some kind of disgraceful junk food?"

Poppy chuckled. "I've got a stash of chocolate somewhere."

"I'll find it. Trust me. I can smell out chocolate better than any hound."

"And after that there was the makeup person. I had a whole afternoon with her. I figured that'd be like torture, but she didn't really goop me up. Didn't even try. It was more skin care. And some basic products. Lipstick and mascara and some blush. Not a whole heavy arsenal. Nothing that was going to take tons of time to do every day…"

Considering she was doing nothing but talking, Poppy wasn't sure why she felt so completely wiped out. She was even less sure how she ended up curled on the couch, wrapped in her mom's old afghan, a tall mug of tea on the coffee table surrounded by a half dozen Kisses wrappers. "The surgery was pretty much the least of it. I can't even complain about that. The day after the surgery, I have to admit, was a little rough. There wasn't pain so much as dis-comfort. I couldn't get my mind off my face, couldn't rest. And all the swelling and bruises were pretty wild. But even though I was all mangled up, I could still see that the changes were there, and pretty much exactly what I'd hoped for...."

"Which was?" Bren had taken off her shoes, put her stocking feet on the coffee table, a mug of tea in her hands, too.

Poppy had to think a moment before answering. "The 'surface' answer is that I wanted less nose, less chin, more cheekbones. But the real answer is that I didn't want to look like Maude Rose."

"Say what?"

"Maude dressed and looked in a way that drew attention to her. There were reasons for that. Which was her business. But I wanted the opposite. To change my looks so that I wasn't...noticeable. Wasn't going to stand out in a crowd. I just really wanted looks that would make me less vulnerable."

"I think you used that word *vulnerable* once before. I didn't understand it then and I still don't. How could your looks make you vulnerable one way or another?"

"It's hard to explain, partly because it took me so many years to figure it out myself." Poppy took another sip of tea before leaning her head back on the pillow. "People always, always assumed things about me because of my looks. Girls in school didn't include me in talks about clothes or boys or fashion—they just assumed I wouldn't be interested in girl stuff because what would be the point, with my looks? But the worst problem was always men. Men always took one look and figured I'd be grateful for their attention, grateful for a date, grateful for a screw. No guy looked at me and thought I'd be a romantic interest."

Bren cocked her head. "So…you felt you were a target for a certain kind of man—a man looking for 'prey'—if you looked different."

"I *knew* I was. And I told you before, I didn't want to be gorgeous—not that that was ever a possibility. But even if I'd had that choice, I'd never have wanted it, because I never wanted that kind of attention. I *just* wanted looks that didn't hurt me."

"You wanted a shot at the right kind of man?"

Poppy snorted. "No. I don't *need* a man. I'm way past those years when having a guy is the only goal worth thinking about. Thank God. But, when I was around males, I just wanted looks where my appearance wasn't always a problem. An issue. The one big thing that always defined me."

"Aw, come on, Poppy. Don't you think that's pie-in-the-sky impossible? I mean, we're all stuck with our looks defining us, at least to a point—"

Poppy nodded. "I know that. I agree. But all my life, my looks defined me in a negative way. Until Maude Rose's inheritance. This whole last week…all the things they did to me…it just totally opened up my world. It was so much more than I hoped. It was fun. And fascinating. I'm so happy."

"Yeah?"

"Yeah, absolutely."

Bren leaned forward, saying nothing for a moment, just looking at her.

"What?" Poppy said, suddenly feeling unnerved and edgy.

"You didn't ask me over to wash your hair."

"I did, too!" Bren fell silent again, so silent that Poppy

felt compelled to repeat, "I did, I did! I can't stand dirty hair!" Still Bren said nothing, aggravating Poppy no end, confusing her as to what the damn woman wanted to hear, what she wanted her to say.

In good time, Bren rose to her feet, disappeared in the kitchen and came back with a square box of Kleenex... which she plopped on the coffee table close to Poppy.

"What's that for?"

"You're upset," Bren said. "I don't know why. Don't even have a clue. But there isn't a prayer in this universe that you'd have asked me over—*me*, Poppy—unless there was something you couldn't tell all the people in your regular life. The dirty-hair story just doesn't cut it. I mean, you don't have to tell me anything. But I'm here, so..." For the second time in as many days—Poppy wanted to take credit for being such a good influence—Bren murmured a soft-as-a-whisper, "Aw, hell."

Poppy couldn't possibly be crying, because she was no prissy sissy. Hit her with a hammer, and of course she'd yelp. But a bunch of emotional tears—or any kind of emotional scene—wasn't in her makeup, never had been.

"Just tell me," Bren said gently. "Talk."

Poppy found a Kleenex wadded in her hand. And then it was waving around in the air. "I just got *scared*."

"Scared of what?"

Cripes. The snot was clogging her nose thicker than the tears were spilling from her eyes. And it hurt like a bitch to blow her nose. Hurt even more just to feel those swollen tissues double-packed because of the stupid tears.

"It's just too *weird*," she said. "I sit here looking at a mirror. Only it isn't *me* looking back. I don't know what to think, how to act, what to do." She pointed a finger at the mirror on the coffee table. "That woman is a complete stranger. Maybe she looks better than I used to look, but that's not the point. How in hell am I supposed to go back to my life? Go to gown, grocery shop, work, see Web and my family? How is *this* woman supposed to react, when she isn't me?"

CHAPTER 8

Poppy couldn't believe she'd spilled all this to Bren. Or that she was blubbering like a baby. Who knew that she had this kind of stupid neediness inside her?

She'd never been a blubberer. For damn sure, she'd never been one to vent on anyone.

But Bren just leaned forward, looking serious and kind, not looking as if she were suddenly stuck dealing with an emotional lunatic—and a lunatic with bruises and bandages, besides.

"Okay," she said gently, "let's get down to what's really happening here."

"There's nothing happening here except for my being a complete idiot."

Hell. She refused to cry any more. It hurt around the eyes. Squinching her face up was *not* an option right now, not unless she wanted every nerve and cell on her whole face to sting and burn like the devil.

"You're not being a complete idiot. But I don't know what you mean...about not feeling you're 'you.' You're the same person you were before this surgery. And heavens, Poppy, honestly you don't look so drastically different that people aren't going to recognize you."

"You didn't!"

"But that's just because I was distracted when I first walked in."

"Well...maybe people will recognize me and maybe they won't. But it's a whole *thing* I didn't think about ahead of time—that some people will talk about my choosing to have plastic surgery."

Again Bren didn't show any expression to indicate she minded dealing with a lunatic, just persisted. "And why would that be so terrible?"

Poppy threw down the tissue she'd been trying to dab her damn eyes with and wildly gestured. "The whole idea was to have looks that *didn't* draw attention to myself. But if I'm that changed, then people will know I had plastic surgery."

"And you're afraid they'll think you're vain or something like that?"

"No. I'm afraid if some people realize I had plastic surgery, they'll also realize...how much they all got to me. Especially the guys."

Bren frowned as if she were hugely confused. She curled a leg under her. "So...if I've got this right...you're happy you went to this spa. Happy with everything they did. Happy with the surgery, as well. It all accomplished exactly what you wanted. In fact, you wanted to change people's perceptions of you—at least, the preconceptions of you they always made because of your looks...."

When Bren stopped talking, Poppy felt prodded into responding. "Right."

"So...the only drawback is that you did exactly what you wanted to do?"

"Damn it. Quit confusing me, Bren. I know I'm sounding goofy. But darn it, at least I knew how to behave with my old face, my old look. Even if I was unhappy, I knew the rules. Knew what to do. Now..."

"Now you're worried to death about something that hasn't even happened yet. Come on. You don't know this is going to be hard or easy, bad or good or anything else. You haven't even taken the new face out for a test-drive yet."

Who could imagine Bren could be so annoyingly full of common sense? "I know. And it isn't ready to be tested in public yet, besides—"

"Oh, yeah, it is," Bren said firmly. "Seems to me it's exactly the right time. If you went now, say, to the grocery store, people would say, 'Oh you poor thing, what happened?' And you can answer them, 'You're not kidding! This was nothing I expected, for sure,' and then just get your milk and cereal and go back home."

Poppy rolled this around in her mind for a minute. "You mean...just let people see the bruises?"

"Why not?"

"I don't *know* why not. I just assumed there was a why not. You're confusing me again."

"I'm not trying to confuse you. I'm trying to suggest that you need a plan. And I think the best plan is to test-drive your new appearance on your toughest problem."

"Right," Poppy said, meaning it. But then she frowned. "Um, what exactly are you thinking my toughest problem is?"

"Your family, obviously. Your brothers. Your dad. That's where you're going to get the worst teasing and harassment, right?"

"Oh, that is so dead, dead, dead right."

"So start there. Do a dinner for your family. Get it over with. Then try the next step—going into town. Hit the grocery store, the gas station, fast food, the bookstore. Wherever your face is familiar, so that you can have some conversation ready to say, all prepared."

"And this prepared conversation would be…?" Poppy pushed.

Bren lifted her shoulders. "I don't know. Whatever you want to say. The point isn't *what* you say, Poppy, it's that you're prepared with some comment so nobody can take you by surprise. You'll be ready."

"Oh…" Granted, she had a headache and her face hurt like a giant bee sting, but the mental wheels were starting to turn. "You mean like…lie." Possibilities suddenly bubbled to the surface. "I could say I was in an accident. Or maybe that the accident ended up turning out for the best—"

Bren interrupted. "Well, personally I don't think you need to lie."

"That's just because you're a preacher's wife. Lies are sometimes good. Lies are sometimes fun. Lies are sometimes a helluva lot easier than the truth, besides."

Bren opened her mouth as if she were about to argue with her, but then seemed to stop herself. "Well, the point isn't what you say. The point is that if you take the lead, you can prepare yourself ahead for how casual acquaintances are likely to respond. You can just joke and evade, if you want. Like…you could say 'You should see the other guy.' Or 'It just doesn't pay to take up wrestling at my age.' I mean…you don't have to fill in the whole story. It's no one's business. You just have to get comfortable fielding some questions. And once you've passed that set of tests, you can move onto test three."

"And what exactly is test three?"

"Since the male half of the population is the group who gave you the most problem, they're the ones that have to come next."

Even though it hurt to shake her head, Poppy did it— hard. "I'm not ready to see Web."

Bren looked at her.

"Web is different," Poppy said firmly. "He's the last test. He's the only person except for you who knew I was going to do this ahead of time and he was really against it." She frowned. "Actually, now I remember, so were you."

"Doesn't matter now. You did it. It's spilled milk. So now the only thing that matters is making it work for you." Bren uncurled her cramped legs. She didn't even blink when Snickers, silent as a secret, suddenly jumped on Poppy's lap and cuddled close. She hadn't said anything when Edward hopped across the room either. Obviously the household had decided to accept Bren.

What surprised Poppy the most, though, was that she did, too. Her brothers claimed she listened to no one, had a head more stubborn than a mule's. But she said, "I'm still listening," to Bren and really meant it.

"Good. Because I want you to listen to me. You look *great*, Poppy. Not suddenly gorgeous or glamorous. Not wildly different. But there's this something. Underneath all those bruises, when you smile, there's something new coming through. I think that's what people are going to see. That you like the new Poppy, that you feel good about yourself."

"You're right. In fact, you're completely right." Poppy couldn't believe how much Bren had made her feel better…when Bren suddenly glanced at her utilitarian watch.

Her face blanched as if it had suddenly been dusted in chalk. She leaped to her feet. "Holy kamoly, I have to get home. I didn't realize how long I'd been here—but before I leave… You're going to have to call me. Let me know how the plan goes."

"Okay." She watched Bren jog for the door, grab her jacket and bag.

"No time to talk about the apartment now, but I've got news on our potential new tenant. Mary Sue needs a place pretty quickly. I don't know if our apartment will suit her, but I blocked out some time next Monday morning to start painting. It shouldn't take long just to do a couple of rooms. So if you have time—or feel up to it—spin over there. And by then you'll be able to give me a progress report on the new-face project."

Poppy had to settle the cat in the afghan before climbing to her feet. "Bren, I feel badly that I took so much of your time. Thanks. For the stew. For the hair wash." She hesitated, then added awkwardly, "And especially for the listening."

"Don't sweat it." Bren grinned. "I like things this way. Now you owe me. So the next time you feel like criticizing me for something, see, I've got brownie points already on my side."

Poppy wasn't fooled by that nonsense. "You never had to do this, be this nice."

"Last I noticed, you didn't twist my arm to come over. I wanted to."

Poppy didn't want to hold her up any longer when it was obvious she was stressed at the time. But she had to say, "It's so weird, isn't it? How those crazy jewels have pushed us together? But…Bren… You know a lot about me. About trouble spots in my life. About how I used the inheritance to try and fix them. So I feel like I'm always monopolizing the conversation. You still haven't mentioned what your plans are…or just more about yourself."

Yet when Bren finally left, Poppy realized she'd still managed to duck any personal conversation. She hadn't mentioned what she was doing with the inheritance. Or, for that matter, what was going on with that husband of hers.

Or whatever other problems she might have.

As Poppy scooped up Snickers and climbed back on the couch, she reminded herself that none of that was any of her business.

Yet it was.

Maybe they'd formed an unlikely friendship, but darn it, they *were* friends. The inheritance had not only brought them together, but it seemed the jewels had brought their most awkward, painful secrets out of hiding. And since Bren had come through for her, Poppy thought—hoped—she had the power to help Bren the same way.

* * *

Two nights later, Poppy pulled into her dad's driveway. Typically the garage door was gaping open—not because it was packed with cars but because her dad used the garage space for a shop. Right now the current projects seemed to be a door getting resanded and stained in one corner, and another corner was filled up with all the gear to water-seal the deck.

Coming home always brushed her mind with memories. She'd grown up in this house, once slept under the dormer window, the shake-shingle roof hanging over her head, her view of the world taller than anyone else's. The boys had slept on the second floor. She'd had to climb the third-floor stairs, but then she'd had that precious room and the tall view all to herself.

Her brothers' vehicles were already stacked in the drive, as was her dad's truck. No one, naturally, had thought to leave her a spot near the door, even though they knew darn well she was carrying the food. Her dad might have asked her over, but Poppy knew there was an understanding unspoken in the get-together—that she'd bring the dinner.

Her men all had archaic ideas about women. Occasionally Poppy went on the war path, but reeducating them was such hard work that often enough she gave up. Besides which, her dad was so darned appreciative of the cooking that she just couldn't mind.

Heaven knew how her brothers had managed to come tonight, but Poppy suspected their wives had pulled a girls' night out…which meant freedom for everybody. She climbed from her VW and immediately felt a sassy wind sneak down the throat of her jacket. She picked up her cell phone, then plopped it back on the seat. There were two calls on there from Web already that she hadn't answered.

She was going back to work next Tuesday—and wanted to—but she just wasn't ready for Web to see her new face yet. Wariness over her family's reaction was making her edgy enough.

She carried the first load of food in, yelling out a hello. She heard hellos back coming from a distant room, but nobody showed up to help her. No surprise. The guys were all wrapped around the big-screen TV, arguing about politics, some sports event screaming on the tube.

She pulled off her jacket, revealing Maude Rose's huge, gaudy jeweled cuff with the bug-eye-sized tanzanite edges. It had taken the visit from Bren for her to think of a trick. No one was going to notice her face with that wild chunk of jewelry to draw their attention.

She hiked back outside twice, hauling in lasagna, apple kuchen, fresh French bread and a spinach salad with mandarin oranges. Her mom's kitchen had never changed. Her dad never moved a thing. A mangy mutt named Lurch was sprawled in front of the fridge—just in case anyone wanted to give him a treat. A cat wandered in so she could get her neck rubbed, too. The oblong table had to have five pounds of mail, tools and newspapers moved off it before she could wipe it down and set it, and abruptly that was the end of the peace.

The guys all moved fast—like hounds, nose-first— toward the smell of the bread and lasagna. They'd brought long-necked beer for them, wine for her. She was kissed and bussed and thwacked, feeling like Snow White dwarfed by mountains. She never felt that way anywhere else, because she wasn't that small. But darn it, her brothers were huge.

Her dad, though, got the warmest, longest hug, and he was the one who first registered a heart attack. "Poppy, for God's sake, what happened to you?"

Her brothers, who could be infamous for not noticing anything, did a spin around and, that quick, were on her faster than ticks. "Hey, if you had an accident, why didn't you call us?"

Naturally they went on and on, she could barely get a word in, much less get them settled at the table before the lasagna started to cool. Because they all grew up in this house, they still went by the laws mom had taught them—which meant they washed their hands before dinner, but definitely expected the woman to do the waiting-on. She didn't put up with that crap often, but damn, she sure couldn't complain that they didn't appreciate her cooking, mediocre though it was.

When and as she handed out blue napkins and started scooping up rectangles of lasagna, she said, "I don't suppose you'd all believe me if I admitted running into a door, would you?" And then slowly, carefully, she flashed the ghastly jeweled cuff as she set down each plate.

"What the Sam Hill is that?" her father demanded.

"That's why I wanted to have dinner with you. Because I couldn't wait to tell you about this, but I only wanted to have to tell the story once. " She had to laugh at their comical expressions. The guys just couldn't believe she was wearing anything so flaunty. "I inherited this."

She spilled out the story—or the part of the story she wanted them to know. The part about Maude Rose. And the jewels. She didn't mention Bren or the value of the loot or what she'd chosen to spend half her money on. Since they'd stopped talking about her face, she couldn't think of a single reason to dwell on what they didn't ask.

Later, driving home, she thought the dinner had turned out to be a piece of cake. She'd been so sure her brothers would tease her, so sure they'd think less of her for doing something so vain as plastic surgery. Instead she realized an old truth, which was that brothers just didn't tend to notice their sisters. Heaven knew, they were the best of family. If she'd asked them for any kind of help, they'd have been there for her—they'd have intruded and bullied and pestered her about running her life their way, but their loyalty and love, Poppy had never doubted.

Zach, because of being a cop, had a couple stories to share about Maude Rose. He knew her, the same way he knew every character in Righteous. Maude had spent a couple nights in the town jail—one time she'd raised quite a ruckus over gay rights. Another time, a pro-life rally had started out peacefully, until Maude had gotten into it and started ranting for the opposite view.

Later, at home, Poppy was still thinking about those stories. No matter how eccentric, Maude Rose was such a stand-up woman, the kind who stood alone for what she believed in, whether others agreed with it or not. Even when her choices cost her.

It was crazy, Poppy thought. To wish she were more like

that crazy, eccentric old woman. To wish she'd known her better. To wish she understood better what made some women have guts…and what made some women afraid.

In the dark, staring at the black dots on the ceiling, Poppy was reminded yet again that Web hadn't seen her face yet. She couldn't wait to get back to work, had enough of this sitting at home and silly recovery routine. She missed the critters, missed the clinic, missed her life. But where everything had gone far better than expected so far, she couldn't seem to stop worrying about seeing Web.

She just didn't want him looking at her…personally. Intimately. Critically.

Not that she was still remembering that kiss. Those feelings. She hadn't given either a second thought.

And absolutely didn't intend to.

Even though Bren had been on a wild racetrack schedule that morning, the minute she opened the can of paint, her heart rate eased. It's not as if the paint smelled good, for heaven's sake. But there was something about the smell that implied freshness, newness, clean starts.

Good things.

Charles thought she was spending the morning with her father, and that was partly the truth, because she *had* stopped by the nursing home. But all those partial truths were bugging her more and more, starting to corrode her stomach and her conscience both. She wanted to come clean. It just wasn't that simple. So for these few hours she determined to just concentrate on painting. On letting herself relax.

Being with Poppy made that easier.

Every time Bren glanced up, she wanted to shake her head. Poppy was slathering paint on the far wall with a roller. In the paint store, predictably, they'd fought tooth and nail over the color. Bren assumed a pure, clean white was the obvious best choice, adaptable to any kind of decor. Poppy had figured a peppy orange would be "fun." They'd stared aghast at each other for a while.

Balancing on the top of the ladder, hand-brushing the ceiling corners, Bren thought the putty color wasn't bad. Not what she'd have chosen, but the white ceiling made a sharp contrast, and it was pretty versatile.

Neither had wanted to leave Maude Rose's pink on the walls for the next tenant. It just didn't seem right to have someone else's pictures go on Maude's walls. That pink had been too private. Maude had only shared her sharp, neon side with the world—not the pastel side.

Kind of like Poppy, Bren thought, who had a terror of anyone thinking she could conceivably have a soft side. "So go on," Bren prodded her. They'd been telling stories since the paintbrushes had come out. "What happened at the tire place?"

"I was just getting new tires, like I said. And Raymond suddenly runs out of his office—beats me why, not like I needed the manager of the store to buy a couple of tires. I mean, sure, we went to school together and all, so we always say hello on the street, but he'd never given me special treatment. And no reason he should have."

Poppy glanced up at the same time Bren glanced down.

Both of them refrained from shuddering, but they could barely tolerate each other's work styles. Bren didn't drip. Her theory of painting was to do the job right and carefully the first time—which meant she worked a little slowly. Poppy already had far more paint on her than on the wall, but heaven knew she covered a lot of ground fast.

"So this Raymond asked you out?"

"Yeah." Poppy kept on, making an exuberant squish-squish-squish with her roller. "I couldn't believe it. I mean, the swelling's mostly gone, but the bruises are sure still there. And it's not like he ever gave me a second look before."

"So did you say yes?"

"Well...no."

Bren climbed down, moved the ladder, climbed back up. "What? Why on earth not? I thought that was one of the major reasons for doing this—to have men see you in a different light."

"Well, it was. It's not like I suddenly thought I'd get more respect. You have to earn respect. But I admit, I admit, I did want some guys to look at me as if I were...potential. Not just a throwaway. But still. I didn't go through this just to get some dates."

"What's wrong with accepting a date?"

"Because dating sucks. It always sucked. Cripes, I don't want to *date*. Anybody. It wasn't about that. It was about not wanting any more men to think I needed a pity date— or a pity f...scre...um..."

Bren couldn't help being amused. In the beginning, Poppy had sworn around her right and left. Yet the more their friendship developed, the more Poppy was trying to desalt her language. "Well, I understand that. But I know Ray. Not real well—he goes to the Lutheran church—but you know how it is. You hear things around town. He seems like an honestly nice guy. Divorced, but that was a long time ago. A young, short marriage."

"Well, he *is* a nice guy. Or he always was. But we were in the same class. I threw up on him in second grade. You can't go out with someone you threw up on. It'd be like…incest."

Her brush was making a fine, precise line in the crease of the ceiling when the absurdity of the word suddenly struck her. It was so Poppy to say something so outlandish. To make it sound normal. But on a sunny October morning, with Monday morning traffic toddling below and her hiding out from Charles and both of them furiously painting, and to hear throwing up compared to incest well, heaven knew what was wrong with her, but an unexpected chuckle burst out of her and turned into another one.

She had to put down the brush. Suddenly she let loose a hiccup the size of a small horse, and that sound was so darn silly that she really started laughing. Then Poppy started in, too, until they were both howling like hyenas.

Finally Poppy caught her breath and gasped out, "What? What'd I say that set you off?"

"I couldn't help it. I just kept thinking that only you would pair *throwing up* and *incest* in the same sentence."

"Hmm. I think you just insulted me, but never mind. How come you don't laugh like that more? In fact, when the hell's the last time you laughed?"

"Hey, I laugh all the time," Bren said defensively.

"No, you don't. Not a big laugh from the belly like that."

"Maybe not." It bit that Poppy was right. She used to laugh all the time, be one of those notoriously sunny people. She still tried to be, but she missed it. That feeling of light-heartedness. The belief that a smile could make a difference. Of course, she'd grown up.

She moved the ladder to a new spot—one perilously close to Poppy's wild roller. "So go back to the progress report. Your brothers and dad were all fine with your new face. You aced that test with flying colors. And so far, every trip to town you described as going smooth as silk."

"Yeah. It's bewildering. Everybody notices, but everybody's just…nice about it. Two guys asked me out. Women I went to school with are stopping to chat as if they always paid attention to me. Couple people have just given me sympathy, like they assumed I was in an accident or something. All this time, I tried to talk myself into believing appearance didn't matter that much. But drat it, it *does*. But whatever—so far, it's impossible not to be happy I did this." She suddenly motioned to Bren with a dangerously dripping roller. "I'm sick to death of talking about myself! What about you? Come on, by now you *must* have some ideas on what you want to do with your inheritance!"

Bren stiffened. She tried to think of something to say, well aware that Poppy had trusted her with her private problems…and that she hadn't reciprocated. She didn't want Poppy to think the trust wasn't mutual. It was. But…the problem was like the difference in how they painted.

Poppy slapped it on, went back later to find the spots she missed. Bren didn't like to make mistakes. Right from the start, she tried not to miss anything. It had to be right. Just as whatever she said had to be right.

God knew why.

Life wasn't paint.

She opened her mouth a couple times, but somehow her vocal cords seemed rusty. She had to try a third time before anything came out. "My dad's in a rest home. Did I mention that before?"

Poppy suddenly stopped all that squish-squish-squishing. "No. I'm sorry."

Bren practiced being a little sloppier with her paint. Contrary to what she'd always believed, lightning didn't strike her dead. "He's in the Righteous Senior Home, the long-term-care wing. He's paralyzed. My mom and dad and sister were in a car accident when I was a teenager. The night…I was being inducted into the National Honors Society, which was a big deal to them. Only they drove separately because I'd already stayed late at school and my boyfriend was driving me home."

Who knew? Who could possibly have guessed that paint would just spill out, slather out, and just maybe she could survive not being careful every single second?

"It was raining that night," she continued. "Really raining. One of those black, shiny nights when the roads are all slippery. Some other driver went through a red light. Not drunk or anything. Just an accident. My dad swerved to avoid him and hit a pole."

"God," Poppy said softly.

"My mom and sister died. I thought my dad was going to die, too…for a long time, in fact. But he didn't. There's some fancy name for the problem, but basically his back was broken. He's got a little use in one hand, but pretty much he's a quadriplegic."

"Damn, Bren…"

But now she'd started, she couldn't seem to stop. She was still facing the ceiling, still painting in splashy, artistic strokes now. "We used to live on Baker Road. Past the hardware and Nel's Grocery, back off the road. Dad was a CPA. Mom started out as a dental hygienist, but she never made any secret of not liking it—she just really wanted to quit and be a full-time mom."

She didn't look down, but she knew Poppy wasn't still painting, because Poppy made so much *noise* in everything she did—cripes, even her smiles were noisy—that Bren knew darn well she was standing absolutely still, just listening. "I didn't realize you'd lost your mom, too," she said.

"Crazy, isn't it? To find another similarity between us?" Bren added, "People who've never lost someone—especially someone as treasured as a mom—it's as if they're in another room. Not necessarily far from you but never quite with you. They can't possibly understand. That loss is like a hole in your life that nothing can fill. As old as I am, it's still there."

Poppy snarled, "If you say one more word like that, I'm going to cry. And let me tell you, I will be really pissed off if I start crying."

Before Bren could comment on that particularly insane statement, she heard Poppy pick up the roller again and start talking. "I know about that stupid, awful hole. I've got the oddest hodgepodge of memories. Like…I remember my mom lying on the grass on a summer evening, laughing. I can't remember why, doesn't matter why. My brothers were all there, too. We were all happy. Rolling around, smelling the grass, laughing with her."

"Hmm." Bren dipped her brush again. "I remember my mom getting ready to go out one time. I don't remember where she was going or details like that, but I was so small that I had to stand on the toilet seat to be able to see in the mirror with her. She was all dressed up, putting makeup on. She put some blush on her face, then on mine. Put some lipstick on, then some lipstick on me. And last was the spritz of perfume. Every darn time I smell that perfume, it's like my mom's right there beside me again."

Poppy said gruffly, "I remember holiday dinners. Especially dinners involving turkey. My mom couldn't cook a decent turkey to save her life. It was either bone-dry or so raw it was lucky we didn't all end up with ptomaine."

"I remember Billy Ray Simpson hitting me in first grade. I hit him back, but then he really slugged me good, right in the stomach. I ran all the way home—and it beats me why I remember this—but she didn't ask me what happened, didn't matter, she just folded me on her lap and rocked me until I felt better."

"Hey, would you *quit* it? Skip the stories like that. You'll make me cry."

For just that instant, Bren let her brush drip. "That's really what I remember most. That even when my mom was mad at me, I knew she'd be there. In my corner. No matter what."

"Yeah. That's how my mom was, too. She just always made me feel like I was the most special person in the universe. Never had any doubt I was loved growing up."

"Neither did I."

Maybe it was by chance they both stopped working and stepped back. Heaven knew the living room was in shambles, between the tarps and naked windows and masking tape. But the actual painting was done. And though it'd be nice to bask in their accomplishment, they were both on a tight schedule and needed to move on.

Poppy started the cleanup, although naturally she was as messy about this as Bren was fastidious. Still, they managed to work at the sink together like two kids sharing the same sandbox.

"Bren...I take it it's absolutely sure that your dad's permanently paralyzed?"

"Yup. They take good care of him. I visit him four times a week...actually, I try to make it every day, but I just can't always." She'd brought over rolls of paper towels to help the cleanup. And dish soap. "There was insurance at first. Good hospital insurance. But that coverage changed once he left the regular hospital, and, well, he couldn't stay in the rehab setup forever either. Once it came down to a long-term-care facility, there was nothing. No money. I mean, I was just a kid. I grew up just assuming I'd go to college, but that was out of the question then—and I sure had no idea how I could possibly afford my dad's health care cost either. It was just huge."

"There *have* to be places—"

"There are. But you wouldn't want to put your dad in them, Poppy. It's like everything else. You get what you pay for. The poor places…you can smell the urine. The despair. You can see how overworked the staff is. See the level of care. And the only place of that kind was eighty miles from here, and my dad was all I had then. I didn't want to be that far from him."

Poppy, being Poppy, stopped working and perched up on the old kitchen counter. "So what happened?"

"Charles is what happened. Charles swooped in just like the white knight in the fairy tale." She saw Poppy stiffen, knew Poppy had formed ugly ideas about Charles. Maybe that's why she'd started this. To get all that out in the open instead of cramped inside herself like a stomachache that wouldn't go away.

"Your Charles had money."

"Nope, not at all. In fact, he was just starting his ministry then, working under Pastor Riverton before he retired. Charles was nine years older than I was…but then, I was mature for my age. Not at first. Believe me, when I was seventeen, I was as ditzy and thoughtless as any other teenager. But after the accident…"

"You aged fast. You had to."

"Yup. And Charles…maybe he felt a spark for me from the start. I'm not sure. What I know is that he stepped in to help. He didn't have to. He just did. The care facility pulls strings for certain people—it's not that they give favors so much as that they recognize certain people in the community have given back, and that's the reason they don't have enough money for their own needs. Or that's my theory. Anyway, they've always been generous with the rules for people of faith. Social Security disability covers my dad's prescriptions and a bunch of basics. And everything we had back then—the value in the house and all—went into his care. But Charles is the one who pulled the strings, got him in, is the reason he's been allowed to stay there even when I had no more assets to give them."

The damp paintbrushes were tossed in a plastic box she'd brought. Damp rags in another. Trash in a bag. Bren could see from Poppy's face that she was thinking. Rethinking her preconceptions of Charles.

"Okay," Bren said finally and straightened up, rubbing two fists at the little ache at the small of her back. "You think we could set a date when this place might be ready for Mary Sue to take a look?"

Poppy was distracted. Went looking for her jacket, which, naturally, she'd tossed in a heap by the front door. "You think her situation is getting worse, that she needs to get in here?"

"I just know that when I saw her a few days ago, I really started to worry about her. It's not like I've met the guy she's with or I'm so sure of all the facts, Poppy. Maybe you'd have a different impression. I also can't swear she'll keep up the place. We could be asking for a lot of trouble. But the only way to decide all that, I think, is for both of us to talk to her together. How about if we set a time, show her the place, then just see how it all goes from there?"

"Sounds like a plan. You want to try for a dinner?"

"No. Not dinner." Bren couldn't do dinner. She did dinner with Charles, period.

"All right, well…how about a coffee, then. Like right after dinner. Say…Thursday? I can't see trying for sooner, because we still need some time to finish cleaning this place up. The painting was the worst mess, but all the same…"

"That sounds fine. Thursday's the soonest I could put it together, too. I'll call her, see if that'll work." Finally all the paint cans were hammered closed and the sink cleaned up and paint clothes exchanged for streetwear. Bren, running late for a Ladies Auxiliary meeting, jogged for the church van.

She was overdrawn on the parking meter and had a pea-sized paint spot on her shoe, but she didn't care. It was her favorite kind of morning—where she felt she'd accomplishing something real and solid. Felt even better that they were moving ahead, doing something about Maude Rose's place and hopefully doing something helpful for Mary Sue.

Time with Poppy always left her upbeat, besides. This morning maybe more so, because it was past time she'd cleared the air about her husband. She felt disloyal that Poppy had formed a negative impression without even knowing Charles. Talking about him had given her a chance to frame him in a more positive light, to make certain Poppy understood he was more than capable of being a warmhearted white knight.

If things were going increasingly rough at home, Bren put that aside.

Poppy couldn't help her with that. No one could. She simply had to find a way to live with her situation.

She kept thinking—had been thinking for weeks—that if there was absolutely no other way, she'd tell Charles about the inheritance. Give it to him. It was just some stubborn, selfish little voice inside her that insisted she stay quiet, that that money was the only freedom she'd ever had.

Knowing she had that inheritance was like holding hope in her hands.

She just couldn't seem to give it up.

Unless she absolutely had to.

CHAPTER 9

Poppy leaned closer to her bathroom mirror, unfurled a thin layer of mascara on her lashes and then stepped back for a judgmental look.

Hot damn, but she looked good. Beyond good. In fact, she looked so damned good that she was risking being late for work if she kept staring at herself much longer, but what the hey. She'd never had a reason to revel in vanity before.

As far as Poppy was concerned, it should never be too late to take up a new vice.

Even after two weeks, the bruises hadn't completely disappeared, but they were pale enough that a dab of foundation easily covered them.

Her clothes weren't odd, at least in principle. Typical for work, she'd donned jeans and a chambray shirt. But the jeans had a boot cut and actually fit, instead of drooping in the seat and bunching at the knee. Who knew that was even an option? And she'd always had chambray shirts in her closet; this new one wasn't even particularly expensive. It just had darts and a slimmer fit.

They were still work clothes. The new version just

seemed to have evolved into work clothes that showed off her boobs and butt.

Hells bells, for years she'd ignored her boobs and butt—particularly when what little she had showed an inclination to sag as of her fortieth birthday. But nothing seemed to be sagging now. The snug jeans miraculously seemed to boost up her behind. And a little wire in a bra did amazing things.

It's not as if she'd never shopped before the surgery. It was just that she'd tended to buy old, reliable brands and products. Apparently she'd been buying the same type and brand of bra for centuries. And apparently she'd assumed that there was no reason to look further when anything she wore was likely to be muddied up and dog haired by the end of the day. But darn, her old jeans weren't even particularly comfortable now that she'd tried on the new versions. Attractiveness was only a part of the picture.

But it *was* a part.

Again she stared intently at the mirror. It wasn't precisely a beautiful face staring back at her. The nose was ordinary. The chin ordinary. The forehead ordinary. To anybody else, that wouldn't seem so…well, so extraordinary. But the little surgical changes were like a miracle. She didn't look wildly different. She'd just lost that distinctive homeliness. The only real extra the doc had put in was some collagen or something or another in her cheeks. Not a lot. Just enough to give the illusion that she had some bones up there, that her face wasn't flat.

The crazy part was that those little bits of surgery seemed to hugely change everything else. Her hazel eyes now seemed huge and oval and striking. A little mascara and they popped even more. A swipe of blush on the new cheekbones brought out more natural-looking color in her face. Her lips…well, she used to think her mouth was too small. Now she thought maybe it just looked wrong in the old face. In the new face, the lips fit. Everything fit.

Her hair used to be her one pride and joy. They hadn't done much to the natural color, just added a few highlights here and there. But the new cut was kind of messy. It seemed to add sassiness. More like her, not less. More astounding yet, she didn't have to spend eons of time to do the style. She'd just had to learn how to blow-dry it and dab a little stuff into it now and then.

It seemed so puzzling…how could she possibly look so completely different? The doctor had actually only changed a few small things. And new clothes didn't really make the woman, everyone knew that. But that face…

Hell, every time she saw that face in the mirror she started smiling.

Maybe that was the difference? That she was smiling like a damn fool all the time? If she got any more self-obsessed, she was going to have to change the name on the mailbox to the Most Shallow, Vain Woman in the Universe.

And darn it, having wasted time this way, now she had to run. Edward and Snickers both needed kisses. She had to make sure they had fresh food and water, that the birds and squirrels and deer outside had their share of fresh goodies…and then Edward got one last petting because he knew darn well she was leaving for the day and he'd gotten used to having her home.

After that, she charged for her car—so antsy about seeing Web again that she could hardly think. He'd helped with the critters when she was in the hospital, of course. And called. And tried to visit one day, but she'd been swathed in bandages then, so he hadn't actually seen her. At least the new her.

Seeing him would never be giving her this crazy heart attack if it hadn't been for that kiss—the one she'd never mentioned aloud again—because before that, it had never occurred to Poppy that Web might have noticed she was female. *Then* it had insulted her mightily to be given a pity kiss—and why else would he have? *Now*, though, things had changed. Now she darn well *felt* pure female, which had drastically created possibilities in her mind that had never been there before. She hadn't gone completely bonkers, but she had to believe Web was going to notice her looks. And like them.

So far, everybody else had.

She zoomed out of the driveway and exuberantly hit the gas pedal. Truthfully it wasn't just Web she couldn't wait to see. It was getting back to the animals, her work, the clinic. For a couple of weeks it had been entertaining to discover this brainlessly vain Barbie-doll side of herself—after all, everyone knew women in that premenopausal phase were entitled to bursts of insanity. But beneath that nonsense, she was just a wee bit tired of looking in the mirror. She was happy enough to look different. But enough really was enough.

En route to the clinic, as she passed the turnoff to Bren's church, she instinctively frowned. That was another thing she couldn't wait for—seeing Bren this coming Thursday. Maybe the excuse was interviewing Mary Sue for Maude Rose's apartment, but that wasn't what Poppy cared about.

Over and over, she'd replayed their conversation about Bren's husband.

Bren had obviously wanted her to see Charles as a hero. Yeah, and slugs flew. Poppy figured she'd gotten the real picture from that conversation. Bren's husband was no white knight but the opposite. The jerk was essentially blackmailing Bren into staying with him. She couldn't leave because of her father in the nursing home, so apparently Charles thought he could do anything he wanted with his wife. And did.

Granted, Poppy had heard nothing but good things about Charles—and God knew, her brothers were a superb source of local gossip. If anyone knew town secrets, it was Zach and Jase. But she'd still seen bruises twice on Bren. Seen something in her eyes that wasn't right. A jumpiness. A defensiveness.

Since Poppy had never been remotely a meddler, she had no clue how to begin.

And right now she had to postpone that train of thought. She wheeled into the clinic and buoyantly soared out.

"Jumping Jehoshaphat, will you look at what the cat dragged in." For once, Lola Mae was earlier than Poppy. Far more startling—and gratifying—was that she took one look and dropped her nail file.

"Man, have you been missed. Everybody and his brother has been calling for grooming. Or training. Actually, mostly training. What is it about fall that brings out bad behavior in dogs? And men." No pause for breath. And Lola was still staring bug-eyed at Poppy's new face. "Criminy, I was prepared to dose out some sympathy. I thought you were under the weather, and instead you look just…incredible!"

"Thanks." Walking into the lobby was like coming home. The voluptuous Pauline was already waiting for Web with her retriever. The golden looked as healthy as it always did. And Barney, the basset hound from hell, was playing the howling diva in the far corner—apparently because of a thorn in his paw. A pair of kittens in cages took up the cat side of the room, pampered on a velvet blanket by a pink-haired woman.

The smells and sights were so luxuriously familiar. "My first appointment's at nine, right?"

"Yup, just like you asked me to set 'em up. But you've really got them back-to-back today, Poppy—"

"Which couldn't be better. I'm so hot to get back to work I can't stand it."

Just past the exam room doors, she ran into Shirley. Web's assistant was rarely here this early, but there must have been a morning surgery scheduled because she was already in scrubs. Her wholesome face broke into a shock of a grin.

"I was just about to banish you to the lobby, tell you that only vet staff was allowed back here—because good grief, Poppy, I barely recognized you!"

"Amazing what a little sloth and feet-up time will do to a girl," Poppy grinned back.

"You've been so missed!"

That was pretty much how it went, everyone at work responding to her just the way everyone in town had. It was fun. Just a little wearing when the only one she really wanted that reaction from was Web. But she had no time right then to track him down.

Howard arrived. Howard happened to be Ruffian's dad, her first customer of the morning. Ruffian had a little problem rolling in dead animals, preferably roadkill. Howard maybe reached five foot four with a lift in his shoes and looked like exactly what he was—a tidy little CPA in a fresh bow tie, doomed to be single, who thought he'd be less lonely if he adopted a rescue dog.

The theory was terrific. It was that pairing Ruffian with Howard was like hoping a stripper could happily room with a nun. Howard adored the dog but was constantly aghast at the terrible ideas the dog consistently thought up. Once, Ruffian brought home a sanitary napkin that it had unearthed from heaven knew where. Howard wasn't the kind of guy who could even say *sanitary napkin* without hyperventilating from embarrassment.

Poppy never said, *Howard, honey, you are so so over your head.* But she did her best to honestly counsel him. "Howard, I can train the dog to behave better. But you're the one who has to follow through."

They'd been through this before, and this was one of those sessions where Ruffian got to snooze and Howard got the training workout. Halfway through, though, she chased to the door when she heard Web's voice in the hall.

She saw him. At least, she saw the back of his leg. From the commotion and back-and-forth between him and Shirl, Poppy gathered he'd just finished one surgical emergency before being called out for another. A Belgian was delivering. Normally a horse didn't need a vet for labor and delivery, but this Belgian had been on the fragile side from the get-go.

Her heart didn't sink—she'd see him later that day, and it wasn't as if she didn't have a full slate of her own. After Ruffian came Killer—an Australian shepherd who was thankfully a lover in temperament, because she was a real bitch to groom. After that came two Bubbas in a row, one a puppy who peed whenever her owner came home and the other a bird dog who couldn't seem to give a damn about hunting birds, a catastrophe for his owner.

The second Bubba was her only new customer. Everyone else already knew her, and they all fussed over her as if she were the most gorgeous thing the town of Righteous had ever seen. No one asked if she'd had plastic surgery. Most of them just seemed to assume she'd done something to herself, lost some weight or put on makeup or something else that had transformed her.

Shirley was the only one who tackled the truth blunt-up, when they were both grabbing a sandwich in the break room. Both ate standing. With Web gone, everything else in the clinic was running behind. Still, Shirley found the time to say, "I always wanted to do it."

"Do what?"

"Have a facelift. I know, I know. You look at this big, old, round face and think what's the point? But I don't care whether there's a point. I never met a woman who wouldn't improve something about her looks if she could."

"Shirley, you look great! You don't have any bad points."

"Neither did you. But you thought you did, right? Otherwise why would you have gone for a change? And more power to you, honey." Shirley shook the crumbs from her hands, tossed out her paper plate and napkin and took off. So did Poppy.

Still Web wasn't back.

A father and son came in without an appointment, bringing their Dalmatian and Chihuahua. The dogs weren't getting along. She heard them out, both the owners' and the dogs' versions. Everyone seemed to realize an intervention was necessary, so she set them up with a training program.

Just after that, she thought she heard Web's voice in the hall, but she couldn't stop to find him. She had two more critters to see. The first was a Maine coon cat, and no one with a brain kept a Maine coon cat waiting. Matilda was getting up there in years and needed help with her grooming. Matilda's owner claimed nobody could handle her but Poppy, which was nice to hear but of course unlikely. Coon cats were just tricky to handle, took a lot of quiet talk and soothing to get the job done.

And last came the only real challenge of the day, and damned if it wasn't a heart-wrenching doozy. Furthermore, it was all Web's fault.

The patient was named Mandy. Josh, his owner, was nine. A very small nine. He brought Mandy in the office via a red Radio Flyer wagon. Originally the dog had been Web's patient—the dog had gotten tangled up in barbed wire and ended up losing her right front leg. Losing a front leg was a ton more traumatic for an animal than losing a hind limb, and Mandy was older, had some arthritis. She was also a Heinz 57. Sometimes mutts were healthier than purebreds, but in Mandy's case, she seemed to have inherited the worse traits of a border collie, a bird dog and heaven knew what else.

For starters, Poppy hunkered down to the height of the wagon, meeting Mandy, judging the state of recovery the dog was in. The question was whether the dog could be trained to function, to cope on just three legs. Some dogs could, but Poppy had her doubts on this one.

She had no doubt why Web had sicced the kid and dog on her. Never mind her hormones and those kisses, Web could be a real stinker sometimes.

Josh was too proud to cry, but his lips shook when he told her the whole story about his dog, and the hope in his eyes was so damned big that Poppy knew damned well she was going to be damned well stuck having to try. Whatever it took. Nobody could face that kid and just say no. At least, nobody with any functioning heart.

"But, Josh…I think the only way this has a prayer of working is if I keep her with me for a little while. This isn't the kind of training we can do all at once or an hour every other day. I need to work with her intensively. You can spend as much time with her as you can. But I'd bring her with me to the clinic during the day, take her home with me at night. I don't know for how long, but I'm guessing at least a week, ten days."

"That's okay. I don't care. And I'll pay whatever you want. Whatever it costs." Josh showed her his wallet, which revealed what was locally called a Virginia bankroll—a bulging wad of one-dollar bills. No fives, no tens, no twenties, but a pretty good chunk of ones. "You can have it all. Everything I got. I can do some more chores for my mom if you want more money than that, so don't be worrying. Do you think it would help if we got her an artificial leg? I mean, that's what they do for people. And she's better than a lot of people. She's better than just about anybody."

And that was when Web walked in, when she was sitting on the floor with Josh, with Mandy snoozing on the wagon between them. Web looked as sharp as a spank of fresh air, all ruddy cheeks and rumpled hair and electric dark eyes. He hunkered down between them. "Hey, Josh. I see Mandy's doing a ton better, isn't she?"

For Pete's *sake*. She'd looked fabulous all day. Well, maybe not *all* day, but at least she'd looked pretty close to sexily attractive that morning. And even after dealing with a few animals, she might have lost the top layers of spiff and shine, but she'd still looked nice. Now, though, hell. When Josh's eyes had welled up, so had hers. She'd been wet and dried and haired up several times. The lipstick was long gone. Unfortunately the mascara was still there, only now under her eyes instead of on the lashes.

Web said something else to the dog and the boy before turning to her. He grinned, then slapped her on the back as if she were a crony from grade school. "Sure missed you, Poppy. Great to have you back." Without giving her a chance to answer, he turned immediately back to Josh. "There's no knowing how far Mandy can recover, Josh. But

I do promise you that if anyone can get that dog on its feet, it's Poppy. But you need to accept that it's not up to humans altogether. It's really going to be on the dog, whether she's willing to live this way."

"I know, sir. You told me. And you told me not to get my hopes up. And I'm not." Josh raised eyes so full of hope that, damn it all, Poppy's eyes welled up all over again.

"I really can't promise, Josh."

"I know you can't," he said bravely. "But we can sure try, can't we?"

"You bet we can try." Web's gaze met hers.

Poppy wanted to swear all over again, this time escalating to the F word. She loved the way his eyes connected with hers, but instead of the female-male electric hookup she'd anticipated, there was only a kindred-spirit connection about the dog. And the boy. When he'd handled the medical side of Mandy's problems, he'd known perfectly well he was going to pawn off the training side of the fence on her.

"Sure looking great, stranger," he said and clapped her on the shoulder again as he stood. But he wasn't even looking at her when he said it. In fact, he was already leaning over to shake Josh's hand. "Tough situation, Josh. Especially when you have a great dog like this one."

"She *is*."

"And between the three of us, we're going to give her the best shot she could have anywhere. So no matter what, we're going to feel good about it. Right?"

"Right," Josh said.

"Right," Poppy said and watched him stride out the door, feeling as if someone had stuck a pin in her balloon.

Okay, maybe that kiss—or series of kisses—had been an aberration. Something she'd built up in her mind as more important, more volatile, more evocative than it had really been. But damn the man.

The entire town—the entire world—had noticed the difference in her appearance. It's not as if anyone could miss that there was a major change. But Web hadn't registered any difference in her at all. He'd just related the way he always had, as if she were a seriously good pal with a lot of common interests and common ground between them.

Cripes, she hadn't changed for Web. Hadn't had the surgery for any man—or woman. She'd done it for herself. But damn, who knew that sneaky hunger for love would suddenly show back up after she thought she'd buried it so well all these years? Who knew she'd had a bunch of sneaky ridiculous hopes about Web, for that matter?

She wanted to kick herself.

Peeling off the old face seemed to have peeled off some old, vulnerably fragile emotions, as well.

Thursday night, Poppy drove to the Heels Up. The sky was darker than tar and pitching sleet, which perfectly matched her mood. Leaving the animals hadn't helped. Edward and Snickers had gotten used to her being home, so now they were ornery that she was back at work all day and had really acted up when she'd left them this evening. On top of which, she'd temporarily added Josh's Mandy to the family now, too.

That wouldn't go on forever, but right now she had her hands too full to waste time—and meeting Bren's young woman friend totally defined *wasting time* as far as Poppy was concerned.

If Bren wanted the kid to have Maude Rose's apartment, that was a no sweat. She didn't have to be here. She not only trusted Bren's judgment, but Bren was the one with the tact and the patience and the counseling talents. Poppy was likely to bungle around and say something stupid. Which she knew.

Possibly, just possibly, she was meaner than a riled skunk because of Web. Web hadn't said a cross word to her in the entire three days she'd been back at work. Not one. Nada. Nothing. He'd been as warm and friendly as he'd always been.

Cripes, she was so depressed she could hardly think. The honky-tonk lights of the Heels Up bar parking lot didn't improve her mood any either. The lot was naked except for a handful of cars and trucks. The minute she stepped inside, she muttered under her breath. There was no sign of Bren or the kid. It figured that she'd be early, stuck in a bar alone, especially in a place she'd never planned to see again.

Probably every single person in a three-county area had been to Heels Up at least once. Poppy had a healthy clutter of bad memories of the place. Nothing traumatic. It was like remembering every cavity you ever had filled—you could probably conjure up the specifics, but why would you want to?

The bar specialized in line dancing, and for years, whenever she felt like beating herself up and finding another loser, she'd sucker in. Still, there was nothing intrinsically wrong with the place. The music was always foot-stomping fun, the atmosphere corny to the nth degree. The plank floor helped make a great dancing racket. The stage was set up for fiddles and a guitar band, with a mirrored wall behind them. The bar was in the center of it all, shaped like an almond. No booths, just dozens of tiny tall tables with stools. The waitresses were all female and all wore the same sexist getup—black short shorts, white shirt with pearl snaps that bared as much cleavage as was legal, fishnet stockings and heels that could kill a girl if she tried walking too far in them.

More than once Poppy had heard the rumor that Heels Up took in more money than the bank. And that was a maybe as far as the bank's being able to compete with the profitable bar.

Poppy just knew what kind of girl got a job here. It was always the same. The girl who'd barely scraped through high school, had no skills, no grades, knew she wasn't moving on and that her best shot was to capitalize on her looks to get a guy. Bars, of course, were no place to get a guy. To screw one, yes. To find losers and one-night stands, sure. But to nail a mate—as far as Poppy knew, it hadn't yet happened in the history of the universe.

"What can I get you, honey?" The bartender emerged from behind the bar with a pencil and pen…but he took a good, long sipping look of her, head to toe, before getting back to the drink question.

She wanted to feel flattered, but damnation, the buzz from the plastic surgery had long worn off. She wasn't looking to attract strangers. Ever. Couldn't imagine why she'd ever thought that might be a kick. "Three coffees," she said curtly.

She realized the order was risky. Coffee could get cold awfully quickly. But it *was* past seven…and then the girl walked in.

Poppy had been pretty sure she knew who Mary Sue was—not that they'd personally met but that she'd seen her around. One look, and Poppy realized that wasn't true. She'd never seen her before.

But she knew her.

The kid came through the back door with that kind of belligerent stride that announced she wasn't afraid of anyone or anything.

Yeah, right. Poppy told herself a zillion times that she wasn't maternal, yet the look of the girl punched a distinctively maternal zone in her heart. It was the look in her eyes. Damnation, was the whole world into whipping puppies these days? The kid—and okay, she wasn't a kid; Bren had claimed she was close to twenty. Still, she was such a baby she didn't have a single wrinkle or sag. The stupid sexist outfit would have revealed any flaw if she'd had one—for damn sure, the grapefruit-sized bruise on her thigh showed through even dark stockings.

There were bruises on her wrist and arm, too. Her hair was a tea-light brown, long, just worn attractively simple and straight, but the girl had painted on pounds of makeup—maybe she'd chosen the first ton of goop to fit in with the bar scene, but the rest was obviously to conceal a swollen lip. And Poppy had news: no amount of eye shadow was gonna match a bruise color either.

The girl spotted Poppy and guessed who she was immediately. She flew to the table and right off said she was Mary Sue Chapman, how are you, but then blurted flat out, "I don't quite get what this test is."

"There's no test." Poppy motioned her to sit down, pushed a coffee toward her, cast a frantic glance at the door for Bren.

"Mrs. Price, she said you two had a place, an apartment. But my shift starts at nine. I got time to see this place, but I can't be late for my shift. And I don't know what you want to hear from me."

"Bren will explain everything better than I can. But speaking for myself, I don't need to hear anything. It's not like a test. We just need to know if the apartment suits you all right."

"Well, that's easy. Any place is better than what I got, because right now I got no place to go but the women's shelter. Been there before. They let you stay four weeks, which is fair, you know, I'm not complaining. Gives you a chance to get on your feet and all, not like it's meant to be a free ride for life. Only it didn't work for me. I mean, I got on my feet and all, got the job here, got a place of my own. And did the same damn thing I did before. Hooked up with trouble."

Again Poppy desperately looked at the door, hoping to see Bren. She'd know what to say. "Believe me, I've hooked up with my share of losers, too."

"Yeah, right." The girl didn't snort, but her tone was humorously disbelieving. "No one who looks like you needs a loser. Me, I'm a bad picker. And it seems I'm never going to change."

How the hell could anyone so young sound so old?

Whatever guy was beating her up couldn't be half as bad as how bad the kid was beating herself down.

"Anyhow," Mary Sue went on, "Mrs. Price, she said this apartment wouldn't cost me rent. But I know that's not right. There has to be a cost. There's always a cost. I just gotta know what it is up front. Then I can tell you, square, whether I can manage it or not."

Poppy almost sprang to her feet when she finally saw Bren sprint through the door. And Bren headed straight toward them, but within seconds Poppy felt a spike of fury shoot up her spine. For Pete's *sake*.

Bren pulled off a jacket as she sat down, immediately smiling, being natural and doing the greeting business with Mary Sue. She was wearing typical Bren clothes—a longish skirt, a bulky sweater. Tonight, though, she had a scarf around her neck—which, on anyone else, would have added a fine little splash of pizzazz.

But it wasn't pizzazzy on Bren. Poppy could see the damn red mark over the edge of the scarf. The discoloring began just under her earlobe and kept building in size until it came to the scarf. It was a welt. A big welt.

Bren had let that son of a bitch put a hand on her again? Damn it! Bren looked worse than the girl!

Poppy wanted to whale off and kick a wall. She glanced at her watch, wondering if she could possibly run home and hide under the bed—now that she knew for dead sure this evening was going to be a complete disaster. She was going to open her mouth eventually and say something ghastly wrong, she just knew it.

Bren caught her looking at the watch and stood up. "I know we're all on a timetable, so let's head over to the apartment. Might as well drive together?"

Poppy drove, because she was afraid if she didn't, she'd be too inclined to knock their heads together. And every damn time Bren moved a certain way, more of that red welt showed, even in the dimness of the car.

Once they reached Maude Rose's, Bren went in first, turning on lights. Mary Sue wouldn't take off her jacket, just slowly walked around.

Poppy tried to see the place through the girl's eyes. Beyond painting a couple rooms, she and Bren hadn't done much. She'd bought fresh pillows, and Bren had come through with clean linens, a bedspread. The old couch had been cleaned up, the cupboards scoured from the inside out and the bathroom shined within an inch of its life.

The only thing the women had completely removed were Maude Rose's personal things—which Poppy was storing because Bren didn't want to take anything home. She hadn't said why, but Poppy knew. God forbid Charles find out that Bren had this apartment and some means of her own.

The immediate point, though, was that Poppy knew the place looked bald. It *was* bald. It had enough stuff for a person to survive with, just absolutely no extras.

Still, Poppy felt oddly good about the place. It was action, that was why. It wasn't talk. It was a way to actually *do* something for someone. Especially since she damn well didn't have a clue what the hell she could *do* for Bren.

Bren seemed as calm as a kindly spring breeze, telling

Mary Sue about Maude Rose. Not any of Maude's private story about the jewels. Just about the old woman's history. "She was someone who seemed to take on every unpopular cause in Righteous that I can think of. I didn't always agree with her, Mary Sue, but I so admired her courage. And when we got this place, Poppy and I just thought…this is what Maude Rose would have liked. For the place to be lived in, used by a woman who needed some help. Just a boost up. Not that big a deal."

"No big deal—are you kidding?" Mary Sue was still twirling around on those silly heels. "Look out those windows. I could walk to any store I needed, carry my food home. I wouldn't even need a car except to get to work, and maybe I could even bike it there. Or maybe I could try to get a job somewhere in town. Then I wouldn't need a car at all and I could really start putting something away." She couldn't seem to stop twirling. "And it's so pretty up here. I can see down into the valley, over the hilltops. And yet it's so nice and quiet."

Suddenly she stopped all that twirling and faced them both, looking Bren straight in the eye, then Poppy. "Okay, now. What's the catch? Really."

"There's no catch," Poppy said.

"Yeah, right." The girl suddenly hugged her arms tight around her chest. "Are you two gay, is that it? Because it's not like I got a whole lot of pride, but there's a limit to what I'm willing to—"

Jesus. Poppy was going to have a heart attack before this damn evening was over. And she jumped in because Bren's expression revealed complete confusion.

"Nobody is gay here, Mary Sue. Nobody wants anything from you. But you're right—there is a catch."

Bren's head whipped toward her, looking confused for a second time. "What catch?"

"I knew there was something," Mary Sue said.

"The catch," Poppy said, "is that we want you to think about something. If you've been to a shelter, I'm guessing you already got a bunch of support and counseling. You can get that from Bren, too, but you sure as hell won't get it from me. If you want this to work, you need to make this apartment a safe place. A place where you start building a different life."

Mary Sue said defensively, "That's all I ever dream about. All I keep trying to do."

"No." Poppy wasn't buying that bullshit. "You've been dreaming about turning losers into good guys. Dreaming that it's your turn for someone to love you. And the next guy who looks at you sideways, you'll start thinking again that he could be the one. You know what I'm talking about?"

"Hell, I wrote *that* book," Mary Sue said.

"So that's the catch," Poppy said. "You get this place, it's yours, rent-free for six months. It's not for us to say who you bring here or not. Nobody can stop you from screwing another loser. But what I want you to think about is…don't bring him here. For your sake. Not for ours. Not because we made it a *rule*. But because this is your shot to have six months that's totally your own, nothing on your back, no pressure, nobody pulling at you to do anything."

"I won't bring nobody here if you don't want." Mary Sue said it soft and low, like a vow.

"I wouldn't know if you did. Neither would Bren. But this isn't about us. It's about you."

Hells bells, by the time they locked up and walked out of the place, Poppy was worn out. She didn't do counseling and pep talks. God knew, she couldn't imagine allowing a guy—any guy—to smack her around either. Yet something in the girl bugged her. The way she thought she could only attract losers. The way she walked and talked defensively.

They drove together back to Heels Up, with Bren making the arrangements for Mary Sue to make a decision, sign an agreement with them, get a key. Couldn't put it all together for another week—unless Mary Sue ran into a crisis.

"That's a euphemism for if the jerk hits you again. As in, don't waste time and wait. Get the hell out of there and call one of us," Poppy said.

"I knew what she meant." Mary Sue climbed out, revealing a long flash of leg in the moonlight. It was almost nine by then, close to her shift time. "Thank you. Thank you both," she said awkwardly. "This is more than anybody did for me in a long time. I won't forget it."

Poppy drove her VW another thirty feet to where Bren's old van was parked so that Bren wouldn't be walking in the bar parking lot in the dark alone.

Bren gathered her purse, put her hand on the door handle. "I think she's perfect. The kind of girl Maude Rose would have wanted to have a shot."

Poppy heard her. Agreed. But when Bren clicked the handle open, she said, "Not so fast. You and I have something damn serious to talk about before you take off."

CHAPTER 10

Outside the Heels Up bar, pickups and cars were starting to clog up the parking lot. Bren hadn't mentioned to Charles where she was going because Thursday evenings he had a regular meeting with a handful of the church elders, some of the major financial supporters. He was never home before nine-thirty, which meant she never had to mention that she was leaving the house in that same time period.

But now it was tipping past nine. She pulled the van key from her purse, snugged her arms around her chest. "It's colder than a well digger's ankle out here," she said to Poppy. "I don't know what you want to talk about, but couldn't it wait until tomorrow?"

"No, it can't wait." Poppy leaned against her VW, obviously not caring whether she got car dirt on her back and behind. Security lights peppered the parking lot—enough so Bren could clearly see Poppy's expression. Which was dark and ornery. "I don't like that bruise on your neck, Bren."

Instinctively her hand shot to the scarf. "I didn't think it showed."

"Don't give me that shit. This isn't about whether it showed. It's about that girl. You knowing she needed to get out of a relationship where she was getting hit. And you staying in one. What the hell is that about?"

"Mary Sue is a girl, like you said. A baby. Too young to know how to help herself. It's not the same thing."

"At least you're not denying the creep hit you this time." Poppy crossed her ankles as if she planned to have a good long talk—even in the freezing night. Even with the time ticking away.

"He didn't hit me. I fell."

"Bren—"

"After I was pushed."

At that admission, Poppy instantly fell silent. She just kept looking at her, her expression intense and unrelenting.

Bren lifted her gaze to the heavens. Seeing stars, seeing a fat silver moon. But not seeing God. Not tonight. She said tiredly, "You want everything to be simple, Poppy. You want right and wrong to be cut-and-dried."

"Sometimes it is," Poppy said furiously.

"Yeah, sometimes it is," Bren agreed. "But not always. Sometimes life is darned complicated."

"But not this time. When someone's hitting you, you get out. Nothing complicated about that."

Bren said gently, "We're not so different, Poppy. You just had plastic surgery. On the surface, you wanted to change your looks. But down deep, what you really wanted to change was how you felt about yourself, isn't that true?"

"I don't get what you mean."

"What I mean is that the surgery didn't work. You look different, but you don't suddenly feel miraculously good about yourself. I've come to believe that nothing is easy, Poppy. Not for either of us."

"I don't *remotely* get what you're talking about—"

Bren said slowly, softly, "You're still not going after what you want. You changed the easy part—how you looked. You haven't done the hard work of real change yet."

Poppy threw her hands up in the air in a gesture of utter exasperation. "Are you trying to talk in parables or something? Because I don't have a clue what *you're* talking about. But what *I'm* talking about is leaving the son of a bitch who keeps hurting you. Why don't you just come stay with me? We'll probably drive each other crazy, but so what? You don't have to stay forever. But I have space. You can stay until you figure out what you want to do. And at least you'd be safe."

Bren sighed. "I can't. I have to…stand up."

"That's *exactly* what I want you to do. Stand up. Get out of there, get away."

A couple ambled past them, snuggling together, kissing even as they walked. Bren said, "It's so darned easy for you to talk, Poppy. So let's make a deal. I'll stand up when you do."

"*Huh?* What the hell do you want *me* to stand up about? I'm not the problem here!"

Bren knew the clock was ticking. Saw another face go by that she recognized, who recognized her. A guy bolted out of the bar doors, staggered toward his car. It was almost funny—because both she and Poppy seemed to instinctively jerk toward the guy at the same time. They'd be stupid to offer a strange, drunk man a ride home. They weren't going to do it. But somehow both had the same instinctive reaction to stop someone from driving who shouldn't. To help someone who needed help, even when it wasn't wise.

"Poppy," Bren said quietly, "I know that you're a gutsy, stand-up person. But for others. Not for yourself. Just like me."

"That's not true—"

"Oh, yeah it is. You desperately want something in your life. You even know what it is—and it wasn't surgery. But you're the only one who can reach out and go after it. No one can do it for you."

Poppy clawed both her hands through her hair in a semi-humorous gesture, as if expressing how hard it was to deal with the demented. "Jesus, I swear, trying to have a woman friend is tougher than going through perimenopause."

That slowed Bren down. "You think we're friends?"

"Don't you?"

Even feeling pressured to get home, Bren didn't want to rush that answer. "I doubt either of us expected it. But I think we've turned into extraordinary friends. Keep feeling lucky Maude Rose brought us together. But lately…I don't feel I'm *being* a very good friend for you. I mean, here Maude gave us this huge inheritance that should have opened up choices for both of us. Instead we both seem to be in worse shape than we were before. Go figure."

Poppy frowned at her, as if suddenly forced to mull that unexpected idea.

It was rare, mighty rare, that Poppy didn't have an immediate comeback for anything—much less anything that worked to shut her up.

Bren, taking advantage, gave her a quick hug and took off.

She begged the van to hustle just this once, but, par for the course, it gasped and teetered and coughed anywhere above forty. There was just no way to get any extra speed out of it. Thankfully, though, when she pulled in the drive, there was still no sign of Charles's car.

Faster than a thief, she jogged in the house, hung up her coat, turned on the TV to the show she would normally have been watching at that hour and then pounced on the answering machine. There were always calls in the evening—calls she would have handled directly if she'd been home. She clipped down the messages and then started calling back.

She was on the phone to one of the parishioners when the kitchen door slammed.

Her pulse jumped ten feet. Her anxiety level soared twenty.

Charles stomped in, red-cheeked, stopped when he saw her on the phone and shot her a dark glower, as if she hadn't already figured out his mood from the slam.

"Now, Mabel, take it easy. You know how teenagers are. That doesn't mean you're a bad mother…." She couldn't cut short the call. Didn't want to, besides. She'd always thought it was her most critical role as a minister's wife to be there for people in trouble. So many people just wanted to talk, to share something they couldn't share with others, or just needed to believe that someone else was actually willing to listen to them.

When she finished the call with Mabel, there was only one more person on the list she needed to connect with that evening. But with Charles home, that last call would have to wait.

She took a breath, then started searching. He wasn't in the living room, not in sight from the hall. The bathroom light was on, but he wasn't in there either. She found him in the bedroom, heeling off his shoes, clapping his belt on the bureau, then slapping down his change. All the sights and sounds neoned the message that his mood was lousy. Yet again.

She tried to sound normal, to say the kind of thing she always used to say when he'd come home late. "Are you hungry for anything? Want me to fix you a snack?"

"No."

"Thirsty? There's some fresh cider—"

"No."

Sometimes he reminded her of a pop can left in the sun, where it sat there and sat there and sat there and then suddenly exploded, froth spitting everywhere. It never took long for Charles to tell her what upset him. She just never knew where or when it was going to happen.

This time it was easy. He said point-blank, "I've had it with you."

Oh, joy. She sank on the edge of the bed, feeling a familiar blend of weariness and bewilderment. Oh, yeah. And fear. She almost forgot that her heart was suddenly thudding as if someone were chasing her down a dark alley. "About what? What did I do? Did it have anything to do with your meeting?"

"Because that's what happened at the meeting. That's all they were talking about. You, you, you."

Initially she couldn't comprehend what he meant, but he readily started listing her crimes. Her talent competition that was culminating on Thanksgiving—the whole community was revved up about that. She'd started a book discussion group at the library for people who wanted to read about other cultures. She'd done a program at the elementary school—nothing new—about kids who thought church was boring. Hospital hours. The kids-at-risk program. The quilting bee in the church basement. The clergy-for-problem-pregnancy group.

"I still don't understand what's wrong. Why you're annoyed with me about any of this." Although she understood quite well, the way he kept pacing, the way the pulse in his temple kept throbbing, that he was on a line. This could go either way. If she could find the right thing to say, the right way to calm him down, this could still turn out all right.

"*You're* what's wrong. Your constantly drawing attention to yourself. Your constantly needing to be a *star*. You used to be my helpmate, the one person I could count on to stand with me. Now you're off on your own, never home, not thinking about the church or me, just thinking about yourself and how important you can make yourself look!"

My Lord. Sometimes he left her speechless when he came to conclusions like this that were so out of left field. "Charles." She tried to make her voice light. "You remember me? The girl who hated any kind of attention drawn to her from the day I was born?"

"Yeah, I remember that girl. That was the girl I used to love."

Okay. That one hurt big. "Actually, I've been doing all kinds of things that I never wanted to do. But this whole last year we've talked constantly about our financial troubles. You said so many times that we have to find new ways to bring money into the church. To encourage people to come to church, to add to the congregation, to find ways to reach out. I thought I was doing what you asked me to do. What you wanted me to do—"

"Yeah, right. Like I want the elders of the church talking nonstop about my wife. I can't understand why you'd want me to look bad. You know what they said? That you were like having a second minister in the church. They were teasing that they sure didn't need me when they had you...."

Some instinct made her tug off the scarf at her throat. His gaze immediately glommed on the red mark, then zoomed away.

For just an instant, guilt silenced him. But that instant was all it took for some of the fire to leave his eyes, his voice, for him to capture a little more calm.

It wasn't an answer.

The next day, when she visited her dad in the Righteous Senior Home, Vane was having a rough morning. Respiratory infections were a constant threat with his condition, as were kidney problems.

"He'll be so glad you're here," the day nurse told her. And then the aide who brought magazines and menus for the day stopped her to say, "Your dad woke up real uncomfortable. He's going to be extra glad to see you."

So she was braced when she walked in. His roomie was asleep, so she could concentrate totally on her dad. Her heart lurched. So quickly, so painfully, she could see his breathing was labored, his eyes weary. As she'd learned every year since the accident, her dad didn't have to fight for health so much as for the will to live.

"Hey, handsome," she murmured. "I hear you've been chasing all the nurses and running down the halls."

"Yeah. That was me." There was his smile. A shadow of the dad she'd grown up with, but still her dad. Her heart welled up with such fierce, sharp love that her eyes stung. She bent down, kissed his cheek and then just sat with him. She talked so he wouldn't try.

It wasn't long before his eyes closed. And while he napped, while she felt the strength of love for her dad, she searched her heart for what on earth she was going to do.

Poppy's words still stung her, because Poppy made it sound so easy to pick up and leave Charles. What bugged Bren even more was that she'd have counseled any woman to leave such a situation, besides.

But it wasn't the same for her.

She couldn't explain why it was so different. Maybe it was the devastating accident, having tasted despair and loss so young. But she took her faith terribly seriously, and that included her marriage vows. Morally or ethically, she just couldn't take off because things had gotten rough. Charles wasn't *evil*. He was becoming more and more jealous and paranoid and downright irrational in his thinking, all of which seemed to create anger. That didn't excuse him lashing out. But she sincerely believed he was a man in crisis...and that if anyone was responsible for helping him, could help him, it had to be her.

If the violence escalated, she knew she'd have to make another choice.

But it was so complicated. No one in Righteous, except for Poppy, had a clue that Charles was anything but how he billed himself. A warmhearted, giving minister who gave tirelessly of himself to the community. No one would guess he was prone to rages. Bren doubted anyone would believe her if she'd told them. She also feared their church would collapse if such a thing came out about its leader.

She gently squeezed her dad's hands, feeling the wrinkled skin, the frailness, yet also the warmth of life. Vane was a terribly important part of the equation for her. Her dad only had so much quality of life left. It would be easy enough for her to take off—but she had no possible financial way to take care of her dad anywhere else.

There seemed no answers. Just the increasingly heavy drumbeat of her heart. Bren couldn't remember a time she couldn't find the sunny side of a cloud, but the mess she was in right now seemed increasingly dark and worrisome.

She couldn't go. She couldn't stay.

But if Charles's behavior continued to escalate, she *had* to do something.

It was after six, and Poppy was close to dying from starvation—she'd only had time at lunch to shovel in half a sandwich. Still, she had one more project she wanted to do before heading for home.

Web was still in the building somewhere. The last patients were gone, and the last staff had locked up and headed out, as well. For a while, Poppy had the clinic to herself with no interruptions, and she wanted to take advantage.

"So it's just you and me, Mandy. And you're not going to like this, but you have to think about it this way—if everything goes well, we'll both get steak for dinner. How does that sound, huh, girl?"

She gently scrubbed the dog's brow, making Mandy close her eyes with pleasure. Josh's dog had gained a ton of strength over the last few days…but every time the dog tried to get on her feet, she gave up. Web had checked her over every morning. The identifiable symptoms of pain, like blood pressure and increased heart rate, had all disappeared.

Mandy just didn't want to try moving without her one front limb. She just lay back down and closed her eyes.

"Now listen, you," Poppy crooned as she jogged around getting things ready. "I've been feeding you by hand. Cleaning up after you. Massaging those limbs. But that's enough of the pity party, don't you think? So we're going to try some real work tonight."

The water treadmill she'd created for arthritic dogs wasn't set up for an animal with Mandy's injuries, but Poppy figured she could make it work for an amputee. It was just that the how was tricky. As she warmed up the water, she took out leashes and harnesses, trying to figure out some kind of sling she could create for Mandy.

Possibly the dog simply wasn't willing to live—or walk—on three limbs. Poppy's theory was to at least get her on her feet, in the warm, comfortable water. To start building up her strength and muscles again. If the dog felt good, felt stronger, she might feel more motivated to try.

The whole time Poppy fussed around trying to jury-rig a contraption that would work, her mind kept straying back to Bren.

She was still mad. She'd been mad all week. She planned to still be mad next year. Nobody, until Bren, had ever accused her of being gutless.

For Pete's *sake*. Maybe she wasn't into hunting, but she could outshoot any guy she'd ever met. She took on critters and people that most people would run from. She lived alone, changed her own tires, cleaned her own furnace. No one, but no one, had ever accused her of being a coward, of not facing up to something because it was hard.

Poppy was so mad she could barely think.

Only the problem was that Bren had forced her to think. This whole darn long blasted week. About what she really wanted and needed in her life. About what she was afraid of.

"Come on now, Mandy. Come on, girl. I'm just asking you to try. Come on, sweetheart...."

Hells bells. The dog was only forty pounds, and Poppy was strong. But the dog didn't like the cushion being fitted around her missing limb, didn't like being lifted into the warm water. Didn't want to participate at any level with this experiment. She splashed and panicked and strained.

In two minutes flat, Poppy was more soaked than the dog. And she could force the mutt into the warm water, but she couldn't force her to walk. And if she kept leaning over, with the dog's forty pounds fighting her all the way, she was going to break her own back, besides.

"I know you don't want to do this, baby. But it's not that scary. Doesn't the water feel good? Doesn't it feel good to be upright instead of always lying down? Calm down there, girl, calm down…."

Mandy didn't want to calm down. She wanted the hell out of this.

"Oops. Looks like you've got yourself in a mountain of a mess there."

She heard Web's voice in the doorway, but he didn't stand there long. He took in the situation, then moved in faster than summer lightning. In seconds, he was bumping-hips close to her, both of them moving swiftly but calmly to stabilize the dog, both talking in the same crooning tones, whether they were addressing Mandy or each other.

"She's trying to give up on me, Web." Damn. It was a relief to share it. Especially with Web.

"If that's what you're doing, Mandy, you might as hang it up, girl. Poppy's more stubborn than a hoot owl. Trust me on this. You'll be sorry if you don't just do what she says…." The pulley contraption Poppy had created had gotten all tangled because of the dog's struggles. Web, darn him, because he was so much stronger, detangled the mess, and between the two of them they fit the dog more securely. In that same lullaby voice, though, he said to Poppy, "I see what you were trying to do here. It's damn near brilliant. But I really think you needed two people to pull it off."

"Well, I didn't have two people. And darn it, sometimes

I just wish I were an engineer. I was trying to create a setup where Mandy could stand and move in a way she was familiar. Where her sense of balance was familiar. In the long run, obviously, she has to compensate for the missing limb. But for right now I just wanted to do something to make her walk, to get her exercising again, so I could build up her strength."

"But…" Web said.

Poppy wanted to shake her head. Web always, but always, knew when she had a *but* in the situation. Her fear came out like water gushing from a faucet. "But, darn it, Web, Josh is counting on me to get his dog on her feet. And I don't think I can make it happen. She's resisted every darn thing I've tried."

As she turned the water treadmill onto its slowest speed, Web crooned to the dog, not to her. "She's not giving up on you, Mandy."

"But maybe I'll have to. If this doesn't work…I'm out of ideas. Unless you can think of something."

"You're kidding, right? If you can't make this work, Poppy, nobody can. You hear that, Mandy? She's your last and only shot, so if I were you, I'd quit giving her a hard time and go for it." And to Poppy, in the same seduce-the-baby tone he said, "I think she just needs more time. She's considering whether life's worth it or not. She's just not sure. She went through hell and a half, Pop."

In the hall, Poppy heard the cleaning crew arrive. Already the night had turned blacker than velvet. Inside, Web was already as wet as she was. She could see the dark hair brushing his collar. The way his long, strong fingers held and soothed the dog. The smell of him…beyond antiseptic soap…it couldn't be testosterone, she knew, because obviously that wasn't actually a scent. But there was a something, this close to Web. The maleness of him affected her like a giddy high…like the stuff she claimed she'd never inhaled in high school.

"The accident was terrible for her," Poppy agreed. It was so much easier with him sharing the dog's weight. She dunked her hands in the water, massaging Mandy's back legs, trying to physically soothe her into relaxing. "But she's as healed up as she can be, Web. And she can't keep going the way she is—if for no other reason than it's close to impossible to handle her digestive system."

Web nodded. "But it's hard to know how traumatized she was by the accident. Even if she's not feeling pain, I suspect Mandy's facing a black wall. A place she doesn't want to go again. She'd rather shut down, close her eyes, than risk something that awful again."

Poppy didn't raise her voice above a croon, didn't lose an instant of concentration. But something inside her seemed to suddenly smoke. Maybe it was Bren implying she was a coward. Maybe it was Web being so wonderful. Too wonderful. Wonderful as he'd always been—great to work with, perceptive about what she was trying to do, accepting of her ideas and opinions. Fun. Dabnabbit, but suddenly she wanted to smack him.

"You could quit being so damned nice, you know," she crooned.

"Huh? What's wrong with being nice?"

"This crap," Poppy sang softly, "has been going on ever since I came back to work. Your being nonstop nice. But unlike everyone else, you haven't said one word about my face. Not one."

"What do you want me to say?"

"I don't know, but how about something wild…like the truth. Just tell me what you really think, for God's sake."

"You want the truth, Poppy?" He bent down, rhythmically stroking Mandy's throat, keeping her calm, his whole being radiating that same serenity. "The truth is that I was attracted to you before. But now…I don't know who you are. It's all different."

Damned if her pulse didn't skitter to a stop and then restart at a breakneck gallop. "You were attracted to me? Before?"

"I swear, you're not always the brightest bulb in the chandelier."

She heard the insult. Somehow it didn't stop her pulse from galloping. "Web, you've been married how many times?"

"Two. Almost three."

"And you told me how many times that you never wanted to hook up with anyone again. Didn't even want to get involved. That's why you were willing to work with me, start this partnership of ours together. I mean, you never *said* it was because I was ugly as hell, but you made it pretty clear that you never had to worry about my being a threat to your bachelor existence." When Mandy raised limpid eyes, Poppy bent down and bussed her furry head. Yeah, it was a people kiss, but sometimes people kisses worked. Besides which, she was damn shaken by Web's comments and didn't want the mutt affected by her rollicking change of mood.

"You always had that wrong. I never thought you were ugly as hell. You're the one who thought that. The only one who thought that." Web, who never lost patience anywhere near an animal, was suddenly starting to sound exasperated. "You're right, though, that I never wanted to get involved. I've flunked every relationship I've ever been in. But then, I never spent time with a woman before where I could just…"

When he failed to fill in the blank, Poppy pounced. "Could just *what*?"

"Could just be myself. I never really had fun with a woman before you. Argued. Talked work. Talked life. Throw out an idea to you and we just go with it. That kind of challenge, enjoyment…was totally new to me." Web took his hands out of the water, found a rag-tail towel on the counter. "It was always…the game. The hunt. The conquest. Meet, admire, woo, seduce. It wasn't about *liking* the woman. Or her liking me."

"That's witless," Poppy informed him bluntly.

"Yeah. Amazing how dumb guys are. Woman are always telling us, but who ever believes them?"

It was a joke she would have laughed at two weeks ago, but not now. "Web, are you actually telling me that you don't like me now? Because I *look* better?"

"You looked fine before. You look fine now. But you're not the woman I was attracted to before. You're not the woman I felt safe and comfortable with. You're more like the woman I flunked the course with. Look."

She stared at him, dumfounded. Bewildered. Upset. Yet for that moment, with her hands full of dog, her hair dripping from the latest splashfest, her makeup long worn off for the day…she realized it was the first time she'd looked at him eye to eye in ages. At least like this. Where chemistry was suddenly arcing between them like an electric rainbow. Chemistry she'd never dreamed of, not with Web. Not chemistry they shared.

"*Look*, Poppy," he repeated.

"Look at what?"

"Look at Mandy. She's walking in the water. You pulled off another miracle, cookie!"

She broke their eye contact, turned her attention back to the mutt. "Mandy, you darling, you darling, you brave, brave girl…" She really was. Doing the treadmill walk on three legs, the warm water helping make her buoyant, the sling helping her balance.

But when Poppy lifted her head to share the moment again with Web, he was gone.

She told herself she was ticked that he'd cut and run. But deep inside, she realized she was a ton more ticked at herself because Bren had been right. She *was* a coward. She *had* been afraid to face what she really wanted and needed in her life.

And no, that wasn't a man.

But she'd had feelings for Web for ages. Deep feelings. Buried even deeper because she hadn't wanted to ruin their working relationship or risk their friendship. Even more— truth on the table—she just couldn't face the humiliation of being rebuffed and rejected.

Yet now his admitting to having felt something for her seemed to leave her holding the ball.

What ball, she didn't have a clue.

What those astounding revelations of his meant, she had no clue about either.

Was she supposed to pretend this conversation never happened? Go back to their comfortable pal-sy, slapping-back ways?

Hell, Poppy thought as she carried Mandy from the water and rough-dried her with towels, life had been easier when she'd been butt-ugly. It had never occurred to her that she might conceivably have a relationship with Web. That it was a possibility. That it could ever be a possibility.

Unfortunately it sounded as if that were still true. Unless she did something to open the door. Fast.

Because it sure sounded as if that door had only opened a crack and Web was already determined to close it again.

CHAPTER 11

It was still dark outside on Saturday morning when Bren wrestled a box from the back of the van. All the leaves hadn't fallen yet, but there was still a spit of snow in the air, a bone-sharp chill as she wrestled the first box, then a second up the stairs of Maude Rose's apartment.

A lone car passed, probably aimed for coffee at Link's. Traffic lights weaved and creaked in the chill wind. It struck Bren as more ghostly than Halloween, not that early November mornings didn't often start out bitter. All the same, she was glad to get inside and under cover.

Mary Sue was moving into the apartment tomorrow. That was Bren's excuse for the visit. She just wanted to bring a few more things to help the girl settle in…and maybe, just a little, she'd wanted a few more minutes in the apartment herself. She trudged up the stairs one last time and, out of breath from carrying the heavy boxes, took her time digging for the apartment key.

When she let herself in, a sigh whooshed out of her lungs. She had to admit it—in the last few weeks she'd come to think of this place as a special haven. It was just…she felt safe here. It was somewhere to go where no one knew her or knew where she was.

Sometimes it felt as if the irrepressible spirit of Maude Rose still clung to the place.

How whimsical could you get, she scolded herself as she filled a teakettle with water and turned on the stove. Maude Rose had been a sinner, not an angel.

Of course, who wasn't?

She'd just hooked her jacket on a chair when she heard vague sounds outside and then the sound of a key turning. Poppy walked in, her gloves between her teeth, her cheeks redder than cherries, carrying a box as big as the ones Bren had carted in.

When Bren caught sight of her, they both seemed to freeze for a good two seconds. The night they'd met at the Heels Up, they hadn't parted on the easiest terms. Neither had liked what the other had had to say. But that two-second lag didn't last. In a noisy bluster of energy, Poppy crashed down her box, shimmied off her jacket, slammed the door closed. And grinned.

"Great minds sure think alike," she said wryly. "I should have known I'd find you here."

"I just thought…" Bren didn't have to finish the sentence. Poppy could see the boxes.

"Yeah, I thought the same thing. So what'd you bring her? And I hope you're heating enough water for two cups, not just one, because I'm frozen to the bone. *Man*, it's cold out there."

As if they'd never fought, never thorned each other's feelings, they pored through the contents of their boxes.

"I just figured she could use some cleaning products," Poppy said. "You know how expensive that stuff is. So it's on her after this, but she'll have a start-up on washing machine soap, scouring powder, Windex…" She lined up the stash on the table. "Then, since I'd started on cleaning stuff, I figured I might as well spring for a few rolls of paper towel, TP, foil, that kind of thing. You know, really get her set up…"

At the very end, Poppy pulled out the pièce de résistance. It was a carefully wrapped handmade afghan. The yarn was snuggle-warm, the pattern diamonds of bright primary colors. "My mom made tons of these. I've hoarded them, but that's pretty selfish because I can't really use them all. And I'm not wasting them on my brothers. They don't appreciate stuff like this. And I just thought…it'd be giving her something personal. Something homemade. Something really like a home, you know? Or do you think that's beyond belief corny?"

"I think it's *fabulous*," Bren said warmly. "Sheesh, Poppy, it's beautiful."

"You saw the purple one I have in my living room. That was my mom's, too."

"It's a treasure…."

"Yeah, okay." Poppy shifted away quickly, the way she always did near too much emotion. "Let's see what you brought."

"Same idea. Just a different road to get there." Bren unpacked her loads. "I was thinking food. Nothing perishable. Nothing great. Just staples to get her started without having to spend too much."

Out came peanut butter. Two peanut butters. Soups. Salt and pepper, sugar, flour. Some home-canned fruits and vegetables.

"We have to give her this?" Poppy grabbed the quart jar of peaches. "What's wrong with me? She's just a kid. I really need this."

Bren laughed. "You're a sucker for peaches, huh? Me, too."

Poppy was still digging through Bren's stuff, came through with a handful of paperbacks and, below them, an easy-read student Bible. "Felt you had to sneak it in there, did you?" Poppy asked wryly.

"Seems like a lot of young women who flounder had trouble in school. So I always figure that the only way they might give reading another chance is·if they get something seriously easy to read. And they don't tend to pick up a Bible because they assume right off the bat that kind of reading will be too hard for them."

Poppy fingered it, put it down. "We'd never have gotten along for three seconds if you'd tried to force-feed me religion."

"I never met anyone who likes to be force-fed anything."

"It's more than that." Poppy was still diving in the boxes. Her voice came out gruff. "You don't need to force-feed anybody anything. You're a good person and it comes through. Wouldn't matter if anyone knew you were part of a church or not."

Bren resisted fainting. "What is this? Why are you being so nice? Are you ill?"

The instant the teakettle whistled, Poppy raced to the

counter for mugs and—lacking coffee—tea bags. Her voice took on another layer of gruffness. "Hey, I've felt lousy about being mean to you about Charles. About making out like it'd be easy for you to cut out of a marriage. I'm not wearing your shoes. I couldn't fit in your shoes in a million years. So I should have shut up."

"It's all right." The minute the tea was poured, they were both burning their tongues. Anything for caffeine.

And once that darn door had been opened on Charles, Poppy couldn't let it go. "But you checked into Social Security, right? Senior citizens' benefits. Disability? All those kinds of things that could help your dad?"

"Of course. Over and over."

"But maybe in a different state benefits might be different."

"They are. But not so different I could afford the care for my dad out of my pocket. There's no miracle job I could get that would come with benefits for my dad."

"Well, shit. That completely sucks."

"Yeah," Bren agreed. "It does. It totally and completely sucks."

Poppy burst out laughing. "I'm so proud of you! I never thought I'd hear a word like that come out of your mouth! You're expanding your vocabulary!"

"It's your influence," Bren assured her.

Poppy laughed again…for a few moments. Then sobered up and pushed again. "I wish there were some way I could help you, Bren."

"I wish you could, too. And that's the truth."

"You *can't* stay there if the violence keeps getting worse."

Bren refilled her mug and started unpacking again. "I know."

"Look, I jumped to judged you before. I won't do that again, I swear. I understand you're trapped because of your dad. But please let me help if there's a way. If I could help with your dad somehow. If you need a place to stay. Whatever."

Bren felt a rush of warmth. She'd never planned to talk about this, didn't feel comfortable. Yet somehow being with Poppy was different than being with any other woman friend she'd ever had. "You know what? You're the only one who even guessed about Charles. I'm with people all the time. People I care about, people who care about me. People who see Charles and I together, who know him. But no one but you saw what was happening, what's been building."

Poppy stopped all her rushing around. "So it *is* building?"

"Yes." Bren couldn't deny it. Maybe it was being in Maude Rose's apartment, but somehow, some way, she couldn't hold it all in forever. "Don't start thinking I'm some *victim*, Poppy. I don't deserve to be hurt. I wouldn't willingly stay with anyone who'd hurt me. But my faith complicates what I can do, what's right to do. So does the situation with my father."

Poppy opened her mouth twice. Closed it twice. "All right. I won't say a single critical word about the son of a bitch. Even one. But damn it, if we keep brainstorming, there's got to be something we can think up that you can do."

This time Bren couldn't work up a smile. "I need to be absolutely sure that he isn't ill. That he's not in the middle of some deep personal crisis where he can't possibly control these mood episodes of his. I need to know if I could do something to make this better. I realize you may not totally agree with me, Poppy, but right now I believe he's a man who's jeopardizing his own soul. It isn't just about me."

Poppy was on her second mug of tea now, too, but she couldn't sit still, jerked to her feet. "Well, heck. Apparently there's a line where I can't possibly shut up, so it'd be a ton better if we don't cross it. Because for me, I don't give a royal screw about him. I care about you. I don't give a rat's behind if he throws his soul into a mud puddle. I only care that he quits hurting you. That you're not in a dangerous situation." She hesitated, looking thoughtful. "You know, I could teach you some serious self-defense. My brothers taught me. I don't have any belts or anything, but I know what I'm doing."

"That'd be good," Bren agreed. "But it's not an answer."

"That's what really pisses me off." Poppy was obviously too restless to stand idle. She started splitting the cleaning supplies between the bathroom and the kitchen. "There are supposed to *be* answers. When you grow up, your parents tell you that doing the right thing is the answer. Everything will work out if you're just a good person. And you know what the right thing is. Or I used to."

"Yeah. The older I get, the more gray shows up. Nothing's quite so clear-cut black-and-white," Bren concurred, only to find Poppy was diving into the boxes she'd brought and she suddenly stopped dead.

She held a box of tampons in her hand. "You really thought you needed to buy this for Mary Sue?" she asked wryly.

"No. In fact, they're not for Mary Sue. It's not what you

think." Bren took the box, opened the side and spilled out the jewels she'd inherited from Maude Rose. "It was the one place in the universe Charles would never have looked. Or any other guy that I could imagine."

"This is *crazy*. Downright ooga booga." Poppy dived in the pocket of her zipped jacket and came through with a Ziploc bag—that held her jewels. The ones that were left after she'd sold the first batch for the surgery. "Why on earth did you bring yours?"

Originally it had just been an impulse. To bring over the housekeeping goods for Mary Sue. Then to sit with a cup of tea and the jewels. Maude Rose's jewels. Just to think for a bit in the quiet of that apartment. And now it seemed Poppy had had exactly the same idea.

When all the goods were put away, they sat with fresh tea on the carpet in the living room with their loot. The sun had long come up. Light streamed in the east window, creating dazzling reflections on the gems.

Bren lifted the dangling earrings that were part of her stash. Mr. Ruby claimed the stones were a mix of tourmaline, peridot, citrine, topaz and diamonds. The second piece, a giant brooch shaped like a flower, was all diamantés with a huge, tongue-shaped pink pearl in the center. The last piece, ironically, was simply a purple cross—a symbol she would have loved if it hadn't been so show-off pretentious-looking.

Still, in sunlight the jewels looked lit from within, as if they had a life and beauty inside that only natural light could bring out.

She handed Poppy her pieces to play with, just as Poppy

handed her a handful of jewelry—most of it junk but also the strange, exotic-looking jeweled cuff with the big-bug-sized tanzanites.

"Every time I look at this stuff, I think it's possibly the ugliest jewelry I've ever seen—or ever imagined," Bren said.

"That's what I first thought. But not now. Now…" Poppy shrugged. "It seems so smart to me, what Maude Rose did. Hiding a fortune in plain sight. No one looked at the sparkle. They were so sure it couldn't be real."

"So many people didn't see the sparkle in Maude Rose either," Bren said pensively, thinking how much she'd changed since the inheritance. How much Poppy had. And maybe because the jewelry made her think of possibilities, she asked, "Did you ever want children?"

Poppy never gave up anything first if she could help it. "Did you?"

"Oh, yeah. Very much. But eventually, when my biological clock was pushing near my late thirties, we had some tests done. Charles was infertile. Once we knew that, I just…stopped feeling bad. I mean, that choice was simply over. The congregation has always been a kind of family, besides. Not the same as having my own, but I've always had children to love, to talk to. Kids who needed me. Charles used to complain that I started the church day care so I could mother the little ones. Probably right." She'd given, so now she pushed Poppy. "You?"

"I don't know." Poppy slipped on the jeweled cuff, twisted her wrist in the sunlight, took it off again. "After my mom died, I was just one of the boys. Never thought of myself as being a real girlie type, you know? No point in trying to play the ultrafeminine role with the looks I had. So I just kind of closed down near subjects like dating and marriage."

"In other words, you wanted kids terribly." Bren didn't say it bluntly, but she thought that Poppy wasn't the only one who got to call a spade a spade. "You probably started mothering animals because you thought you weren't going to have children."

"Maybe."

Bren wasn't fooled by the scowl. "Poppy, you could still have a child."

"At forty-two? Not for me. I know women are doing it. But I think the risks are too great for birth defects."

"So you could adopt."

"So could you."

That wasn't strictly true, because Charles had been unwilling to, but Bren was tired of churning up her own troubled waters. Poppy had made her think about a lot of things she'd happily buried for years. It seemed to Bren that she should be doing Poppy the same uncomfortable favor. "It's bothered me," she said gently, "that I was pretty rough on you the last time we talked."

"Hell. No, you weren't. You couldn't be mean if you tried, Bren." Poppy heaved a gusty sigh. "Besides, you were right. It ticks me off to say it, but…I was a coward. I *am* a coward. I never did admit—even to myself—what I really wanted in life."

"Which is?"

Poppy slipped the cuff back in the bag and zipped it back

in her jacket pocket. "The same old thing every other woman seems to want. A life with a guy. A marriage. A family, even if it's only a family of two. It was only a secret because..."

"Because you thought you could never have it," Bren filled in.

Poppy nodded. "And over the years...there was never a guy I really wanted to be with. Not someone I wanted to wake up every morning to. Not the kind of guy I could trust. Really trust. I like men, for Pete's sake. Always have, always will. I get on better with men any day of the week than with women. But as far as that serious thing—"

"That love thing?" Bren didn't smile but thought there was only one four-letter word Poppy didn't easily use—the one that started with an L.

"Yeah. It's the truth. I just never met a man who wanted me—or who I wanted either. Not at that level. Until—"

"Until Web?"

Poppy blinked. "How'd you know I was going to say his name? You don't even know him."

"Don't have to. Whenever you talk about your job, his name comes into the conversation. And you talk about him differently than anyone else."

"Well, sure, because he's the vet—"

"No. Because he's special to you." Both of them started to move at the same time. One glance at her watch and Bren knew she'd stayed a half hour later than she'd planned. And Poppy, naturally, was antsy to leave now that she'd been forced to talk about herself.

"All right, all right. I admit it," Poppy said. "Anyway, that was the secret. The one I'd been hiding from myself for a good long time, that I want the same, boring thing everyone else does. The mortgage. The dog barking in the middle of the night. The someone to fight about money with. The someone who snores next to you—"

It only took a few moments to wash up the cups, give the rooms a last glance, cart the empty cardboard boxes to the door. Bren made it before Poppy—who was still folding the afghan on the back of the couch—so she could block the door for another second. "What are you waiting for, Poppy?"

"What do you mean?"

"Go after him. You got your face fixed. You're not that woman anymore who was afraid to believe she had a chance. You like this guy. You've liked him forever." When Poppy opened her mouth, Bren knew damn well she was going to protest. So she just said, "Go after him."

And led the way down the stairs.

An hour later, Bren was in the middle of a Ladies Auxiliary meeting in the church basement, planning the details of the Thanksgiving event. The ladies were charged up because T-day represented the finale of their Righteous Idol competition, and the winner was going to sing the hymns in church that day. Several of the women had children and grandchildren who'd made it to the top-contender list. They weren't even halfway through the discussion when a phone rang and Bren was called away.

Charles was up at the house. Coughing and sneezing, suffering a sore throat and a fever almost to a hundred and two. The morning with Poppy had brought revelations and thought-provoking ideas and traumatic possibilities. Yet it struck Bren's sense of humor…on a day of high drama and a thousand huge things roiling around in her mind and heart, certain interruptions were guaranteed to bring a woman straight down to earth. And a sick man always headed that list.

Typically for an early Sunday morning, Zach and Jason were behaving like pigs, eating everything they could scare up—and that was after they'd completely demolished the fresh coffee cake she'd just made, almost before she'd gotten a piece herself.

"So I'm just saying…when you're driving by there, take a glance, okay? She's only been in the apartment a week. And she's younger than spring."

"What's the part you're not saying?" Zach opened the fridge for the third time. This time he emerged with a chunk of fresh cheddar. He tore off a piece and, without looking, handed it to an unseen feline mouth in the top cupboard.

"That she was hooked up with a loser. I'm not sure of the guy's name. I think I heard her say Spanger. Springer. Jimmy—"

"Spivey. Jimmy Spivey. Not surprised to hear it. He's been in the system. Not for knocking a woman around but drug crap and domestic calls that he always slithers out of. But, Poppy, we can't do much if she doesn't call, doesn't file a complaint."

"I know that. I'm just asking you to do an occasional drive-by, watch over her a little." It was just a week ago that she and Bren had handed over the apartment keys to Mary Sue.

All week, that moment kept replaying in Poppy's mind. Mary Sue had tromped up the stairs carrying two trash bags bulging with clothes and stuff, huffing from the trip, her hair matted from the drizzling rain.

Neither she nor Bren had wanted to stay long. They'd both figured Mary Sue needed to settle in her own way. So they'd just helped bring in her things and then simply handed her the key.

Who could have guessed Mary Sue would burst into tears? And damn, but who could possibly guess she'd throw her arms around Poppy?

Poppy had patted and patted and patted her back. And then, when the girl had kept snuffling and gulping and dripping more tears, simply hugged her back. What the hell else could she have done?

"Hey, earth to Poppy." Zach snapped his fingers to get her attention. "Just wanted to mention that I think you're nuts to take on that girl. For all you know, she could be bad news to the nth degree. And you'll be on the hook if your name's on the lease."

"Well, she'll sure as hell turn out bad news if no one gives her a chance." Poppy and both brothers stopped talking when Mandy got up on three legs and negotiated her way over to the counter. Steak was waiting. A girl did what a girl had to do, Poppy figured. The dog had started to down-right thrive—with the right motivation.

"I can't believe that dog's walking at all," Zach said with a whistle. "The kid is going to take him back, right?"

"It was all I could do not to give her back this week. Josh

is chafing at the bit. But she wasn't doing this great until a few days ago. I figure the more head start she gets, the better Josh'll be able to cope with her…." Outside, Poppy heard the crunch of leaves as a vehicle pulled into the yard.

Her heart hiccuped even before she lifted her head to glance out the window and saw Web's truck. Instead of wondering what he was doing there or why he would have popped by without calling, her first thought was a trumpet in her mind: Go after him.

Bren had put that idiotic idea in her head, so it was entirely Bren's fault that the idea kept popping up at totally inappropriate moments.

"Web's here," she said calmly to her brothers, who immediately surged to their feet and dug in their pockets for their car keys. "For Pete's sake, you guys. You can stay. He's not bringing wood this time. You're safe. No one's going to ask you to do any manual labor."

But they weren't going to risk it. She got smacks on the head and thanks for the coffee before they pelted out the door. Poppy wasn't far behind them, but she had to push on shoes and a jacket first. The morning was so chipper, she'd put on thick socks with her jeans and a bulky blue sweater, but as the locals said, there was frost on the pumpkin this morning. For sure, she couldn't run outside without shoes.

By the time she caught up with Web, her brothers had exchanged greetings and were climbing in their cars. Web was dressed Sunday-morning-style, wearing old cords and a thick buffalo-plaid flannel shirt, boots. He'd obviously been outside a while because his eyes had that dark sparkle and his skin the brush of ruddiness.

Go after him echoed in her mind again, which was so damned mortifying that she crossed her arms tightly under her chest. One look at his expression and Poppy knew darn well this wasn't a social call.

"What's wrong?" she asked swiftly.

He led her to the back of his pickup and opened the cab window. Inside, nestled on a ratty old wool blanket, were twin fawns snuggled together. "Oh, God, oh, God," she whispered. They were both shaking—scared, colored with the same soft cinnamon with white spots, their eyes softer than love.

Instinctively her voice calmed, seducing their trust, willing them to take it easy. It only took one look for her to be in love—not that that was news. Not with Web and not with her. Neither of them had an ounce of character when it came to saying no to a critter in trouble.

Web filled her in. "I was driving back from White Hill, saw the doe hit in the road. She'd been dead for hours, and these two were right in the middle of traffic, trying to suckle from her. Hell. Rut season's on. As soon as she'd have gotten around to choosing her buck, she'd have stopped nursing, and they wouldn't be so dependent. But I could see how it was. These two weren't just hungry. They weren't going to leave their mama. Lucky they hadn't been hit by the time I got there—"

"I've got formula." She was already moving.

So was he. "I knew you would. It was closer to your house than mine. Actually, I was right by the clinic, but—"

"But the babies would only have been more freaked out near the smells of dogs and cats and antiseptics."

"Yeah. Exactly. They shouldn't need that much care. They're not newborns, but they'll have to be weaned. If you can't keep them, I'll take them home—"

"Don't give me that horse spit. You knew the minute I saw them that I was going to sucker in."

"Well, yeah," Web agreed.

"You were never going to take them on if you could get me to do it."

"Well, yeah," Web agreed again, as if these things were so obvious they didn't need saying.

He was so damned cute she almost kissed him right then—but that was just because Bren's advice was branded in her brain like an ill-advised tattoo. "Back your truck up to the barn, okay? I'll start pulling stuff together."

Web caught up with her while she was still gathering up supplies from the utility room. On a top shelf, where normal women undoubtedly would have stored soaps and cleaning supplies, she had Bag Balm and sealed containers of dry formula and various-sized bottles and nipples.

It's not as if she hadn't suckered into problems with wounded critters before. In this case, the fawns were hardly newborns. They were spring born, ballpark six months old, so they didn't need the sterility that a newborn would. Still, if they were still suckling, they'd need to be bottle-fed. She could pick up corn and deer feed over the next week to start the weaning process. Right now, though, especially because of losing a mom, they were likely to need all the extra nutrition she could pack into them, any way they'd take it.

"I'll stir up the formula," Web volunteered.

"Good. I'll get some bowls and blankets and all. Next week, I can pick up some straw."

"There's some in the back room of the clinic. And I'll go for a bale—don't be buying it when I'm the one bringing you the problem."

The talk was easy, natural, the same way they always talked while working through problems at the clinic. No kisses between them now, Poppy thought. No memories of that awkward conversation about his wanting her/not wanting her either.

At least on Web's side.

Arms full, they both pelted out to the barn. The wind was picking up, slapping her cheeks pink. The last of the leaves were sailing down in the yard, making crunchy sounds underfoot.

She pulled open the old barn doors. Inside, it was darkish and musty. Since she'd—never intentionally!— fostered a few wild creatures in the past, she'd already isolated a couple zones for special care. Usually, though, she was stuck with a raccoon or opossum, and the small cages that worked for those size animals wasn't remotely the kind of containment the fawns needed.

"Every time I get in here, I think you're crazy not to pursue it," Web said.

"Pursue what?"

"Doing this full-time. Working with training animals.

Not wild animals. But you already have a terrific amount of space. It wouldn't take that much to fence and reorganize and fix up the grounds specifically for training. And you're so damned good with them—"

"Oh, quit being nice. You're just buttering me up because I'm getting stuck with these babies instead of you." And he wasn't making it easy to concentrate, she thought dourly. It wasn't fair, to be hip-bumping close, working side by side, teasing the way they always did, when she felt an incessant ton of voltage between them…voltage that he either didn't feel or wasn't remotely bothered by. And darn it, she needed to concentrate on the orphans.

She opted for space in the barn shop. The shop wasn't pretty, just a long, narrow room with a lot of historic bangs and dents. But it was still the best spot she could think of, had two doors, good light, a heater high in the wall. Until she got straw, she settled several rag-old blankets to make a nest. Filled two bowls with fresh water.

No one needed to sell tickets to Web. He saw what she was doing, figured out the plan and added to it, pushing out the lawn mower and lawn tools to a different room, setting up a staging area for feeding. "They'll make too much mess in here long-term."

"I know. But I can open up that one door, set up a yard with a snow fence on the other side, so they can be in or out, whatever they want. Then they'll naturally do their business outside, besides."

"You already have the snow fence?"

"Yup."

"I can set that up before I go."

"Okay. That'd help a ton, because those rolls of snow fence are mighty heavy. And for now…let's bring in the babies."

"Okay. You want to try carrying them or use a harness?"

"They're going to try to bolt on us, no matter what," she said thoughtfully. "But my vote is to try carrying them in." In the clinic, she tended to defer to Web for the obvious reason—not because he was the boss but because he knew tons more than she did. He'd earned her respect. Here, though, she seemed to naturally take charge. "They'll be less freaked if they're not separated. So let's carry them slowly, together, keeping them touching and in sight of each other if we can. In other words, not walking butt to butt, but with their noses facing each other."

"You're the boss."

"And let me talk to them for a minute first." Again Poppy couldn't help but think that she wouldn't have said that to another living soul. But Web already knew her. She didn't have to worry about hiding the less sane sides to her character.

She climbed in the back of his truck quietly, slowly, starting the talk. She didn't speak the same way to dogs and cats as she did to wild animals, because they represented totally different kinds of problems. The sound of a human voice was never going to be reassuring to a wild critter, but still, there was a tone of sound that seemed to soothe a frantic heart rate, no matter who or what it was. The words didn't matter. She just kept up the tone, humming how much she loved them and promising they were safe and how she knew how scared they were.

By the time Poppy crawled back and actually picked up the first fawn, it made a single panicked move and then just went still in her arms. Web shot her a silent thumbs-up and picked up the second fawn. The babies weren't happy, that was for damn sure, but Poppy kept talking the talk, and the orphans stayed good enough to settle them in the shop nest.

After that, Poppy and Web backed off a few feet. The fawns almost immediately stood on spindly legs, shaking hard, their flanks touching, clearly examining their new environment—and not liking it. They looked around as if desperate to find an exit to flee from yet finding no place to go. Still, Poppy kept up the talk, but she and Web leaned against the far wall without moving.

"Now?" Web whispered finally.

"Not quite yet," Poppy said. "I know they're hungry. But I don't think they'll really settle down until they've accepted that they can't get out of here. And that's the point when they'll likely relax enough to eat."

Minutes passed. Then more minutes. There was just no hurrying them—no way to even *try* hurrying them. Yet finally they just stood still, facing Poppy and Web with those big, soft, frightened eyes as if waiting for more hell to get heaped on their heads. Slowly Poppy picked up the bottles and squeezed out a little of the formula milk so they could catch the smell.

Both babies leaned forward—then skittered back, too afraid to come closer. Poppy waited another minute, another two.

Then she slowly moved to the blanket and sat down. She talked for another four or five minutes, her voice starting to feel hoarse, her shoulders feeling knotted from the effort of carrying the two sluggers. Finally the first one edged closer. Not close. But closer.

Poppy didn't look at Web, but she could *feel* him next to her. Maybe it was goofy, but she knew they were sharing the same feelings. Willing that first fawn to take a chance. Needing to communicate the same calm and safeness to the orphans. And then there was just a sensation of connection knowing Web cared exactly the same way she did. How many people would devote a Sunday morning to sitting absolutely still and cramped in the cold for an hour or more—and be thrilled at the chance to do it?

When it came down to it, Poppy thought, he was as bonkers as she was.

But then the first caramel fawn lifted its head and took the terribly frightening risk…and came closer. Damned if Poppy didn't feel her eyes squeeze with tears when it finally latched onto the bottle and then latched good and tight.

The second one finally edged forward. Web, silent and slow, was ready with a bottle for that one.

Poppy felt his shoulder rubbing hers. His knee rubbing her knee. The only sound in the musty old shop was those two orphans guzzling milk like there was no tomorrow.

When they finished, they left the fawns on their own for a bit. Poppy headed inside to make some coffee while Web unfolded snow fence to make a makeshift outside yard. Warming up, waiting for the coffee to brew, Poppy stood at the kitchen window—and as she watched Web work outside, she felt a sudden lump in her throat.

Nothing was wrong. There was a smile on her face, she could feel it. She'd loved every minute of working with the fawns with Web. Was still happy. But that happiness seemed to be the whole cause of that lump.

She stared outside, judging Web's progress. The make-shift fence was going to take another twenty minutes to finish, she figured.

But then, Poppy thought darkly, it was past time that push came to shove. She could relate so well to those fawns—they'd been so scared, so brave, so furiously unhappy at having to take a frightening risk and trust. She knew. She really did. But the more she looked at Web's tight butt in his worn cords, his rumpled hair shining dark in the wind, she felt a scared sinking deep on the inside.

Damn it and double damn it, but it was about time she took the scary risk herself.

CHAPTER 12

"You didn't have to come outside in the cold." Web, bent over the snow fence, glanced up when he saw her walking from the house. "I was coming in for coffee in a blink. Only one question left. We have to set up some kind of opening from the outside. You don't actually have to have a formal gate, but you're going to want some kind of latch—"

The closer she got to him, the more he straightened. Wiped his forehead with his jacket sleeve.

Even when she kept coming, he didn't seem to guess there was anything amiss. His mouth cocked up in a welcoming smile. He kept talking about the type of latch he could set up for her. "And the height of the snow fence— that'll only contain them for a few more weeks, you know. But that's probably enough until—"

All this time, she'd never taken the terrible risk and reached out to him, and here, Poppy thought, it was so easy. All she had to do was pop up on her boot tips, clench her hands on his flannel jacket to tug him closer and lay one flat on his mouth.

It wasn't that she wanted to do this. She'd *never* wanted to do this. Years before, she'd quit taking risks where the odds were high she was going to get kicked in the emotional teeth. But, darn it, Web had brought this on himself. He's the one who'd said he'd wanted her back when she was butt-ugly. Once he'd put that idea in her mind, it was like dislodging glue. And if he'd wanted her then, how could he possibly want her less now that she was downright decent-looking?

Or close enough to decent-looking.

Hells bells, right then she didn't care what the Sam Hill she looked like. Looks weren't the point. Taking terrifying risks was the point. And because Poppy didn't enjoy risking humiliation or rejection, much less a double dose of both, her hands were shaking and she seemed to be feeling more belligerent than sexy. But that was only when she kissed him the first time.

That first smack nearly knocked him over. She was a little afraid that kiss was hard enough to loosen teeth. And she hadn't considered any tactical problems ahead of time—like having the good sense to take a breath, because now she was out of breath before that collision of a kiss was even half done.

Heaven knew what happened next.

Web didn't cooperate, that was for damn sure.

Here she was gasping for air like a beached fish, and suddenly his big, cold hands were framing her face and he was bending down for another one. Or…not exactly another one. The kiss he took had little in common with the train wreck she'd attacked him with.

His lips sealed on hers, sank into hers, then seemed to nestle right in. Cripes, now she was not only short on oxygen, she'd completely forgotten how to breathe. In fact, her brain short-circuited every rational synapse she'd ever had and then some.

She just stood there in the freezing wind, her blue sweater jacket flapping, and closed her eyes. Good grief, but that man tasted better than hot mulled cider in a blizzard. Better than a double marshmallow sundae with chocolate ice cream. Better than fresh-whipped cream over hot, sweet cherries. Better than…aw, hell. It wasn't about food. It was about him. His taste that went straight to her head.

She wrapped her arms around his neck because she'd have fallen if she hadn't. Eventually, finally, his mouth eased away from hers. He grunted something impossible to understand, like, "It sure took you long enough."

And then he went back for some tongue and tonsil.

She pulled at his flannel jacket, trying to tug it off his shoulders. Undoubtedly they'd freeze to death if they stripped down, but Poppy couldn't seem to worry about it. It was just like the fawns. The fawns knew it was stupid to trust humans, but hunger won out over the risk. She knew, same way, that it was crazy to make more of this than it was—whatever it was—but darn it, once she'd thrown her line in the water, it was too late to pull back, so she might as well go for the whole tuna.

When she pulled on his jacket, he pulled on hers. Since hers was just hanging loose, it slipped off right there, in the leaf-strewn yard, with the wind doing that whistling, whispering thing it did in the fall, the sun dappling through the clouds from one second to the next.

And then, although he seemed intent on still kissing

her, he started back-walking her toward the house. "I don't mind the exhibitionist thing, but not today, no hypothermia for you," he warned her.

"Huh?"

"We're going inside."

She was relieved he explained. Right then she doubted she'd comprehend anything that wasn't spoken to her in simple, short words. Walking backward proved treacherous. She nearly killed herself backing up the steps, then almost bumped hard into the back door—Web yanked her away in time, but when a woman was bent on self-destruction, it was hard to always save her.

Inside, Edward and Snickers and Mandy all rushed them, because that's what they always did—rush her when she came in, expecting petting and attention and a lot of baby talk. This time, the poor darlings got nothing. Not even a glance.

"I'm hoping your bedroom is close, real close, because I can guarantee we're not going to make it much farther," he said.

She didn't ask *Does that mean we're going to make love?* because even in her dim-witted state of mind, some things didn't need major clarification. Still, her blood pressure kept suffering astounding shock waves. Who could have guessed that taking The Risk could result in complete and instant annihilation of the world as she knew it?

He yanked off her jacket and sweater as if he'd had practice stripping women all his life. Then claimed another kiss. This time he got intensively busier with his hands—which were still colder than just-thawed ice cubes and raising gooseflesh on her throat and sides and fanny and breasts and everywhere else he touched.

When he fumbled for her bra strap, she broke free from somewhere around their thirty-third kiss to say, "They're pretty darn small. And not sagging, exactly. But if you were expecting—"

"My God, if this is another discussion about how you aren't physically perfect, I might have to punch a hole in your wall."

That was such an outstanding thing to say that she stared at him blankly for at least a second. That was all there was time for before he was skinning off his shirt, unbuttoning his jeans and then diving for hers.

If she was supposed to be registering second thoughts, they never surfaced. She wasn't about to waste time on nonsense like ethics or morals or rational thinking. Who knew if she'd ever get another chance to see him naked? It's not as if she had many shots at guys who were a feast for the eyes, much less a feast for the senses like Web.

One of the few advantages to picking some losers over the years was that she sure as Pete knew the difference. And she wasn't about to let a winner go free if she could help it even if she only had him for a night. Or a few hours. Or hell, for a few minutes.

So she peeled as he peeled. His eyes seemed to darken, the more clothes strewed on the carpet. He stopped leaving frostbite marks on her skin. Thankfully as they progressed, her skin seemed to pick up a fever that rivaled imminent loss of brain function.

Damn, but was he built. Not as if he didn't have a few

years on him, too, but his shoulders and upper chest were sleek and solid. Her eyes and palms both savored the patches of dark hair on his chest—no gorilla thing, just those sprawly, springy patches of hair, enough to charge up her feminine senses another notch. When he yanked off his cords, hell, the man had no shyness to him. His briefs were abandoned at the same time.

That wand could have weaved spells all on its own.

She knew the "wand" thinking was a cliché. But that was a wonder of it. For the first time in her life she owned all those delectable clichés. The making love in front of a fire on a big old rug—not a bear rug, true; but then, a bear rug would have been scratchy, and the fluffball of a rug by her hearth was almost thick as a pillow. The phone rang a couple of times, but it wasn't as if either of them paid any attention. The critters initially seemed fascinated with the strange sounds and actions of the humans, but after a while they went off and napped elsewhere. She had the man, the crackling fire and the magic all to herself.

Of course, there came that moment when she was naked and suddenly remembered all the faults of her body and in- stinctively clenched up. She tried not to let Web know so he wouldn't be annoyed again…yet he did know. She could tell from the way he looked at her, and damn, but her inse- curities this time just seemed to inspire revenge in him. Web seemed to have the preposterous idea that making love meant letting everything hang out. Heart, soul, vulnerabil- ities, the whole kahuna. Being really naked, not just phys- ically but verbally and emotionally and every other way.

Who'd have ever guessed that making love to a winner could be so completely different than making love with losers?

An occasional thought seemed to squeeze through. Like, how stupid his ex-wives must be to have given up. Like, was there a chance in the universe this afternoon could go on forever? Like, why the hell hadn't anyone told her it could be this good?

She'd never tried it before, making love side by side. She'd never tried the position where she spooned against him and fit that way either. She'd never tried closing her eyes and just soaring on a man's wings before, either.

When it was over, her hair was surely plastered to her scalp. She was sex- and sweat-slick and had surely used up her quota of oxygen for the next three weeks and yet still couldn't seem to catch her breath.

Yet when Web murmured, "Am I too heavy?" she just wrapped her arms tighter around him and refused to let go.

She vaguely remembered their intention to make it to her bedroom. The living room had certain disadvantages. The fire had long died in the hearth and the floor draft was starting to chill them both. Edward and Snickers edged closer, peeking around chairs and couches to check on the humans but not bothering them. Nothing could have bothered Poppy right then.

Eventually Web said, "I can hear wind really picking up outside."

"I can, too."

"We've got to finish putting up the snow fence before dark."

"I know," she agreed. Her fingers threaded the hair

from his brow, still wanting to touch him, needing to touch him. Any which way she could. "We should probably see if the fawns will go for another bottle, too. There's no telling how long they'd gone without when you found them."

"Yeah. Need to do that, too."

"You realize it's almost four o'clock?"

He opened one eye. "You trying to get rid of me?"

Her answer was instinctive and swift. "No. God, no, Web."

He smiled, but it wasn't a grin of a smile. It was something softer and more dangerous. And then he kissed her as if there were no tomorrow.

Maybe there wasn't. For them. At that instant, she didn't know or care. She figured she'd be too sore to walk tomorrow or she'd be walking bowlegged for the next week. But, man, what a way to suffer.

She roped him in her arms and took him down for another round.

She heard his throaty laughter…but he wasn't laughing for long.

It was only later, after they'd both stuffed on warm jackets and hats to head back outside, that she felt a harsh wind slap her cheeks. What had she done? He hadn't said anything huge or portentous. She hadn't said anything huge or portentous.

But she was so damned happy it was as if she'd crossed over to the other side of the sun—the dangerous side of the sun. Because what Web wanted from her—and what she wanted from him—was still unspoken, buried deep inside a locked Pandora's box.

She tried to convince herself it didn't matter. This time with him was euphoric. She'd always have this—a man who'd made her feel incomparably beautiful. Sex better than she'd ever dreamed of. A chemistry that had been beyond perfect for that moment. Love. And no, she wasn't afraid to use the word with a man, for a man, not this day.

But what was going to happen on Monday?

"You're going to have to do the service." Charles suffered a fit of coughing, had to stop talking. The dullness of his eyes told the fever story. The bubble in his coughing told the rest of the tale. It wasn't pneumonia. But the antibiotics were only starting to dent a plain old rotten case of bronchitis.

"I can do most of it," Bren readily agreed, "but I can't give your sermon—"

"Would you *stop* arguing with me?" More coughing. "I want everything about the church service to be exactly like always. We're not changing anything. Not when things are finally going so well."

"I understand. But—"

"You need to read all the events going on. You can do that with no sweat. And as far as the sermon...it's all written out. You just have to read it aloud."

"But I won't do it like you do it—"

"Of course you won't. No one would expect you to. But there isn't anyone else to ask, Bren. It has to be you. Now just *do it*. And don't mess it up. Just read it exactly like I wrote it."

By the time Bren walked over to the church, a half hour before service, she was rattled times two. Having a sick

Charles wasn't all bad. He'd needed a lot of caretaking, but it was a ton easier to feed him chicken soup and do some fetch-and-carry than worry about his temper.

But pulling off the Sunday services was another world.

Charles thought of the church as his firstborn. His own private child. Something he owned. Nothing was right unless it was his way.

Through the years, Bren had been forced to get up in front of a podium for various causes. Minister's wives had to. Most of the time, all she had to do was say a few kind words and sit down again. She could do that. But treading on Charles's territory was like asking a wren to keep up with an eagle. Nothing she did or said—or how she did and said it—was likely to be right. Not by Charles's standards.

She parked her spineless body outside the church front door as of ten-thirty, ready to greet church comers, the way she and Charles always did before service. The morning was unseasonably frisky, even for November. The grass was still frost-white, the branches still silvery with hoarfrost. The sun started to peek through as she started shaking hands, but it was still cold enough to make her nose feel like a mummified ice cube.

She'd tried to give herself some confidence by wearing her dark burgundy dress. A scarf at the neck spiced it up a bit. And she was having a good hair day—in spite of the cold, there was no wind at all, so the soft, pulled-back style stayed tidy enough. Beneath the scarf at the neck, she wore a cameo. Charles didn't approve of jewelry, especially on Sunday. But she needed luck today and she loved that piece of her mother's. And anyway, it was out of sight under the scarf.

"How are you, Mrs. Franks? Recovering from that fall? Bobby, you're taller than me. How'd you do that since last week? Thanks for coming! Thanks for coming! Thanks for coming. George, you're looking so good, no one would ever guess you had that stroke, you handsome devil. Susannah." Her hands were actually warming up just from all the shaking and clasping. "A sad time for you, but let's see if we can scare up some time together next week. I'll be thinking of you when we sing."

By the time Bren headed inside, she was startled at the huge turnout. Actually, it seemed close to a record turnout, judging from the filled seats, but the crowd jangled her nerves even more. The greeting part of the service had gone well, but criminy, that always went great. She knew everybody, cared about all of them. All she had to do was offer a hand to hold, clasp a shoulder, share a smile. Give of herself.

Giving had always given her strength.

She just didn't feel strong as she made her way to the pulpit. By then, of course, she'd told folks that Charles was ill, but there were still looks of surprise when she climbed up there. She was surprised herself—that she hadn't fallen over. Stunned mute was more like it.

"Good morning, everyone! First, I want to list all the events we have coming up."

The rummage sale. The craft show. Caroling in the hospital and rest homes was being organized by Marge Fenwick this year. The last Righteous singing competition was only a week away, and the winner would be singing the hymns on Thanksgiving Day…. Bren looked up. "As well as being broadcast *live* on both radio channels 3470 and 1138."

The congregation burst into applause, startling her but then naturally making her smile. "Yes, I'm as tickled as all of you with how much we've been doing lately—for our community, as well as for other causes in need. It's too soon to tally the amounts, but I can give you a ballpark of what you've managed to bring in so far. I think you'll all be pleased and proud at how much you've helped raise."

When she named the figure, the congregation burst into another round of spontaneous applause. Right after that was when Bren suffered a tiny crisis in judgment. Charles had picked a rather sober hymn, but now…well…everyone seemed so *connected* today. So happy.

So she switched the hymn to "On Eagle's Wings"—one of those songs that everyone loved and no trial for the organist, who could play it in her sleep.

After that came a little larger crisis in judgment. Following that first hymn, Charles usually did his sermon. He'd never missed, not once since they'd been married. It's not as if he was never sick—of course he was—but somehow by Sunday, even if he wasn't at his best, he always managed to make it to the pulpit.

Bren stood up there, shuffling through his typed-up sermon. She'd practiced. Gone down to the basement, read it aloud four times, studying it to get the words and the pacing right. But it was such a somber talk about disasters striking us all and how no one could or should ever feel safe, all we could do was trust in God. That sort of thing. The sort of thing Charles did very well. It's just…she didn't.

Still, when she opened her mouth, she just assumed his speech was going to come out. Instead she said, "I know you're expecting Charles. And he left me this wonderful sermon for you. But since you're stuck with me today…I'd just like to share something a little different. Do any of you remember an older woman who used to live in Righteous…Maude Rose?"

Maude Rose was so notorious that at least a third of the congregation nodded yes. Another third, when Bren relayed a few more comments to jog their memories, recognized who Maude Rose was, as well.

"She wasn't a member of this church," Bren said. "As far as I know, she wasn't a member of any local church. And she certainly wasn't a popular personality. So…you're wondering why I'm bringing her up, hmm?"

Little Billy Baker in the third row was fussing and whining, until his daddy picked him up. Lily Stone, on the far end of the fifth row, always slept through sermons, but she cocked her head toward Bren. Robert Kachanov, one of the church pillars, had a disapproving scowl on, and when his wife—Bertha, a good woman and a super church participant—nodded at Bren, he threw her a quelling glance.

"Charles would be annoyed for my bringing her up, too," Bren confessed to the congregation, which ignited smiles in a lot of the women. "He's always telling me, 'Bren, you can't save everyone.' And I know he's right. We all try to be good people, but there simply has to be a limit. You can only spread yourself so thin, right? So why feel guilty if there's someone just so totally different from you that you can't find a way to relate to them?"

She could see from their faces that they didn't get where she was going. They weren't alone. She didn't have a clue. The only thing in her mind was this wicked flash of light…the wicked, flashy realization that Charles really *wasn't* here. That even if he killed her later, she could say anything she wanted to right now. And that, obviously, she'd never have another opportunity to talk about Maude Rose.

"If you happened to pick up a piece of coal," she said thoughtfully, "I doubt anybody'd be very excited about it. It's dirty. And it's the kind of dirt that rubs off on your hands. It doesn't smell very good—doesn't seem to have anything appealing about it. So who could possibly guess that if you compressed a piece of dirty ole coal right down to its essence that you could produce the most sparkling jewel on the planet?

"I'm not saying, mind you, that Maude Rose was a diamond. But we seem to live in a world today where we're extra afraid of those different than us. A world where everybody, all sides, are quick to judge. A world where everyone seems to think God's on their side and yet they use that as an excuse to shoot those who don't agree with them."

She talked a bit about Maude Rose. About a woman who'd had few choices. Little love. Little means to protect herself or build any kind of security. Yet a woman who was stubborn enough, had enough soul and heart in her, to stand up for what she thought was right.

"I honestly can't imagine someone who rubbed more

people wrong in this town than Maude. She couldn't seem to take on a single popular cause. As far as I can tell, she only picked the fights that she couldn't possibly win. In fact, if any of you knew her, there was every chance you didn't much like her."

She waited a moment. They were listening to her. Their attention was weirdly energizing but weirdly innervating as well. "What I'm suggesting to you is that we were all richer because she lived in our town. What I'm suggesting is that none of us were harmed because Maude Rose spoke up, loudly and sometimes obnoxiously, for causes we all didn't agree with.

"What I'm suggesting is that Thanksgiving is coming…a time when we remember all the things we're grateful for. And maybe it's an extra good time to give a thought, just a little thought, to coal and diamonds. The next time you run across a piece of coal, think about it before judging. Before kicking it out of your way. Before feeling all self-righteous because you're the one who's right and God's on *your* side. Think about how there might just be the sparkle of a diamond under that coal…if we can just see it. If we remember that people could have reasons for their behavior that we never know. If we can open up our hearts to be more, just a little more, wiser and kinder than we were yesterday…"

Holy kamoly. She was out of breath when she finished, and the congregation was just staring at her. No one was asleep, she could see that. But she couldn't tell if they were annoyed or bored or interested in her little impromptu sermon. For darn sure, Robert Kachanov looked grim. But then, if she'd stood on her head and done cartwheels, he'd have responded with that grim look of his, too. He thought of himself as just under God, with a far more direct line than most people, so there was no pleasing him.

She quit trying. And since she'd already screwed everything up, she figured there was nothing more to lose by beating to the same drummer. After the sermon, Charles always did a universal prayer for people in need in the congregation. She read that list, too, but asked everyone to hold hands, to make a prayer "connection" for those folks in need.

She held her breath when nobody moved, certain they weren't going to pay her any attention—but then they did. One by one, hands stretched across to the aisles, lifted to each other. And when everyone was hand-holding, she read through the list....

"For Mabel Lee, struggling with lung cancer...and our prayers go to John and Jimmy Sanders and their parents, hoping their safe return from the Middle East...and for Mr. Robert Samuel Hawkins, the newest member of the church, born last Thursday at a whopping ten and a half pounds..."

Near the end of the list, a two-year-old broke loose. Most Sundays, Bren missed part of the service because she ran the Sunday school, but the very little ones always stayed with their parents. This particular little squirt was Barb and Joel Smith's first. He was one of those kids that should have been named Born to Run.

Bren heard the giggle before she saw the ripple of movement. While everyone was standing, praying together, the tyke got loose, jumped on top of the pews and took off.

Hands reached out. Nobody could catch him. And when he got to the aisle, he ran straight up to the altar at a breakneck pace, still giggling. He was wearing a white shirt and short pants and a tie, give or take that it was all untucked and unstrung and unbuttoned.

She stepped aside from the pulpit and caught him midgallop. He was definitely a heavyweight little slugger, but he quieted instantly when she scooped him up—certainly not out of fear. Maybe because he was still having fun.

"We're going to finish our community prayers in a minute, but I think, given the circumstances, that young Mr. Smith and I are going to lead you in a song first, all right? A prayer about the joy of love and thanksgiving."

The two-year-old got to touch one chord on the organ and then just stayed snuggled in Bren's arms while she swayed and sang with the congregation. The whole time she thought, *Please don't let Charles hear about this. Please, please, please.*

Because she'd lost track of time, the service ended after noon. By then, the two-year-old had been reclaimed by his parents, and Bren made her way out to the porch steps. She and Charles always said goodbye to everyone after the service, same way they greeted them. Only today, she was startled by the unexpected response of the congregation.

"That's the best service we've had in years, Bren. Thanks so much."

The couple after that took turns pumping her hands as if she were a faucet on a hand well. "That was so inspirational and uplifting. More about *us* and who we really are in Righteous."

The next group out was a family. "Bren, the way you handled the Smith hellion had us all laughing. But it really showed how we can all be together. Not critical. Just helping each other. A real church family."

On and on. Two more people called her "inspirational." Three couples told her she should do the sermons instead of Charles.

One man said flat out she should be the minister instead of Charles. Robert Kachanov brought up the rear, herding his clan—wife, kids and grandkids. He paused, because he always paused to deliver a grade on the service as if he were the most important final judge. "An unusual service," he said curtly.

Which was almost praise. At least it wasn't condemnation.

By the time the church was empty, Bren strode back in for the cleanup…but her heart was soaring somewhere near the stratosphere. She couldn't help doing a little boogie-woogie up the aisle. When had she last felt crazy euphoric like this? Giddy happy. Laughing happy.

Of course, it was pride. She'd just expected to flunk her absentee-minister role, and instead…somehow it just felt great. To reach out. Her own way. To feel she'd brought people together in a way they needed, a way that made them feel good about themselves.

It was like tasting a dream she'd never known she had.

CHAPTER 13

Bren arrived at Link's first. It was the fast-food place next to Ruby's Rubies, and she knew Poppy grabbed a meal there now and then. Neither could steal more than a half-hour lunch today, though, they were both swamped. Bren, now that she'd discovered vice, was practicing greed, chugging down a roast-beef-on-rye with Link's special sauce, then pigging out on Link's special chips. And she wanted dessert. One of those little crème brûlée that must have about fifty million calories. Poppy had gone straight for pastrami and packaged one to take back to Web.

"Why are you so damned surprised they loved you?" Poppy demanded.

"I'm not saying they *loved* me. It's just…I never felt like that before. As if I were really making a difference. The kind of difference I want to make. I don't want money—"

Poppy waved a french fry at her. "Oh, quit being so damned good. There's nothing wrong with money."

"I know, I know. I'm just saying that my best highs are when I've helped someone. That's my champagne. That's my money."

"So…you've had all those people encouraging you for two Sundays now. Why don't you go for it?"

"Go for what?"

"Go for being a minister yourself."

Bren laughed. "I can't do that, Poppy. I don't have the education or theological background."

"Does your Charles have a degree in theology?"

"Well, no, actually. You don't necessarily have to have a degree to start a church. But a church has a right to expect a pastor with experience and real knowledge and qualifications—"

"Well, I think you're more qualified than he is. By ten times. No matter what education he's got. But speaking of the devil—how's he taking to this success of yours?"

Bren ducked her head. "He doesn't know. That bronchitis really took him under. He just got out of bed yesterday, and today's the first morning he's even trying to catch up. It'll be a while before he's really back to snuff, but I know he'll find a way to do the Thanksgiving service. And since you've nagged me nonstop since we got here…" Bren stole one of her fries. Stole. Right off Poppy's plate. Proving how skilled she was getting at this new vice thing. "It's your turn to confess. What's going on? You're glowing like a lightbulb."

"Am I really?"

"Yup."

"It must be the hot sex," Poppy said thoughtfully.

Bren's jaw dropped. "You did the deed? With Web?"

"Now don't jump all over me."

"I wasn't going to."

Poppy rolled her eyes. "Yeah, right. I know what you were thinking—that sex goes with marriage, that whole moral thing. But you know what? I don't know what's wrong with me, but I've never been this happy."

"He's good to you?"

"More than good. Bren, I feel like I'm living a dream. And I don't do dreams. But…he just comes over. We feed animals and do some training with them. We crash on the couch, still talking, while we chow down some kind of dinner. We talk and talk and never seem to run out of conversation."

"Never?" Bren teased.

"All right, all right, I admit, we quit talking when we're doing the deed. And as far as that…" Poppy shook her head, obviously too high to eat. To think. Her beam could have lit the entire block. "The bubble has to burst. I know that. But right now I admit, I'm just floating with it."

Bren didn't press further. She could see Poppy was testing out this new happiness, the taste and smell and texture of it. It was hard not to worry for her. No relationship could sustain that level of euphoria without some solid substance underneath it. But surely she and Web would talk soon, and right now Bren figured that Poppy just plain needed and deserved this stretch of happiness. So she switched subjects before they ran out of lunchtime.

"I heard from our Mary Sue that she got a job with Cal Asher. Just filing, receptionist stuff, that kind of thing. Cal keeps saying he's going to retire, so I don't know how long the job can last, but he's paying her good money. And the contacts she gets from him could really give her a boost up, offer other opportunities. If she'll just stick with it."

"I told my brothers to watch out for her. Especially Zach."

"Have you heard if the boyfriend's still coming around?"

Poppy shook her head. "I don't know. But she's gone out of her way to tell me she's slept alone in the apartment since she moved there."

"It sounds good. Like having the apartment really is making a difference in her life. But she's not totally out of the woods yet."

"Hell, Bren," Poppy said wryly. "Who is?"

Bren was still smiling when she drove back home. She and Poppy hadn't been lunching every week, but almost. It wasn't when or how often they met that mattered but the chat that buoyed Bren. Honesty and Poppy went together. So did talking about things—thinking about things—that Bren never might have without a friend. At least, without a friend like Poppy.

Once home, she went in search of Charles. He'd left a note on the kitchen table telling her he was doing some paperwork in the church rectory—a super sign, she thought, that he was feeling better, out and about again.

She popped over there, hearing the phone ring in the rectory just as she opened the door. Charles didn't answer it. She found him standing by the window, the phone ringing behind him. He spun around when he heard her come in.

In a glance she could see he was white-lipped and tight. "I've been waiting for you," he said. "I heard all about this Mary Sue Chapman. About how you got her into this apartment on Willow, are paying her rent. How on *earth* did you manage to do this?"

Her soft, buoyant mood started crumbling. "How did you hear about this?"

"Apparently this girl has been talking all over town about how good 'these two women' have been to her. Standing up for her. Being her 'guardian angel.' The first call I got this morning, I said that couldn't have been my Bren. My wife would have told me. It has to be a mistake." The phone stopped ringing. In the silence, Charles said very quietly, "But then there was a second call. And a third. You made me out to be a liar, Bren."

"I didn't know you were getting those calls—"

"*Where* did this money come from? The money to support the rent on this place? What else have you been doing behind my back? And that's not counting the endless, endless calls I've been getting over the last two days about your standing up in the pulpit, making out like you're a better minister than I could ever be."

The sunlight was behind him, making his expression hard to read. But unlike other times he'd been mad, this time his voice was quiet. Slow. Something was different, so ominously different that she instinctively wrapped her arms around her chest. Weeks had been building to this. Maybe months. Maybe her whole life—not that she had time to dwell on past history.

She said, "Charles, please, sit down with me. I'll tell you how all this happened. Believe it or not, I've wanted to tell you for some time."

"You're damn right you'll tell me. I heard you were even asked to serve as cominister! Somehow you neglected to mention that to me, too."

Quickly she shook her head. "I never thought anyone was serious about that, Charles. I just thought they were trying to be nice. And you were ill. I didn't think it was important—"

"Give me a break, Bren. You've been full of your own pride and glory, thinking you could fill my shoes. Thinking everybody loves you. Everybody loves little Bren. They don't know you're manipulative and ambitious and conniving behind my back, now do they?"

Oh, God. It was going to be bad. Something inside her went still, as still as an impossibly close summer day when you just couldn't catch a fresh breath. Yet even as fear rollicked in her pulse, Bren felt something different than fear, more than fear. Maybe it was just that she'd been living on this cliff edge for so long. Whether she fell off or found a way to safety almost didn't matter. Anything was better than living in that limbo forever, never feeling safe, never being able to breathe.

"Charles, I was trying to be there for you when you were sick. You *asked* me to give the sermons. In fact, you insisted—"

"Yes, I certainly did. Only you never gave the sermons I told you to."

"No, I didn't. And I'll tell you why. I'll explain all of it—"

"I know you will. Right now. Immediately. Starting with this inheritance you held back from me—"

She nodded, trying to nod slowly, not quickly, trying to look calm. To be calm. "But it's not a short story. There's a lot to it. So please try to calm down enough to listen."

He didn't want to calm down. Or sit. The phone rang yet again, eventually playing a message on the answering machine that both of them could hear, both of them ignored. Charles paced in front of the window, fingers restlessly jingling the change in his pocket. He was thinner than he'd been three weeks ago. Paler. But those eyes of his burned dark and hot.

"I did conceal this from you," Bren admitted honestly. "Maude Rose left me an inheritance—"

"No one leaves just *you* an inheritance, Bren. We're married. What's yours is mine."

"I understand that's how you feel—"

"That's how it *is*. Not how I *feel*."

"Maude left me some jewelry. For being kind to her when so many other people in town weren't. In her will—"

"And how did you find out about this inheritance?"

"From Cal Asher. He called me after she died, because he's the one who handled Maude's will. He told me the terms. And he read me her express wishes—which were that I keep the inheritance to myself."

"That wasn't your call. This is a marriage. You don't have things 'to yourself.' How much was it worth?" he grilled her.

She had fault in this, Bren reminded herself. Lots of fault. For omission. For lack of loyalty. So she wasn't going to duck this, not anymore. "I didn't do anything with it. I just decided to wait a while. Think about it. For one thing, we were in the middle of so many projects with the church that we already hoped would turn our financial situation around. So if we didn't need the money for that—"

He was only listening to one drummer. "How much exactly was this inheritance worth?"

She continued trying to explain. "And those projects have gone even better than we ever dreamed, Charles. We've been out of hock, running in the black. We've brought in new members, have a half dozen projects and services that are bringing in—"

He stalked over to her chair, clenched his hands on both sides of her and said very quietly, "I'm going to ask you one more time. How much was this inheritance worth?"

She tried to take a breath. Tried to suck in a little extra oxygen. Said just as quietly, "Does it really matter if it's ten dollars or a hundred? The reason I—"

The punch came toward her faster than she could duck. A shake was one thing. A slap was another thing. Throwing something that may or may not have accidentally hit her was yet another thing.

But a punch…it was like an explosion in her cheek. A rocket of pain that echoed through all the nerves in her body. She understood in a single sharp flash that morals and ethics and principles were all very well and good, but when a woman was afraid, fear changed everything.

He said, "You're going to tell me how much it is. And then you're going to hand over every cent of it."

And then came the second punch.

* * *

Poppy pocketed her cell phone with a frown. That was the second time she'd tried to reach Bren today.

Bren was busy. Nothing new about that. The two often didn't catch up with each other on first try. But Bren's voice mail wasn't working. That was the odd thing. Bren carried her cell phone like a third hand. God forbid anybody in that church not be able to reach her for two seconds. She was *always* reachable by phone or message.

Well, Poppy thought, it wasn't as if she couldn't catch her later. She'd just wanted to share some news. Zach, her grapevine expert, had told her that Mary Sue's worse-than-a-guppy of a boyfriend had pulled up stakes and left town. That didn't mean, of course, that Mary Sue wouldn't pick up with another troublemaker. But it was still good news that the jerk was putting miles between them.

Good enough news to share, anyway. But it would wait. Heaven knew, she had a crazy schedule of an afternoon ahead.

Josh had finally taken Mandy home that morning. And Poppy had come in late—and left for lunch late—because of feeding the fawns. Then her first grooming job had been interrupted because of an emergency—a puppy had tangled with a woodchuck, and Shirley hadn't been in when Web had needed an assistant, so she'd stepped in.

One way or another, the day was turning into one of those nonstop chaotic Fridays. Nothing was that terrible. It was just impossible to keep any kind of schedule, so that by three she was feeling on the rattled side.

Booger Matthews was next. Poppy didn't know the dog.

Lola Mae had made the appointment and jotted down notes—that Booger was a mixed-breed terrier, ten months old, here because the dog refused to be potty trained.

It was another one of those cases where it was the owner who needed training, Poppy thought wryly. But not as if that was unusual. She checked the file to make sure Web had seen the dog first, that the dog didn't have a kidney infection or other physical problem. And before heading to the lobby to claim the dog, she glanced again at the name.

Some dogs weren't fancy. And some owners had ghastly senses of humor. But something told her an owner who'd named a pet "Booger" was more than half the problem.

She headed for the lobby. As it happened, she was on her second set of clothes for the day. She'd started out in jeans and a yellow sweater, but they'd trashed out before lunch. Her blue striped shirt and jeans were no fancier, and certainly they weren't taking critter hair any better than her old outfits, but she wasn't going back to ill-fitting clothes and no makeup.

Even on challenging days like this one, she felt better about her looks than she used to. Maybe it was the clothes. Maybe it was the surgery. Maybe it was feeling loved by a wickedly wonderful man. Who knew? Who cared?

She strode in the lobby with a welcoming smile and looked around for the woman who owned Booger. But then her stomach clenched into a sharp spike. There were no women in the lobby. There were three guys. Two with cats.

The third man held a leash on a worried-looking mixed terrier. Poppy didn't know the dog, but she sure as hell knew the guy.

"Hello, Mike. Come on back, you two." She didn't lose the friendly expression, but her cheeks were already starting to freeze just trying to keep that smile in place.

Mike Matthews stood, scooped up the terrier on his arm and immediately followed her—but she noticed the quick frown on his forehead. He didn't recognize her.

"I was told you were the one who worked with problem dogs," he said.

"Sometimes," she agreed. Once in her room, she closed the door to the lobby. "You can let Booger loose. Let's see what's what, okay?"

She crouched down, wanting to see how the dog behaved, how it related to a stranger. That proved easy enough to figure out. The dog was shaking like an aspen in a high wind. The instant Mike let it down, the dog promptly squatted and peed.

"Hell," Mike said and made to cuff the dog—until Poppy said firmly, quickly, "Don't. That's what we need to see. What's going on. So we'll know how to fix it."

"I'm gonna drop her off in the backwoods, she doesn't quit pissing and pooping all the time," he said gruffly and stared hard at her again.

She focused her attention on the dog, but she was mentally kicking herself for not making the connection. Matthews was such a common last name that she just hadn't thought about Mike.

For that matter, Mike didn't *look* like a sleaze. She hadn't seen him in, what, two years? Closer to three? Still had a nice head full of blond hair, a booming infectious laugh, shoulders big enough to make a girl feel safe. He also had great moves on a dance floor—but that should have been her first clue.

Nice guys always had panic attacks near a dance floor. If that wasn't a universal truth, it was close enough. But three years ago, she'd just been so happy to have a chance to dance, to kick up her heels and let it hang out a bit.

"What you've got here," she said, "is a nervous dog. If you yell, she pees. If you scare her, she pees—"

"My God," he said suddenly.

Annoyingly.

"Some breeds," she continued, "like dachshunds and Jack Russells…they're just tough to potty train. Always have been, always will be. In this case, though, I don't think you're dealing with a case of stubbornness. This—"

"Poppy? Is that really you?"

"—this is pretty clearly about her giving you submissive behavior. And unfortunately, when you scold her, you exert your dominance, and that prompts her to give you even more submissive behavior. No matter how much of a nuisance her leaking is for you, the more you yell, the more you need to understand that you're encouraging her to do the same—"

"Wow. I can't believe it. I'd never have thrown you over if I'd known you could look like this. What in hell did you do to yourself?"

Poppy kept her voice pleasant, but it was becoming an effort. She'd always, always had patience with animals. And Mike Matthews was certainly an animal. But the human kind was so much more exasperating than the animal kind.

"Are you listening to me? I thought you came here to talk about your dog—"

"I did, I did." He put on his slickest smile. The one she'd thought, once, was the genuine version. "Hey, Poppy, no hard feelings, are there? I mean—"

"Good grief," she said, "your cheating on me was the best thing that could have happened. Saved me from caring about you. And wasting any more time."

"Like, I'm sorry. But honestly, honey, who'd know you could look so…sharp. So sexy. I mean, maybe we could talk about this over a drink—"

She didn't want to hit a man in front of his dog. It had to be hard for Booger to be proud of her owner as it was. A dog needed to believe someone higher than pond scum owned her. But Poppy stood up because she wasn't willing to continue this asinine conversation while she was hunkered on the floor and he was standing over her, looking down her shirt.

And at that precise moment she spotted Web in the doorway.

"I knocked," he said. "I just wanted to tell you thanks for helping this morning, Poppy. And our baby bloodhound just woke up. Doing great. She's going to make it. I just thought you'd want to know."

"That's great news. Thanks, Web."

"Need any help in here?" He didn't look at Mike. He looked at her.

Making her wish she could disappear in the Bermuda Triangle or somewhere she could positively never surface again.

"Everything's fine," she assured him.

When Web was gone, she turned to Mike-the-idiot Matthews and said, "We're done here. No charge for the visit, since I won't be taking on your dog. As far as Booger, I wish her luck. As far as you—I can't think of a circumstance where I'd have a drink with you, unless I lost my mind. I hope the next woman you ask out can see right through you, Mike. Out."

She motioned toward the door.

"Still holding a torch, huh?"

She looked at the dog, thinking maybe she could make an exception. But Booger had so much stacked against her future already that Poppy just couldn't see slugging him. She opened the door, motioned to the exit with her thumb.

He started to say something else, with that supercilious grin of his. With rare pleasure, she slammed the door very close—not close enough, but very close—to his nose.

Then felt her heart sink faster than a lead ball off a high cliff. Web had seen. No, he hadn't been there more than two seconds. But enough. She'd seen the way he'd looked at her, offering help. He couldn't possibly know the details, but still, somehow he'd guessed it was an old boyfriend.

In itself, that wasn't a sweat. At their ages, obviously, they both had history. But a single glance and Web would have been able to see that her old lover was a loser. The kind of jerk she used to fall for. The kind of loser she used to attract. The kind she'd go with because, damnation, no one else ever gave her the time of day.

Web couldn't understand. In a zillion years he'd never

have been anyone's pity lay. He'd never have taken on a woman who wasn't decent, because he'd never been that…lonely. That just totally tired of being alone. That just totally needing to dance, to get out, to just have some opposite-gender company because too many nights of TV and reality shows had made her want to take up drinking.

Aw, hell, there was no point in her dwelling on her past mistakes. Her life then was what it was. It was just…she'd never wanted Web to know she'd slept with losers. Or that she was the kind of woman who'd attracted losers.

The front desk buzzed her. "Scarlett O'Beara is out front waiting for her haircut," Loretta said.

She heard. There was no chance she could hide for the rest of the day in the back room. And it was really just Web she didn't want to run into…Web, who'd been treating her like a cherished love. Like a desired cookie. Like a red-hot mama he respected. Like everything she'd ever dreamed a lover would treat her, for several weeks now. Damn it. She didn't want Web to feel ashamed to be with her.

She turned around to wash her hands and faced her reflection in the small oval mirror over the sink. Nothing new in the reflection. It was the same new face. Same cute haircut, effective light makeup, new clothes look. Same new confident tilt to the shoulders, in the smile.

So why the hell was it so hard to change herself on the inside?

She went to fetch Scarlett. The Newfoundland was an old favorite patient. The dog spent all summer and fall swimming and getting matted up. She had to be clipped in stages, just because the job took hours and even an angel couldn't sit still that long. So Poppy clipped for a couple hours, let her rest, then packed in another client, an arthritic hound who needed the water-bath treadmill. Then back to Scarlett.

The day had been running late anyway, but cripes, it was almost seven before she got her work area cleaned up and she could finally call it quits. Just before pulling on her jacket, though, she dialed Bren again. Obviously she could have waited to call at home, but it had been like a background itch in Poppy's mind that she'd had such a hard time reaching her.

Bren's phone rang. And rang. Yet no one picked up, and voice mail again failed to kick in.

She was just about hang up when she felt a warm, long hand snug around her chest and a wicked wolf take a bite out of her neck from behind.

The phone, once clicked off, was removed from her hand. Her whole body was spun around, secured into a position where she didn't have any place for her hands, it seemed, but hooked around the wolf's neck. Her wolf.

"It's been a helluva day," he murmured between taking bites.

"You're not kidding."

"I'm starving."

"Me, too."

"Not for food."

"Me either."

"No one's still here but us. And I'm pretty sure it's my turn to do the seducing."

"We're taking turns? Who knew?"

"Shut up and be seduced, woman."

"Well, shoot. If you insist."

She was still rattled about Mike showing up, about what Web might have seen or thought. But just then Web didn't seem to be looking for conversation…and if he was upset over anything he'd seen earlier, it sure didn't show. Kiss followed kiss. Caress followed caress. Nips turned into bites, sighs into groans.

Fluorescent lights—who could guess that she'd ever willingly get naked under bald, unforgiving light like that? But Web, the devil, never gave her a chance to think about idiotic details like where they were or what the lighting was.

He'd stayed over a half dozen times now, didn't even seem to mind the cat sleeping between them. She hadn't stayed over at his place, but that was only because she had such a herd to feed. He'd started bringing his strays when he came over so he could stay without worrying about his menagerie being hungry or needing attention.

But right now neither of them was home, and for darn sure, she wasn't thinking about feeding pets. Except for her wolf. She just wanted to give solace and succor to her favorite wolf…and to be succored in return. The only level surface in sight, unfortunately, was the gurney. It was too hard and too skinny to be comfortable, but who cared?

Laughter bubbled up, wicked and soft. A groan when she couldn't bend the way she could have at twenty-one. A frustrated growl from him when he couldn't reach where he wanted. There was no time or interest in thinking, but a quick, sweet thought drifted through her mind that she was so glad she hadn't met him when she was twenty-one…and just as glad she hadn't thought about him this way when he first hired her. It wouldn't have worked then, not a relationship, not a friendship, not anything this real or intimate.

But, man, it was sure working now. Their tummies tucked perfectly together. Her breasts cleaved exquisitely against his chest. By the time he was pumping hard, her heart was slamming need. And his face…she loved watching his face, his eyes dark with desire, his expression so grave when he was on the crest and then easing, finally, when they both tipped over.

Then, of course, came more laughter. The place was a mess. Clothes were strewn in every direction. The gurney rolled and parked cockeyed against the far wall. Her bra was missing completely, although obviously it couldn't have walked off too far. She was damp and sticky. So was he. Her hair was ruined, and his looked like a warlock's in a high wind.

"You are so, so what I needed tonight," she admitted.

"Yeah?"

From nowhere, his easy smile faded. The rush of lust and satiation faded, too. And suddenly those darned fluorescent lights became what they were—harsh, unyielding light that was hard to hide from.

"Poppy, is this it? All you want?"

"Huh? What do you mean?" She hopped around on one leg to face him, still trying to tug on her jeans. As he was tugging on his.

"You were upset when that guy was here today. Matthews. You two obviously had some kind of history together."

"We did. But it was short and a long time ago," she said straight out.

"But you wouldn't have told me if I hadn't asked, would you? Even though you were upset."

"There was nothing to tell, Web. I wish I hadn't run into him. It was uncomfortable. I'm sorry I was ever involved with him, no matter how short a thing it was." She buttoned her shirt quickly. "All right. If you want the total truth, I didn't want you to know about him. I wouldn't have said a word if you hadn't specifically asked."

"And there's the problem." He spun around, looking for his shirt. It seemed to have dropped in a wrinkled ball on the other side of the gurney. He walked over to retrieve it, every stiff movement showing Poppy that he was uncharacteristically tense and unhappy. "As close as we've become—as many hours as we've spent together—apparently nothing has really changed. Not for you."

"Wait a minute." Seconds before, she'd suffered nonstop bliss. Now her stomach felt as if a wrecking ball had lodged there. "I don't understand. You were happy with me a minute ago. Now…it's like you stored this up. What did you think, that I'd give you the details of every guy I ever spent any time with?"

"It's not about details. It's not about lists. It's about getting down to something that matters. I've had two failed marriages. You know that. I'm nobody's good risk. You know that, too. But you haven't brought any of that up."

"What did you want me to say?" She watched him thread his arms into his shirt, still facing her squarely, still with that strong, harsh glint in his eyes.

"It's not what I *wanted* you to say. It's that…it's hard not to notice. If you thought we had any future together—if you wanted any future—I'd think you'd want to get down to a deeper level. Talk about what we both want from life, where we're going from here. Look, you don't have to care at that level. Nothing wrong with what we're doing. We can be lovers. We can be the same friends we were before this." He finished buttoning and tucking, stood near the door with hands on his hips. "As far as I can tell, it's pretty obvious that you don't want more than that from me."

"Do you? Want more?" she whispered. The wrecking ball in her stomach was bad enough. But now she had this sinking feeling, as if she'd just suffered a huge, unbearable loss.

"Come on, Poppy. You know that stupid chick flick where the girl says, 'You had me at hello'? That was me for you. I took one look and thought you were the first real woman I ever found—real for me, real with me. But you never saw it before and still don't. You're still looking in a mirror, worried about self-image, self-worth…hell, I don't know what all you're worried about. I just know I'm too damned old—and so are you—to waste time on someone who doesn't love me back."

"My God, Web. I never realized that you thought about me that way. Before. Or now. Or that you were thinking about a life together or—"

"Exactly. You never thought. The surgery, this whole appearance thing that you're so hung up on—if you wanted it to give you confidence, go get your money back, Pops. Because it hasn't changed a thing. And I can't keep singing in the wind."

She stood there frozen, even after he'd walked out, after she'd heard his office door close, and she knew she was alone.

Of all the selfish jerks, she thought furiously. Beating her up for not having confidence? Expecting her to read his mind and realize he cared? Hells bells, he seemed to be telling her he was in love with her.

A man should at least give a woman time to recover from a heart attack after dropping something that huge on her. For Pete's sake, they'd both just had an exhausting long day. And wasted each other even further by making love as if they were the only two lovers in the entire universe.

What a jerk, she thought again. But she didn't mean Web. She meant herself.

She'd blown it. All this time, she'd known darn well she could survive without a man. Hell, any woman could. Living alone wasn't half as lonely as being with the kind of guy who made you feel lonely.

Only Web wasn't like that. He was the one. The one she'd been afraid to dream of all these years. The one she'd been afraid to hope might ever be in her life.

And it was just as he'd said. She'd looked, but she'd apparently never opened her eyes.

CHAPTER 14

Bren had barely dialed the phone before Poppy picked up—and immediately started yelling at diva volume. "*Finally*, Bren! I've been trying to reach you for *days!* Where the hell have you been? Did you know your voice mail wasn't working? I didn't want to go barreling over to your house when Charles doesn't even know me, but damn it, I've been worried. *Really* worried. It's not like we talk every day, but for heaven's sake—"

"If you'll take a breath, I could get a word in sideways."

"I don't want to take a breath! You *always* have a cell phone or voice mail on somewhere! What the hell happened? Are you okay? I—"

"No."

"I'm telling you, this friend thing is the pits. If you're going to disappear like that again… *What* did you say? *No?* You're not okay?"

"Nope, I'm in a pretty darn awful mess," Bren said cheerfully. "To be honest, I could use some help."

Poppy dropped the diva thing immediately. "Just say where and when. And what."

"Outside of Ruby's Rubies. Around four-thirty or five

today if you could possibly make it. I know those are working hours, Bren, but there's a reason why I—"

"Don't waste your breath. I can cancel work in a blink. I'll be there."

She was. Bren had finished her meeting with Ruby but waited inside until she saw Poppy's bright VW pull up right at the dot of four-thirty. She promptly charged outside. The weather had turned crazy, not cold so much as wildly windy. She'd already pulled a knitted white hood scarf up over her head and neck. Her shoulder bag flopped against her side, significantly lighter than before the meeting with Ruby.

A few parking spaces down, Poppy climbed out of her VW and started hiking toward her. Her head was down as she battled the wind, but then she glanced up—and did a double take when she spotted her.

"Damn it, Bren. Damn it times ten. Damn it times fifty."

Bren suffered a fleeting hope that Poppy might consider behaving more subtly in public, but that was pretty silly. Poppy was Poppy. She grabbed her as if she were a child and framed her face—gently—with gloved hands, then just looked at her face.

"He's the reason we have gun permits," she said fiercely.

"Take it easy. I'm all right."

"The hell you are. And you're never going back there. I'd offer to call Zach and Jase and the entire police force, but I don't want to leave this up to some damn fool men, even the good ones. Besides, I'd rather shoot him myself—"

"Poppy, calm down. It's healing. No long-term scars. But I do need help," she said. She'd stayed out of sight for a week, claiming to any and all that she had a flu. That worked for a short stretch—but it wouldn't work now.

Thursday was Thanksgiving, a huge service at the church. And tonight at eight in the high school was the last competition for the final winner of the singing pageant. It was Bren's baby, so there was just no one who could step in and take her place.

"So I need makeup," she said. "But I don't want to go in and buy it because I don't want anyone seeing me like this. I have lipstick and some blush. Obviously. But not foundation. I just never used it. So I'm not sure what to buy. What would cover—"

"Okay. We'll head right to a store."

"I don't really want anyone to see me, Poppy. And I don't want you paying for it. I'll buy. But what I need help with is knowing *what* to buy. And then how to use it."

"Any other time, this'd be hysterical. Talk about the blind leading the blind," Poppy said with a shake of her head. "Of all the women in the universe, we have to head the list of underachievers in the face-paint department. But I didn't go through all that spa and makeover thing for nothing. I know what we need. Foundation. Eye makeup, shadow and all…"

Bren saw the wheels turning in Poppy's mind and winced. "We don't have to go overboard. It's been a week. The bruises are almost gone, but I still thought—"

"He did this to you a week ago and you still look this bad? Screw the makeup. I'm going to kill him—" She made an impatient gesture at Bren's face. "All right, all right. I won't say another word about the son of a bitch. For the next five minutes. We'll just talk makeup and how to get you fixed up. What are you wearing for that shindig, what colors and all?"

"Brown skirt, brown-and-camel top."

Poppy's hand flew to her heart. "You almost shocked the breath right out of me. That's awfully wild for you, don't you think?"

For the first time in ages, Bren let out a laugh. "Shut up, Poppy. I love those colors. And besides, it's about fall." Bren felt herself being herded into Poppy's car as if she were a kid who needed caretaking. But by then she'd seen Poppy's face close-up, too. There were no scars, no bruises. No one had punched her. But something was sad and lost in those soft eyes. Abruptly she said, "What happened?"

It seemed a measure of what good friends they'd become that Poppy didn't dissemble, didn't pretend to misunderstand, didn't even try to hide the sudden stark misery in her face. She pulled out on the road and kept going. "I blew it with Web. That's what happened. And to be dead honest, I wouldn't mind telling you about it. But if I start talking right now, I'll get all upset, and then we'll risk a car accident and then we won't get your face all fixed up before the deal tonight. So my problem will have to wait."

Bren studied her a little longer. "You want me to drive?"

"If I can't quit crying, yeah. But give me a minute. Damn it. I do just fine until I start thinking about him again. And what a mess I made. You told me to go for it, Bren."

"And that turned out to be bad advice?"

Poppy shook her head fiercely, tears flying. Someone honked at her, possibly because she'd been sitting at a green light for some time. Eventually she put her foot on the gas pedal. "It was great advice. It was what I needed to do for years. Go for what I wanted. What I needed."

"But…" Bren didn't try to finish the thought, only encouraged Poppy to say more.

"But I went at it half-assed. Still trying to cover my butt, protect myself. I wasn't honest. With him or with myself. I tried to show him I cared. But I didn't *tell* him that I'd fallen in love with the damn man. That I actually wanted a life with him. You can't just go from zero to sixty in a jalopy, you know? And I'm a jalopy. Not that easy to risk rejection when you've got a ton at stake. Like your heart."

Bren checked to make sure both their seat belts were buckled tight, since they seemed to be arbitrarily weaving in and out of various lanes. When a car honked at them, Bren turned around and, for the first time in her life, raised a finger to the other driver. "Poppy, those kinds of things were never to be easy for you to say," she said gently. "You couldn't expect yourself to change a whole life of habits— and fears—in one fell swoop. And if Web expected that from you, then he was being unfair."

"He wasn't being remotely unfair. He expected me to be a grown-up. To bring grow-up behavior to the table. The problem is, for God's sake, that I'd never been in love before. Not like this. It's the *pits*," she said furiously.

"Yeah. Heaven knows why we tolerate that half of the species at all. They're hopeless."

"I don't need a damn man! I've been running my life for almost four decades without a bunch of testosterone cluttering everything up! And he's had two divorces. It's not like he's virgin-clean in the successful-relationship department himself."

"Kick that mother right out of your heart," Bren said feelingly. "Who needs him? Forget the idiot. Move on." And then gently, "So…have you called him yet?"

"No. But I will."

"You're going to take another chance."

"I *have* to. I was the one who blew it. And maybe I blew it for good. But I've got to try one more time, and this time I'm going to do what you said. Go for it, for real. Risk all the potatoes." Poppy shot her a narrow-eyed stare that threatened traffic patterns again. "And don't you be saying 'mother' and shooting the finger at people again. People are going to start guessing that someone's been a terrible influence on you."

Poppy parked a few spaces away from Pete's Pharmacy, flew in and emerged fifteen minutes later with a hundred and fifty dollars' worth of cosmetics.

"What on earth *is* all this?" Bren said in a faint whisper, which was all she could manage from the shock.

Poppy took her to her house, where she was set down in front of a mirror at the kitchen table with a rabbit snuggled on her foot and the cat purring on her lap. "I have to feed the fawns," she said, "but they can wait for another twenty minutes."

Bren heard about the fawns. Heard about the three-legged Mandy and Josh and how the two were getting along. Heard about Mike Matthews and the mistake Poppy had made a few years back, the kind of mistake Poppy considered herself famous for. Heard about her brother Zach expecting another urchin come summer and all about the rest of Poppy's nieces and nephews.

She heard about everything but Web.

The whole time, her face and neck were being slathered with various lotions and potions. She was brushed, sponged, poked and penciled. And finally Poppy whisked off the kitchen towel around her neck and let her look in the mirror.

"This is the first I've seen proof there really are miracles," Bren said. "Who is this dazzling woman?"

"Damn, but I'm good, aren't I? Of course, it was a pro who taught me at that spa. I was stuck putting the foundation a little thick, Bren. Nothing less would completely cover the..."

She saw Poppy's change in expression and tried to cut another tirade off at the pass. "Don't say it."

"Please, *please* tell me you're not going back to that man."

Bren stood up and started to clean up the mess they'd both made. "He crossed a line," she said. "I won't live with it anymore. But I had to figure out some things before I actually make a move, Poppy. First, what to do about my dad. And second, there's a congregation of wonderful people who shouldn't be hurt because their minister is involved in a personal scandal. I don't want to cause talk. It's just all been...challenging...to know what to do."

"More than challenging. You've had impossible problems thrown at you right and left."

"Not impossible. But...if it came down to my dad's welfare, then I just would have to stay. It's not that I'm a victim. It's not that I can't or won't speak up for myself. It's that I love my dad. And Charles was essentially blackmailing me, because I couldn't see how I could leave him without sacrificing my dad's welfare."

"You found a way out?" Poppy asked fiercely.

Bren nodded. "Maude Rose's inheritance opened up a choice I hadn't thought of before. But more than that...when Charles hit me this last time, that was when I finally figured out I had the same problem as you, Poppy."

"Huh?"

"Both of us have always stood up for people—or animals—more vulnerable than us. What we never did was stand up for ourselves. And it's not easy for two leopards to change our spots, but shoot, I think we both actually are managing to do it."

By the time Bren arrived at the high school, she was early, but the parking lot was still already packed to the gills, with vans and pickups and cars trailing down the side of the hill, as well. The gym was exuberantly decorated in blue and silver, the school colors. Every seat was filled and the bleachers were overflowing.

She aimed straight behind stage and spotted Charles almost immediately, chatting up some parents of the contestants. Now that the event had turned into such a moneymaker, of course, Charles was all about how much he was behind it...and, for that matter, how much he appreciated what a wonderful minister's wife Bren was. She caught him saying, "Bren's just a bit under the weather tonight. If she's not able to make it, though, I'll easily step in. No one's going to miss the finale—"

She paused next to him. "I'm here, Charles." She smiled at him and at the couple he was speaking to. "We're going to have a great time tonight, aren't we?"

Charles did a double take when he saw her face, but he never lost his smile—and she never lost hers. All the contestants were waiting backstage. One of the contestants was so excited she threw up. Another was so excited he'd already sweated through his stage makeup and his costume. She did the obvious—talked to them about all being winners, all being wonderful and all doing something for others in participating.

And then the competition to pick out the one and only winner began. The first competitions, with the chalk-screaming voices and off-key beats, were long over. There wasn't much singing talent in Righteous. No Hollywood careers ahead of anyone. But there were a lot of hams. A lot of kids with dreams. A lot of people who loved music.

It didn't end until eleven. And by ten after, a reporter from *Our Way* had taken a dozen pictures of the winner—Julia Mae Quince, fifteen, doing her rendition of "Climb Every Mountain." Unfortunately Julia's parents and extended family wanted more pictures after that and then so did all the rest of the runners-up. People started filtering out, but the judges were the last to leave, as they got kudos and criticism and commentary from almost everyone in town.

Finally, though, the crowd was good and gone. There was still a mess to clean up. Although the school had volunteered the use of the gym for the cause and the janitor had agreed to do some extra cleaning, there were still extra chairs to put away, trash to be picked up. Bren didn't mind. She was too wired to try sleeping tonight anyway.

From the other side of the gym she saw Charles doing the same thing she was…pushing a trash bucket, picking up debris, stacking chairs. A small crew from the church stayed to help for a while, until Charles finally shooed them home. That left the two of them alone in the ghost-silent gym.

And that was more than enough silence between them, she thought.

As if he sensed her walking toward him, he suddenly straightened and turned around. And then stopped still. His face looked worn, like a man who'd spent too many hours away from fresh air and sun. And he studied her face intently, but she felt him looking at the bruises, the makeup. Not her. She'd realized for some time that Charles had stopped seeing anything deeper about her years ago.

"The church women put all the receipts together," she said. "The cash box is sitting on the stage for you."

"It's been unbelievable, the community support for this." He said awkwardly, "Thanks to you. I was wrong about this."

She nodded. "Yeah, you were. But your church is in the black again. Which is what you wanted. I'll be attending the Thanksgiving service—"

"Of course you will," he said as if he couldn't fathom her not.

"But after that, Charles, the congregation is going to discover that I'm not living with you. You'll have to decide how you want to deal with that."

The tightness in his jaw reflected how close anger was to the surface. She'd come to realize that the stronger she became—as a woman, as a leader in the community, even as a wife—the more anger showed up in his character. The realization made her sad and unsettled.

But she was through denying it. Through trying to pretend it would go away or that she had the power to control his anger.

"You can't leave me," he said flatly. "You know you can't leave me—"

"I won't stay with you, Charles. I wouldn't stay with anyone who hits me. That's done." Her voice was as calm as water. Once she'd figured all this out, the stress of it had dissolved. Inside, she felt a sense of sureness she'd never felt before. "I've bought a piece of property on my own. It's not big or fancy. But I'm going to use it as a shelter for women and children. I've looked into grants and agency funding. It's a real need in this area. And that's where I'll be hanging the clothes in my closet."

For a moment he looked stunned. Then color shot up his neck. "You got the money from that damned inheritance."

"Yes."

"Anything you get is mine, too. We're in a marriage. Mutual assets. You don't get to spend that money anywhere you felt like, Bren. And as far as living there…somehow you seemed to have completely forgotten about your father."

There now, the threat she'd been waiting for was finally out and on the table. "I haven't forgotten my dad. But I don't think you'll want the community to hear that you would actually withdraw support from my father. Because you would have to tell them why. I also don't think you'd want to publically criticize my opening a women's shelter. Because of how it would make you look."

"How it would make me *look*? What do you think people are going to say if they find out you've left me?"

She said quietly, "I don't know or care, Charles. I finally figured out…I don't have to care about the details. I only have to do what I have the power to do. Right now I can't imagine living with you again. I don't necessarily need a divorce. I don't envision ever wanting to remarry. And I am going to stay in Righteous—for my dad's sake and also for mine, because I love this town. It's my own. But those are my decisions. You'll have to figure out what you want to do about your own situation on your own."

"You can't do this, Bren. I won't let you."

"You can't stop me," she said gently and then picked up her coat and aimed for the door.

Outside, the air was crisp, but the wild wind had died down to a whisper.

Her lungs took in gulps of fresh air as if they'd never experienced freedom before. And maybe they hadn't.

The road she was choosing wasn't remotely easy. She saw bumps in every direction. Problems she couldn't fix. Problems that were going to be touchy. But she was claiming her life again.

Actually, maybe for the first time as an adult woman, she was owning her life.

And she walked toward the van with her head held high.

* * *

Trust the weathermen to get everything wrong. After a week of wild winds and freezing nights, Thanksgiving had dawned balmy as a spring day. Even though it was soothingly sunny, Poppy felt an edgy chill as she walked up the steps to the Church of Peace.

She didn't like churches, and as far as she could tell, churches didn't like her. She did the God thing in the woods. And the praying thing when she was alone in the dark. But the money-grubbing judgmental thing a lot of churchgoers did drove her crazy, and since she sure as hell had no use for Charles, she specifically didn't want to step foot inside *his* church.

But damn it, this was for Bren.

It was a weird thing, this woman's friendship business. In some ways, she and Bren hadn't remotely changed. They still looked like Mutt and Jeff, were never going to share a common lifestyle or common tastes. Possibly they shared a love of purple. And possibly they were both inclined to protect the underdog, even if Poppy preferred to define *underdog* within the canine rather than the human species. Some of the time, anyway.

Still, the thing about a woman friend was that you could really let loose with big, silly belly laughs—because you wouldn't be embarrassed to death if you laughed until you peed. And you could fall apart the way you just had too much pride to do around a man.

All of which meant that she was stuck sitting through this stupid service, so Poppy told herself to bite the bullet and go in. She wasn't about to let Bren sit alone or be alone through this service. Not today. Not because it was Thanksgiving but because Bren had been through hell and a half with Mr. Self-Righteous. And because Julia Mae Quince was singing in the service, and that whole competition thing had been Bren's personal baby.

Poppy didn't know what Bren planned to tell the congregation about her personal situation, but she suspected—not much. But if people were catching wind that there was something amiss with the minister's marriage, Poppy intended to stand in front of Bren if need be.

From the outside, the church was pretty nondescript. But inside it wasn't quite as aggravating as Poppy had been prepared for. The church was decorated to beat the band. Lots of gourds and pumpkins and colored leaves. Lots of things smelling like cider and cinnamon. Lots of candles.

And good grief, the whole town had stuffed the place for this. Mary Sue was there—fifth row, next to Cal Asher and his wife. No guy. Just a couple young women on the other side of her. Pauline—as in, voluptuous Pauline with the golden retriever—sat with her husband and a stair-step set of soccer kids. A couple of caretakers from the Righteous Senior Home were there. Pete from Pete's Pharmacy and Marcella from Marcella's Expert Hair Salon and Nel from Nel's Grocery.

All these people went to church? Surely there were other self-respecting heathens in town besides her family? Other people who had church allergies?

She didn't slip in a back pew, because that could have

been cowardly. She searched over all the heads for Bren, already resigned to sitting visibly close to the front.

And there she was. Second pew. Before Poppy reached that far, Bren rose and went to say something to the organist—who Poppy thought was Mrs. Merriweather, but who could tell underneath that fifty-pound hat with all the fake berries and cornstalks on it? When Bren turned back around to take her seat, she spotted Poppy.

Thanks. Her lips shaped the word. And then she reached out a hand.

Poppy took it, offering a fast squeeze of support, and then just took the seat next to her—the aisle seat. Just in case she had to get out quick.

"I can't believe you're here," Bren said.

"Yeah, well. I'll cut out if I do anything that embarrasses you. You know, like suddenly swearing. Or sitting down when I'm supposed to stand up."

"You couldn't embarrass me, you idiot. We're friends."

"Yeah, I know." She tried to steal a tactful glance at Bren's face. Bren had on a little plum lipstick, maybe a little blush. All that god-awful bruising was gone except for one spot near the eyes. "He giving you a hard time?"

"He's sure not happy," Bren said quietly, "but it's all right. I'm doing fine. Better than I have been in years, in fact."

They couldn't keep talking because Charles walked up to the podium. The service promptly began. And then— how rude could you get—a tall man nestled in, taking the aisle space. Worse than that, she felt a sudden hand patting her behind.

In church!

She whipped her head up with a shocked swear word ready to drip from her tongue, only to recognize Web. Close. Hip-bumping close. And even though the church was packed, the second pew had ample room, so he just plain had no excuse for the fanny patting and hip gluing.

"You never said you attended this church," she whispered under her breath.

"I don't. But I heard what was going on today. Also saw the article in the paper on Bren buying the land, opening a women's shelter. Lots of speculation around town. So I figured one way or another you'd be there for her."

"Yeah. But that doesn't explain why you're here."

She felt another frisky squeeze on her tush, which surely everyone in the whole pew behind them could have seen. "You know damn well why I'm here, Poppy, so don't mess with me."

At least his voice was a whisper. And so was hers. "Don't say 'damn' in church. And I don't know why you're here, so don't you mess with me. *I'm* the one who screwed up."

"No, you didn't. I did."

"It was me. I…" Cripes, people were turning around from all directions to stare at them. Possibly this wasn't the time or place to discuss their fractured relationship. She clutched Web's hand.

He clutched back.

A young teenager walked up the center aisle—a girl maybe fourteen or fifteen. The kid had to be fifty pounds overweight and was stuffed into a dress that looked like living cotton candy, lots of pale pink and poofy organza and bows.

Someone had troweled enough sparkly makeup on the girl's face to block her pores for all time...but then she started singing.

No one spoke. No one fidgeted. The kid's voice blew out the whole church. Hell, even Poppy felt tears forming in her eyes.

When the corny hymn was over, it startled her to find Web still holding her hand. And that she was still holding his.

For Pete's sake, she couldn't remember holding hands with a boy even when she was a teenager. It struck her as pretty absurd to do it for the first time when she was past forty.

But she didn't let go.

And neither did he.

And she abruptly realized that there was probably a key reason she'd avoided churches all these years. Places like this made a heart hope. Made a heart think. It was unnerving and disruptive. She had a raging headache by the time the service was finally over and she could finally walk out— only to discover she and Web were still holding hands, for Pete's sake.

Outside, on the front steps, Bren had already installed herself by the door, shaking hands and wishing people a happy Thanksgiving as they walked out. Charles was there, too, but across the ocean of people, on the other side. Bren took one look at Poppy and then Web and started to laugh.

"I'll catch up with you later," she said to Poppy.

Poppy answered, but she was increasingly distracted. She wasn't sure what Web had in mind, but they both kept walking—at least until they reached his car, when she was the one to abruptly halt. "All right," she said as if they were in the middle of an argument. "All right. I admit it that I thought we were headed somewhere serious. That I wanted you to feel serious. For me. Maybe I was afraid to admit that. Maybe I was even more afraid of admitting I'd come to care about y—"

"Care?"

If he didn't start being nicer, she was going to smack those Clooney lips in front of the whole darn church crowd. "All right. I meant *love*. But we just came out of church. I don't like to use four-letter words this near to a steeple. They make me feel wicked."

"Yeah," Web said, slow and soft. "That's what I'd hoped. That we could both get into that kind of wicked behavior. For a few decades. Together. But right this minute, I'll settle for all those maybes, Poppy." He kissed her on the nose. Then climbed into his car.

"Wait a minute," she said and leaned in his open window. Just in case he wanted to give her another kiss. Which he did. "I suppose you could come over for turkey and meet the family. But wear body armor. You'll need it around my brothers. Say, around three o'clock."

"Was that another maybe?"

"No, that was an order not to be late."

She watched him back out of the parking lot with the most confounded, silly grin on his face. But then, she seemed to be wearing a grin that she couldn't peel off either.

She just might never take off that smile ever again.

"So what do you think?" Poppy asked Bren. Spring was exploding in her backyard. The fruit trees were a froth of blossoms, from the white pear to the pink cherries. An exuberant hedge of yellow forsythia bordered a walking trail. Even from the distance you could see the soft beds of violets in the woods. But it was fences on her mind.

Bren had come over for a girls-only lunch—meaning that they'd had quiche and three kinds of chocolate.

It had taken Poppy a while to sell her last jewel, but she finally had. Some of her inheritance was visible back here. The old barn had a fresh coat of paint, inside and out. New lighting had been installed. She'd set up a small pond with a bridge. And the most recent construction project had been some fancy fencing, set up in circles and mazes and containment areas.

Naturally Bren had no way to know what all the stuff was for or how it would be used. But where Poppy had the dream, Web had the practical engineering brain to help her plan it and then either to create what she needed or buy it. Almost all of it they'd created together.

"I'm just amazed at all you've accomplished in such a short time," Bren said. "Are you getting some customers?"

"More than I ever dreamed of. I can't believe it. I just started by sending out a mailing to the people I was already doing dog grooming for. But then the Righteous Senior Home called…they had some funding, I guess, and they'd wanted to try some therapy dogs for some time. And then the hospital kicked in, got a grant for their rehab center, wanted dogs to work with the elderly and those in wheelchairs. And then there's just the usual run-of-the-mill families who pick the wrong pet and need to know how to get better behavior from the critter."

Bren kept looking at her. "I hate to tell you this, but you're radiant. And I'm not talking anything the plastic surgeon did to you. You're over-the-moon happy."

Poppy heard a car door slam, knew Web was home…and knew he was a good part of the reason for that radiance business. But for another long moment she looked only at Bren. "I hate to tell *you* this, but you look just as happy as I am. The shelter's got to be going good."

Bren nodded. "I've been picking up funding right and left. Now I realize…I should have been doing this for years. It's not just the women. It's the kids. Not a day goes by I don't feel needed, like I'm making a difference. I can't wait to get up in the morning."

"Charles…?"

"We did a legal separation. There had to be some kind of paperwork, just because I can't take on both his debts and mine—and that's vice versa, as well. Otherwise, though, he's pretty much let me alone. It's awkward sometimes, but awkward isn't that hard to live with. Several people keep counseling me that I need a formal divorce, should be giving myself the chance to marry again. But I don't see that in my cards and I don't see a reason to worry about it." She smiled. "I'm happy. My own way. Maybe no one else would want my life—but I'm loving it."

"You sound like me. I could never seem to conform to what other people thought was important. But right now I just feel like I've found the path I was meant to walk."

Bren turned pensive. "I just keep thinking about Maude Rose. If she had any way to realize how much she did for us. How those jewels turned our lives around."

Poppy nodded. "That inheritance…it really wasn't about the jewels. Or the money. It was about somehow seeing things in a different way. Opening up choices I never thought I could have."

The back door opened, and there was Web. He shot her a grin, the kind of wicked, unwholesome grin that made her feel all mushy on the inside. She suddenly got a bad feeling. Generally when Web looked at her that way, he was either two seconds away from jumping her…or had brought yet another stray for her to adopt.

"Oh, boy, does he look like trouble," Bren murmured in a teasing whisper.

"Yeah. He is. Best trouble I ever had." But before going in, Poppy hooked her arm with Bren's. "And you've been the best friend I ever found."

"What is it about this day? The quiche? We're both turning corny."

"Sick, isn't it? Maybe we can blame that on Maude Rose, too. Gave us those darn gems, and we found all the sparkle on the inside."

"You've got that right," Bren agreed.

Stability is highly overrated....

Dana Logan's world had always revolved around
her children. Now they're all grown up and don't
seem to need anything she's able to give them.
Struggling to find her new identity, Dana realizes
that it's about time for her to get "off her rocker"
and begin a new life!

Off Her Rocker

by Jennifer Archer

Available August 2006
TheNextNovel.com

HN53

Life.
It could happen to her!

Never Happened just about sums up
Alexis Jackson's life. Independent and
successful, Alexis has concentrated on
building her own business, leaving no
time for love. Now at forty, Alexis
discovers that she still has a few things
to learn about life—that the life unlived
is the one that "Never happened"
and it's her time to make a change....

Never Happened
by Debra Webb

HARLEQUIN®
Next™

Life on Long Island can be murder!

Teddi Bayer's life hasn't been what you'd call easy lately. Last year she'd never seen a dead person up close, but this year she discovered one. And it's her first paying client.... But Teddi is about to learn that when life throws you a curveball, there's no better time to take control of your own destiny.

What Goes with Blood Red, Anyway?

by Stevi Mittman

HN54

Available August 2006
TheNextNovel.com

Sometimes you're up...
sometimes you're down.
Good friends always help
each other deal with it.

Mood Swing

by Jane Graves

A story about three women who discover
they have one thing in common—they've
reached the breaking point.

When life gets shaky… you've just gotta dance!

Learning to Hula

by Lisa Childs

REQUEST YOUR FREE BOOKS!

2 FREE NOVELS TO INTRODUCE YOU TO OUR BRAND-NEW LINE!

NeXt ™

There's the life you planned. And there's what comes next.

It's the time for courage, to love and be loved.

Francesca Bond has been surviving her life much more than she has been living it. Late one summer's night, things take a dramatic turn and she finds herself running from her bleak existence and into a welcoming new world. Francesca soon awakens to her heart's desire and discovers the courage to live.

Awakening
by Kate Austin

HN52

Available July 2006
TheNextNovel.com